The Braided Tongue

# The Braided Tongue

a novel

Roshni Rustomji

We acknowledge the support of the Canada Council for the Arts for out publishing program. We also acknowledge support from the Ontario Arts Council.

Selections from this novel have appeared in: *Our Feet Walk the Sky: Women of the South Asian Diaspora* edited by the Women of South Asian Descent Collective. San Francisco, Aunt Lute Books. 1993
*Her Mother's Ashes and Other Stories* by South Asian Women in Canada and the United States. Edited by Nurjehan Aziz. Toronto, TSAR. 1994
*Growing Up Ethnic in America: Contemporary Fiction About Learning to Be American.* Edited by Maria Mazziotti and Jennifer Gillan. New York, Penguin Books. 1999

National Library of Canada Cataloguing in Publication

Rustomji-Kerns, Roshni
    The braided tongue / Roshni Rustomji.


ISBN 1-894770-07-2


    I. Title.


PS3618.U88B73 2003         813'.6         C2003-902900-X


Printed in Canada by Coach House Printing


TSAR Publications
P. O. Box 6996, Station A
Toronto, Ontario M5W 1X7
Canada

www.tsarbooks.com

For

Amy Ling-friend and mentor-with gratitude
Chuck aka Charles and Carlos-compañero-con prem

Rosa, Victoria, Rachel, Amy , Shakira, Tahira, Panna, Lu and
Linda,  JJ, Susan/Kukii, Lucía, Leny, Chitra, Meena, Annie/Betty,
Carlo, Federico, Moazzam

And Ed-wherever you are
Thank you for reading the stories

# I.

## Half Moon Bay, California—Lakewood, New Hampshire

### *Friends and the Possibility of Relatives*

Vegetarian vampires, an old woman wondering around barefoot in New Hampshire, an unexpected, unknown birthplace on the back of a photograph and pelicans dive bombing into the Pacific Ocean a few blocks from my house. I was trying to sound reasonable. But the heft, the settled comfort of words were awkward for me. They carried no colour. They couldn't bend, curve or implode into unpainted silences.

The two women sitting in my living room were my audience. Browns and reds, saffron and tumeric, black and green. Carmelita Gutierrez's hennaed hair reflected the fluid amber of the late afternoon light. Ratna Sharma's hair absorbed the darker shades.

I tried again. "Carmelita, it really is the old woman's fault. She pushed me, I broke the photograph and now I have to go all the way to India. Do you know how enormous India is?"

Ratna laughed at the surprise in my voice.

Very few things surprised Carmelita. But quite a number of things exasperated her. She seemed especially susceptible to exasperation that afternoon. She wanted to know how I, who knew India only through art, mythology and food, knew anything about India's measurements. She didn't pay any attention to my comment about possessing an atlas.

In her khaki jeans, which according to her were specially tailored for the middle-aged body, her black T-shirt with a hand-embroidered Virgin of Soledad on the front and a picture of Caesar Chavez on the back, and her hair springing out all over her head like short, rusted wiry serpents, Carmelita was a post-hypermodern Medusa. She was known to refer to

1

herself as "una morena-post-modern-toastie." Medusa? Not quite. I would not include serpents and snakes in any painting. Not even in a portrait of my gorgeous-haired friend Carmelita who was shouting that just because I had discovered, in my middle age, that I was born somewhere called Devinagar, somewhere in India and not some place in England as I had been led to believe, I couldn't blame the old woman. Especially not after all the trouble the old woman had taken to wander across the United States of America with me, "From New Hampshire to California—back and forth, back and forth—only God and His Mother know how many times. She even lives with you here in this foggy, chilly town. Barefoot in Half Moon Bay. Such devotion. And you blame her for a little accident like a broken photograph frame!"

Ratna commented on the level of sound and melodrama in the room. "There you go again, Carmelita! Mahagarbarwali! What a tamasha!" Ratna's statements usually calmed Carmelita. But not that afternoon.

Carmelita continued to yell. She said that she was not at all surprised by my connection with India. She demanded to know why I had never realized what she had known all along. I could not possibly be a "proper little English muchacha . . . por favor, mira! Your skin, your eyes, your hair, Katy! Brown, brown, brown all over. Quite a morenita. You are an artist! Don't you ever look at yourself carefully? Didn't your foster parents tell you where you were born?"

Theresa and Gregory Sanders could not have told me where I was born. The only legal information they had about me when they brought me from Oaxaca, Mexico to New Hampshire was the formal paper that named them my guardians in the case of my father Freddy Cooper's death. Gregory Sanders had been my father's employer in Mexico and I, Katy Cooper, was described as "Female baby born on October 29, 1958. The only child of Freddy Cooper and Margaret Shriver Cooper." No place of birth for me. No further information about my mother or my father.

My foster parents and I had always believed that I was born in England. After all, my father constantly spoke about England and my English mother. He had also taught me to sing "The White Cliffs of Dover" and "Rule Britannia" when I was a very little girl. Songs he and I sang together in Mexico, every night before I went to sleep. They were the closest I knew to bedtime prayers. I had to hum "The White Cliffs of Dover" my first year in New Hampshire because I had forgotten the lyrics after my father died. I decided not to reproduce "Rule Britannia" in Lakewood. It sounded silly without my father's sweet tenor to bolster my voice. I also realized very early in my life in New Hampshire that this would be one song that my new family might not appreciate hearing. I was now expected to learn "America the Beautiful" and "Yankee Doodle." Gregory Sanders had announced that the "Star Spangled Banner" had too many bombs and too many changes in pitch for enjoyable singing. As far as I knew, this was the only song he didn't like to sing. Anything else in the way of a song or a tune that he encountered, he sang. Off-key. The only time Theresa Sanders sang was in church. Softly. She believed that New England was created for soft, muted sounds. She believed this in spite of her husband's boisterous singing and the thunderstorms that crashed through Lakewood and the surrounding countryside every year. I wondered if there were thunderstorms in Devinagar, India.

I turned to Ratna for help. I hadn't been able to find Devinagar anywhere on the maps of India, Pakistan, Bangladesh and Sri Lanka in my atlas.

Ratna, who had said very little since I had announced the discovery of my birthplace, answered that as far as she was concerned, maps and documents—legal or otherwise were not always trustworthy. Carmelita was inspired to begin a complicated creation myth in which she equated all cosmic explanations to an eternal fraud. An "Ur Fraud" that according to her was the cosmic root of "our Big Bang Planet." As she meandered through her theory about creation and frauds, I looked out the window of my living room. I had not expected to see the hawk circling over the cemetery across from my house in late July. Hawks were at their most visible in autumn over the town of Half Moon Bay. And on winter days, when the rain stopped for a few hours, a pair of hawks soared over the cemetery where the grass had at last turned green, the wild sorrel had begun to bloom, and the Christmas poinsettias placed around the graves in small plastic containers were still bright red. I watched the wings of the hawk turn transparent in the sunlight and remembered the restlessness of the jays and the sparrows in my foster parents' home in Lakewood, New Hampshire. The house where I had grown up was surrounded by tall slender trees and enormous rocks. And the constant presence of the lake. We could see the lake from every window of the house. In every season of the year.

I had very few memories of the house I had lived in with my father in Mexico. I remembered the colors that surrounded that house. The reds, pinks, yellows, magentas and purples of bougainvillea and roses, the greens, browns, grays and whites of raucous birds and the silver of the morning mists rising from the soil which promised fertility even when it was completely bare. I tried to picture Devinagar and was disgusted at my lack of imagination when I came up with NATIONAL GEOGRAPHIC landscapes photographed in Kodachrome. A village at the foot of mountains drenched by monsoon rains in which the drops of water were aligned perfectly. Nothing looked believably wet. Or a town in the midst of a desert with nomads, gypsies, and camels moving against the background of crumbling forts that looked as if they were especially constructed for a faux-documentary. What form did water take in my birthplace? Rivers? Oceans? Lakes? The hawk flashed by my window. I wondered about the flight of birds in Devinagar and heard the keening of a high-flying bird. I hoped there weren't any snakes slithering around unchecked in Devinagar.

I used to have a recurring nightmare for many years. I was about thirteen years old and a white snake appeared out of the ground and drank the menstrual blood pouring out of my body. That nightmare used to scare me more than the old woman who had haunted me since I was eleven years old. She was everywhere. At all times. Actually by the time the nightmare began, I was quite used to the old woman. Since the idea of being haunted didn't appeal to me, I decided that she was my shadow. A shadow that didn't quite follow the shape, the lines, the size of my body. A shadow of an old woman who had no idea about the laws of physics, of the angles of light, of the relationships between light and objects.

Ratna shook her head in bewilderment at Carmelita's creation myth. Four or five lethal looking hairpins fell out of her chignon and onto my living-room rug. "What's wrong with being born in India?" She asked quietly. "What's so bad about not appearing on a map? Devinagar is between Bombay and Karachi. On the coast. Facing the Arabian Sea. A small town that has grown up around a fishing village."

Carmelita made it clear that she was arguing with me about blaming the old woman. She had no arguments regarding my place of birth. She declared that she found much to say in favor of India. India had the good sense to confuse Christopher Columbus into getting lost and Ratna as well as Mahatma Gandhi were born in India.

Ratna didn't thank Carmelita. She pointed out that India wasn't spared Europe. "Vasco da Gama did arrive in India. As well as those Kipling people. And much as I respect Gandhiji, he did write the ultimate chapter on the passive aggressive personality. True, I was born there. What made you think that you were born in England, Katy?"

Where else could I have been born? As I reminded my two friends, I had sung "The White Cliffs of Dover" and "Rule Britannia" when I was a child and my father had told me that Margaret Shriver Cooper, my mother, was a beautiful woman with the smile of an angel and the perfect manners of an Englishwoman. Whenever I cried or pouted, he would say, "Please Katy, behave like your mother. How will I ever take you to England to see her when you are grown up if you don't have perfect English manners just like her?" I had no memories of my mother. Nothing except her presence in the only photograph my father had left me. A photograph of me as a baby with my parents. I decided that the old woman was not the only one to blame. I said, "It was also the fault of the photograph. That's why I have to go to India. But the old woman bears some responsibility."

The old woman with her bare feet and the ghastly scar on her neck was said to be a ghost. And apparently following the way of all ghosts, she manifested herself only to a select number of people. I was among the selected. Carmelita, who prided herself on knowing all about ghosts, was not selected. But even so, she had taken it upon herself to champion the old woman.

Carmelita was relieved when I moved the fault from the old woman to the photograph. She said that my father should have left me a larger legacy. Something more than just one photograph and a paper naming the Sanders as my guardians.

My father had also left me a personal song. He always sang "K-K-K-Katy beeauutiifuul Katy" to me. He was stammering "K-K-K-Katy," as he lay dying in front of our house.

Ratna bent down to retrieve her hairpins. While sticking them back into her hair with some semblance of precise order, she told Carmelita to quieten down and asked me to explain why I was blaming the old woman and the photograph for the discovery about my newly discovered place of birth.

I told her that it was also Carmelita's fault.

Poor Ratna. She shook her head again in complete bewilderment, those infernal hairpins fell out again, she retrieved them once again and sat in her chair looking at me. She didn't even try to put up her hair again. It just lay there all along her shoulders and down her back, fanned out against the green and yellow of her sari.

"It's Carmelita's fault. She sent me that large print of Remedios Varo's 'Vegetarian Vampires' two days ago." I pointed to the print hanging on the wall behind Ratna. "She should have known that it would provoke the old woman into some kind of bizarre, ghoulish action. It's a perfect picture for ghost-type creatures. I was standing on a chair, trying to hang the print when the old woman crept up behind me. She surprised me. I fell off the chair and grabbed on to the small table next to it and then this one and only photograph I have of my parents and myself fell off the table. The glass broke. I had to pull apart the frame and that's when I saw the inscription on the back of the photograph."

Carmelita picked up the photograph from the small table and examined it. She turned it upside down. And then she turned it over and stated that I was correct. The three people in the photograph were, she read out, "Freddy Cooper and Margaret Shriver Cooper with baby Katy Cooper born in Devinagar, India, October, 1958. Are you sure she was your mother, Katy? You really don't look like her. You don't look much like Freddy either. Except the smile. And don't blame only me. Ratna helped me choose the print. She has always been amused by the idea of these vegetarian vampires. She likes all that wonderful red, vegetarian food. I have been looking for a print of a work by Remedios Varo as a gift for you. After all, you introduced us to her obras. Thought you'd like this one."

"Very civilized vampires," added Ratna. She started to putting the pins back in her hair. "Sipping their food through elegant straws. These are not your usual messy, blood-dripping-from-their-mouths-and-fangs-and-chins vampires. Even your English mother would have found them well mannered."

I did like the print. But now because of my friends' gift, I had to rethink my life. The old woman had liked the vampires' pets the best. She had pointed at the multilegged roosters on leashes and laughed. That's what had really surprised me into losing my balance. I had never heard her laugh or seen her smile.

The familiar pain in my knees started off again. Zigzagging like slivers of lightning across my knees and down to my ankles.

Ratna looked at the photograph in Carmelita's hand and decided that the old woman had deliberately scared me off the chair so that the frame would break and I would look at the back of the photograph.

Carmelita didn't agree. Ghosts, she explained, can't push or touch. They walk through walls, objects, people. At best, they terrify people and pictures into falling down. They can't move things and people.

Although I had told Ratna and Carmelita about the old woman a few months after the three of us became good friends, I had not gone into details about her first appearance. I decided that it was time to tell them about that first visit when the old woman had touched a television screen. Carmelita revealed that she had been waiting con mucho patience to hear about that first visit.

I was in the living room of the Sanders' home in Lakewood watching television, the curtains drawn against whatever light was left of that November evening, the front door tightly closed against the cold, when I first saw the woman. It was about two weeks after my eleventh birthday. That last piece of information caught Carmelita's interest. "Around Halloween and the dia de los muertos. What do you think Ratna?"

Ratna wasn't overly impressed. According to her any day could be the day of the dead.

I hadn't paid any attention to the particular timing of the first visitation. I most probably didn't even know about the Day of the Dead during all those years in New Hampshire. The Sanderses, Catholics that they were and having lived in Mexico, may have known about it but they considered themselves civilized Catholics. Theresa Sanders often told me about how embarrassed she had been by the "enthusiastic passion" displayed by the Mexicans for everything religious. She used to say, "I suppose I can understand their enthusiastic passion for poetry and flowers and love. But for death? For religion? But then, they are such beautiful people. I suppose passion comes easily to beautiful people." One day I said to her, "You too are beautiful." And she replied, "Thank you dear. But they live in such a hot land! We are in a cold, sensible place. We must behave appropriately."

There was nothing sensible about the old woman's first visit. Or for that matter, there was nothing sensible or appropriate about any of her visits. On that first visit, she had walked over to the TV set and changed the channel.

Carmelita said that she hadn't met anyone else who had experienced celestial censorship and insisted again that ghosts couldn't move things manually.

I assured her that the old woman had touched the television. With her right hand. I was watching a Thanksgiving Special and was confused. New Hampshire was cold, television seemed like a miracle and I didn't know what to make of the program I was watching. Turkeys talked and sang, pumpkins chattered. Just as the turkeys joined the pumpkins in a dance, the old woman walked into the room. Without opening the front door or a window. There was no draft, no cold air. She was dark like me and had braids with bright ribbons wound around her head. She was wearing a long, blue skirt and a white blouse with flowers embroidered around the neck. No shoes, no boots, no coats, nothing covering her feet or her arms or her head. And she didn't look cold. A large translucent, black butterfly was perched on her left shoulder. A jagged scar ran across her neck. A puckered, pink seam against her brown throat. She nodded at me. No smile, not a word. Walked to the television and did something. I didn't know if she turned knobs or merely touched the screen.

The turkeys and the pumpkins disappeared and I saw a group of people performing a strange dance.

The dancers on the screen wore tall, straight white hats and thick white robes that flared away from their feet as they danced in a circle. Round and round. Each dancer danced alone. Spinning around a private, individual axis. In solitary silence. Eyes closed. There was no music. They danced in a room with earth-red, high, curved walls. There was no top, no roof to that room. And as far as I could see, there was no audience.

When I described the dancers, Carmelita wanted to know, "No explanation of who they were, what they were doing, why? A voice-over? Writing on the screen?" Carmelita was in recovery from PBS.

"No. The old woman seemed to step into a corner and a few minutes later my foster mother walked in. She looked at the dancers and said that they were circling around themselves in an ecstatic search for God. I didn't tell her that I couldn't see the dancers anymore. They had become a circle of white, whirling candles. Threatening to burst into flames, smoke, a silent melting, a collapse. I think Theresa Sanders only saw the dancers."

"Did the dancers really burst into flames? Right there on television? In front of Mary, Mother of God, the television, your foster mother, Theresa Sanders of Lakewood, New Hampshire and you?"

Neither Ratna nor I commented on Carmelita's certainty regarding Mary's presence in that room in New Hampshire with me, the turkeys, the pumpkins, the dancers, the candles, the old woman, the butterfly and Theresa Sanders.

Early in our friendship, Carmelita had confessed to us that she suspected that God didn't always exercise his powers of omnipresence at all times, in all places. Too busy. But Mary, Mother of God, was present. Always. Everywhere. And it was usually to Mary as Nuestra Señora de la Soledad, the Virgin of Soledad, Queen and Protectress of Oaxaca, Mexico that Carmelita addressed her prayers of praise, gratitude, or complaints. She often carried on a markedly one-sided conversation with Mary. Since Carmelita's ancestral home was in Oaxaca, her madrina Glafira, who lived in Oaxaca, had insisted that Carmelita be baptized in Oaxaca, in the Church of La Soledad. Carmelita told us about seeing her own guardian angel in that same church when she was a very young girl, right there in the presence of the Virgin of Soledad. That was the first time. I took it that she saw her guardian angel quite frequently after that. It was a subject I preferred to leave unexplored.

Carmelita insisted that the talk about angels being sexless was all nonsense. Her guardian angel was definitely female and was "two parts in one form." One breast had Mary revealing the sacred heart, "plump, not surrounded by barbed wire, not bloody," the other breast had a Mixtec warrior queen descending from the clouds. The angel apparently appeared to Carmelita in glowing neon colors. Carmelita saw that angel and the Virgin of Soledad as her special aunts or older sisters, with incredible powers and inexhaustible love. I found that rather presumptuous of her but then the only unusual visitation I had was the one by the old woman and her butterfly. And I definitely never thought of either of them as any kind of relative. Or even as a special protectoress. At least not until the photograph fell down, the glass broke and I found out that I was born in India and not in England.

After about a year of presenting Carmelita with traditional portraits of Mary, Ratna and I found out that Carmelita felt more at ease with irreverent, exotic versions of Mary. "It shows that Mary is real and not a figment of some holy, frustrated male's imagination," she said when she first saw Yolanda López's paintings. Her favorite was the artist's self-portrait. Yolanda López with her short, wild hair, her short red dress, clutching a snake in her right hand, stepping with her sneakered foot on the angel trying to hold her up. It took Carmelita nearly nine days to stop talking about the artist tearing right out of the bright nimbus and into the real world, the Virgin's starry mantle slung jauntily over her shoulder. Another favorite of hers was the portrait of the bespectacled elderly lady surrounded by the familiar nimbus, sewing endless reams of the Virgin's mantle on an old sewing machine. One Christmas Eve, Carmelita told us the dream she had on her fifteenth birthday. In Carmelita's adolescent dream, Mary refused to ascend to heaven, her blue mantle flowing gently in the breeze. Instead, Mary wrapped her mantle around herself in tight but graceful folds, opened her eyes and dived into a frothy green ocean. To swim with the dolphins and the whales.

I imagined Carmelita and Ratna swimming with dolphins and whales while I remembered that day of turkeys and pumpkins on the television when I was eleven years old. I told my friends that I didn't know if the dancers really turned into candles or not. Theresa Sanders said nothing about it. So maybe only I saw them as turning into candles. Anyway, my foster mother told me that television time was over and I had to go to bed.

I didn't go straight to bed. After I closed the door to my room, I drew a circle around the pink carnation on my rug, with a yellow coloring pencil; I took off my shoes, found a place in the middle of that pink flower and danced. Turning round and round, the toes and heels of my right foot so close to the toes and heel of my left foot that the two feet barely moved away from one another.

I thought that if people could dance in search of God, I could dance in search of the memories that I had lost. I wanted concrete memories of my life with my father. Of my life before I came to New Hampshire. But even though I turned faster and faster, I could not add anything more to what I already remembered. Nothing more than what I already knew. My father's face, his smile, his voice singing and then stammering as he fell down. And the green plants and birds and insects, the landscapes of Mexico which were so very different from New Hampshire with its startling colors of fall, the frozen lake and the ferocious winter storms. I didn't need to dance that dance on the carnation to know that I hated wearing shoes and that the pain in my knees did not exist before I came to New Hampshire. I never did tell the Sanderses about the shoes. Only about the pain in my knees. I had to stop dancing on that carnation because of the sharp pain in my knees and because I thought the old woman who had entered my room would join me in the circle.

I jumped into bed and pulled the quilt over my head. That's how my foster mother found me the next morning. With the quilt covering all of me, even my face. She turned up the thermostat on the heater a bit more.

As I spoke to Carmelita and Ratna about the old woman, the dance, the pain, I remembered how I had to deal with the loss of my father, the appearance of a strange old woman and a butterfly no one else saw, and the pain in my knees, at the same time as I was trying to understand the new people around me. And no matter how hard I tried, I was never able to call Theresa and Gregory Sanders anything but Mrs Sanders, Mr Sanders. I knew that they would have preferred to be called mother, father, mom, dad, but they didn't force me. When I turned twenty-three, they requested that I call them Theresa and Gregory.

Theresa Sanders, made anxious by the pain in my legs, took me to at least four doctors. All four declared that there was no reason for the pain. The pain should not exist. In order to end Theresa Sanders's anxiety, I decided to believe the doctors. I stopped talking about my pain, stopped using it as a reason for my physical awkwardness and asked if I could take ballet classes. I thought that ballet classes would force the pain out of my legs and help me to move with some degree of grace. I knew that the ballet classes would please my foster mother. I always wanted to please her. I was very dear to her. The pain did seem to be more bearable during the classes, I did learn to move with grace, and Theresa Sanders was definitely relieved and delighted. She considered ballet the pinnacle of art and culture. When I didn't complain about my pain anymore, she assured me that it had disappeared because my body had become accustomed to the New England weather and had accommodated itself to an eleven-year-old girl's natural growth of bones and muscles.

She attributed my earlier pain and my slow physical growth to the diet in Mexico. "Corn, corn, corn and more corn," she would tell her friends and her husband. "And then those beans and more beans. Meat from scrawny chickens or goats. No real vegetables or milk or cheese. And of course the other extreme. You should have seen Katy's father's version of good English food in the midst of a Mexican plantation! That horrible, humid coffee finca with nothing but trees and bushes and plants that never seemed to stop growing! Can you believe it, in that place, Freddy Cooper ate soft boiled eggs, which most probably came from diseased chickens, and boiled rice, which was of course, never free of bits and pieces of ground up stones and husks! And stale bread. And that is what Katy ate. As well as all those spicy corn and bean things the Mexican woman who took care of their house cooked for herself. What a diet for a child! Thank heavens, Gregory and I didn't have to live out there. It was hard enough living in Mexico City. But at least we could get some edible food there. I know that Katy's knees do not hurt her anymore because of her good, healthy diet here."

She had no idea about how much I missed the foods of my childhood. The hunger for corn tortillas, beans, tamales and the occasional mole had transformed itself into a silent obsession. Many of the doodles in the margins of my notebooks had started out as attempts to draw the hunger I lived with as I ate the foods Theresa Sanders served me with such loving care and generosity. I ate those healthy New England breakfasts, lunches, dinners, snacks, and special treats and longed for the rich textures, the complicated tastes, the rough fragrances of the food I had eaten in that small house in Mexico set in the midst of trees and vines which were always filled with birds and insects. That was another hunger. The sound of birds and insects. Sounds that I couldn't paint or draw.

I stopped talking about my pain. I couldn't describe my hunger for my childhood food to anyone. And I didn't tell anyone about the transparent, black butterfly and the old woman.

As I grew older, I relegated the presence of the old barefoot woman with the butterfly to the part of my life I had decided to call, "Can't understand. Can't be very important." By the time I was twenty years old, I had convinced myself that I didn't really see them.

But the pain in my knees continued. I never denied that to myself. I even went to a series of doctors in Berkeley when I was a graduate student there. And I consulted at least three more doctors when I became a professor of art history at Sierra College in San Mateo. The doctors told me, once again, that there was no reason for my pain. As far as they were concerned, my pain did not exist. Physical therapists and chronic pain psychologists taught me exercises and relaxation techniques. Those worked well when I was dealing with confused students, difficult colleagues, the long trips back and forth from California to New Hampshire and the sorrow of the final illnesses of my foster parents. But the exercises and relaxation techniques didn't help the pain in my legs.

When one of my students noticed that I constantly rubbed my left knee with my right hand, my right knee with my left hand, he persuaded me to go to a psychic.

He was quite serious when he said, "The pain might be something from one of your past lives, Professor Cooper. Anyway, what harm can come out of visiting a psychic? I know of a good, sensible one. She doesn't charge a lot. Only fifty dollars. Come on, this is California! How can you tell your folks back home in New Hampshire that California is now your home if you haven't visited a psychic at least once?"

I didn't tell him that even in Lakewood, New Hampshire there was a shop, The Mystical Journey, which carried books dealing with paranormal events and spiritual journeys and advertised readings by a psychic every Wednesday afternoon from 2 PM. to 5 PM. Theresa Sanders didn't quite approve of that shop. She felt that its wooden sign with dragons and arcane symbols and its sunflower-patterned awning were far too garish for our sedate, small town.

The sensible psychic I went to in San Mateo reminded me of Carmelita. She wore a long black tunic that carried an announcement over her ample breasts, "Marilyn. Psychic. Member of the Ladies Sewing Circle and Burrokicking Society."

Marilyn told me that alas, I would never be a very famous painter but I would always have wonderful friends and that— "glory be!"—I would somehow get just enough money to retire soon. The psychic was very honest. She had no idea about the cause or the cure for the pain in my legs. And she noticed neither the old woman sitting next to me nor the butterfly, which had hovered above my head throughout the session.

Two years after my visit to Marilyn the psychic seamstress-burrokicker, my foster parents died. Theresa Sanders died first and Gregory Sanders followed her within four months. I gave up teaching and began to make some kind of a living off my painting. Four years after my visit to the psychic, I found out that I was born in Devinagar.

# II.

## Half Moon Bay

*Cunha's Store and Trabajadores Cemeteries at Christmas
and Dinesh the ice cream vendor*

When I learned about my birthplace I was living on the Pacific Coast of Northern California trying to come to terms with the fog that could change within two minutes from a transparent stretch of gray vapor to an unyielding dark cloud settling down on the ocean and the land.

I had bought a small house across a cemetery in Half Moon Bay with the money the Sanderses had left me as their sole heir. After ten years of teaching art history to sophomores and juniors and after two years of leave without pay so I could take care of my foster parents in Lakewood, New Hampshire, as they struggled against cancer, I retired. I had not yet turned forty. As the psychic would have said, "Glory be!" I was free to paint as much as I wanted and tend to as many types of roses and vegetables as I wished in my garden.

Greenhouses stood all along the winding, mountain road leading to the town. They sold clay and ceramic pots and garden statuary together with the usual flowers, plants, fruit trees, herbs and dried flower arrangements. The garden statuary came in the shape of Buddhas, bunny rabbits, owls, Virgin Marys, lions, griffins, little boys peeing, little girls holding baskets of flowers, Saint Franceses, Kuan Yins, ducks, elves and other creatures from nature, mythology and history. In the fall, pumpkin fields stretched green, yellow, gold, and orange right up to the edge of the ocean. The acrid smells of brussel sprouts and broccoli often permeated the fields and spread over to Highway 1 and the edges of the towns along the coast.

The Christmas tree farms close to Half Moon Bay offered train and pony rides throughout the year and were decorated from Thanksgiving through Christmas with Santa Clauses, his helpers, and his reindeers. For some reason, Snow White with her Seven Dwarfs was sometimes included among the decorations. Carmelita, true to type, always referred to the dwarfs as "the seven deadly sins transformed into seven unsuspecting dwarfs by Mr Disney's warped mind." She refused to change her opinion of Mr Disney even when I told her that the story was pre-Disney. One Christmas, the fancy cemetery on top of the hill on Highway 92—not the cemetery across from my house—had Santa Claus, his sleigh and the reindeers, all in bright lights perched on top of its signboard. Even Carmelita didn't know what to make of that.

I decided to live in Half Moon Bay because of the nurseries, the cemeteries and its one main street sensibly called Main Street. And because on that Main Street there was Cunha's Country Store which reflected the town's population. It sold Portuguese foods, Italian breads, Mexican tortillas and salsas, packages of spices and herbs for instant Indian curries, English biscuits, Greek cheeses, cilantro, chilies, avocados, flowers, newspapers, and chocolates. Upstairs in the store there were All American Levi's, turquoise and silver jewelry, ceramics, beautifully stitched children's clothes, and kitchen items that reminded me of my foster parents' home. Songs of the 40s, the 50s, the 60s followed the shoppers through the narrow aisles of grocery and the meat counter at the back of the store. They were the songs Gregory Sanders had sung and hummed. But the deeper, darker fragrances of the spices, the fresh breads, the wines, vinegar and meat were from the scattered memories of my childhood in Mexico.

Men in search of work in the fields, the green houses, and the construction sites along the coast gathered early every morning in Mac Dutra Park across the street from Cunha's Country Store. They talked among themselves in the Spanish of Mexico, of Guatemala, of El Salvador, of Peru. When the pick-ups and the trucks pulled up to the curb, the bargaining and the hiring were carried on in English with a few words of Spanish, or Spanish trying to form itself into English. Sometimes the Spanish and English were used by speakers more at ease with Italian or Portuguese. Walking by Mac Dutra Park during the early morning hours, an observer on the periphery of a private world, I would watch this daily ritual of hiring, the gestures and words among men who hired, and those who would labour.

The women from Mexico, Guatemala, El Salvador, and Peru seldom stood in one place. They were seen all over the town, pushing other people's babies in state-of-the-art baby carriages, cleaning houses, working in stores, bagging groceries, stitching clothes. As they worked they traded the sounds, the rhythms, the meanings of their language with those of the women they worked for, the children they took care of. Voices and languages wove into one another, clashed, sometimes spun out of control into a world of new, hybrid languages. I moved through Half Moon Bay nurturing my own desire for long silences, comfortable with the life of the town the campesinos called el pueblo.

In my small house on the east side of Main Street, I could hear the water in the creek across the dirt-paved road after a satisfying series of strong winter rains. The stand of Eucalyptus trees on the banks of the creek shielded the stuccoed house from the cemetery and during the high windstorms dropped lethal-looking branches all over the street. The cemetery, of course, had the best view in town. It also had the usual broken crosses and angels, granite slabs and new graves covered with mud which threatened to slide down the hill during heavy rains, year-round plastic flowers, faded American paper flags and teenagers excited by the idea of drinking beer among the graves.

Carmelita who was born in Corpus Christi and who remembered stories that crossed three generations of her relatives, explained the presence of amorous teenagers in graveyards as proof that sex and death were truly related. Ratna who was born in India and was Carmelita's apartment mate in San Francisco, laughed and said, "If people would just be sensible, burn their dead, and dispose of them, there would be no such need to bring sex and death together."

At the time when the photograph revealed to me that I was born in Devinagar, Ratna was teaching English literature at Sierra College in San Mateo. She wanted to be a filmmaker or at least write a novel that could be turned into a movie. Ratna also remembered stories about her relatives, those who still lived and those who had been cremated and consigned into the waters of the rivers of India many years before she was born.

Quite a few things happened the month after the old woman surprised me into pushing the photograph off the table. I sold a painting of pelicans flying over the cliffs. A crow had managed to penetrate the pelicans' perfect flying formation. The man who bought the painting said that the ocean beyond the cliffs looked thick, "As if the backs of whales and dolphins and sea serpents have become these heavy waves." I smiled while inwardly shuddering at the thought of serpents inhabiting my paintings. My favorite restaurant, "Original Johnny's" closed down for remodeling. Carmelita went off to Oaxaca to visit her Tía Lucía and her companion of many years Tía Elena. Ratna began to write a novel about a man she had met on one of her visits to Half Moon Bay. He was named Dinesh and was from India. He drove an ice cream truck that played the introductory phrase of "Turkey in the Straw" over and over again. Ratna thought to save him from a life-time of "Turkey in the Straw" by making him the protagonist of her novel. Dinesh was to discover a corpse among the ice-cream bars in the back of his truck and thus be transformed into an amateur detective. A Marx-Lenin-and Gandhi-quoting detective. Ratna would not tell us anything more. Carmelita said that the man certainly needed to be saved, even if it were in a novel, from the financially ridiculous position of trying to sell ice cream from a truck in the constantly chilly city of Half Moon Bay.

While Ratna was working on the novel in isolation, Dinesh became tired of selling ice cream and went off to Taos, New Mexico to become an artist. He was not heard from again but continued to live on in Ratna's novel. I decided it was a good time to go to Devinagar, India, to begin my long deferred search for my mother.

# III.

## Devinagar, India

### *A Cousin, An Aunt, Camels and Eleanor Roosevelt*

There was one hotel in Devinagar and it was called Hotel Niketan. It had ten rooms, four bathrooms—two Indian style, two European style—and a restaurant that served tea, chicken puffs, and onion, eggplant, and potato pakoras. The Niketan rooms were usually vacant since most people who visited Devinagar had family or friends in town.

The verandah of Hotel Niketan was the best place to collect news and gossip about everyone in town. Given the appropriate amount of time, some news became myths and legends. Ancestresses who had defied their mothers-in-law, raised children single-handedly, or those who had fought with Gandhiji became avatars of warrior Goddesses or wise women with mysterious powers. Ancestors who had renounced the world or taken on the world as soldiers or successful businessmen were transformed into saints, sages, or heroes of epic proportions. They possessed chariots that flew and swords that spoke. Children lamented for their early deaths became dream spirits or shape changers. Normal events such as marriages, births, deaths, family feuds, the demise of an export-import store, the appearance of Europeans and Americans in search of drugs, took on the language of elaborate, stylized dramas. The Hotel Niketan verandah was a Carmelita kind of place.

Hotel Niketan survived mainly on the numerous cups of tea and the platters of pakoras that were purchased every evening to accompany the daily gathering, dissemination, dissection, and recreation of Devinagar news.

I did not find my English mother in Devinagar but I did find my paternal aunt, Agnes Driver, born Agnes Cooper. I found my Aunt Agnes through

Devinagar's self-styled "leading lady lawyer" Roxanne Japanwallah. Roxanne Japanwallah walked into the Niketan restaurant for her weekly dose of pakoras and gossip half an hour after I arrived in Devinagar from Bombay. Following Ratna's instructions, I had eaten cheese sandwiches on the train and no meat, fruit or vegetables. I was hungry by the time I checked into the Niketan. I had barely finished giving my order for pakoras when I was joined at my table by a woman with intelligent eyes, an unforgettable voice, and graying hair cut short by the bluntest pair of scissors. She was wearing a red sari with a border of beautifully embroidered birds and flowers. Without asking for permission to sit at my table, she sat down across from me. There were at least four empty tables on the Niketan verandah that evening. She turned out to be Roxanne Japanwallah who was not only a lawyer in Devinagar but also a cousin of mine. A few times removed.

Roxanne Japanwallah had never been known to encounter a stranger in Devinagar without initiating a conversation. It usually began with a strong handshake, which startled foreigners who had been instructed never to offer a handshake to an Indian woman, accompanied by, "How do you do? I am Roxanne Japanwallah. I am from one of the oldest Devinagar families. If you need a lawyer, do please come to me. Even if you have no money. I am the leading lady lawyer of Devinagar. And if you need help in locating anyone in Devinagar, come to my house. My companion Nanibai will help you. She was at one time the founding president of the Devinagar Lady Thieves' Union. She is quite reformed now, but she still has a very useful network of friends and helpers."

Most Indians did not find Roxanne's introduction too lengthy or overly disturbing, but I was quite taken aback by her extravagance. It also took me some time to get used to her habit of echoing words in strange forms— "family-bamily," "English-finglish," "martyr-tamartyr"—practice appropriated from her mother language Gujarati and frowned upon or denied by the more genteel members of her family and community. Some of her fellow members of the Devinagar judiciary had tried in vain to tell her to speak clear, regular English. Apparently whenever they asked her to keep to one language, by which they meant, "Use the Royal English," Roxanne spoke in Gujarati and then mixed English forms into the language. Whenever it was announced that Roxanne Japanwallah was going to defend a client in court, residents of Devinagar came to witness the drama. They sometimes sent her notes offering her their own versions of deformed, re-formed words. I understood all this about Roxanne and language much later, after I had begun to learn Gujarati and after she had led me through a terrifying labyrinth of relatives.

When she sat down at my table uninvited—I introduced myself as "Katy Cooper from America, the daughter of Freddy and Margaret Cooper." Roxanne replied, "How very interesting! You are the niece of Agnes Driver. She is one of the reigning matriarchs of Devinagar. You and I are cousins." And then without waiting for any response from me, she went on to tell me that my family name was not the English "Cooper" but the Parsi "Cooper" and that my father was not a man from Europe who had spent a short time in India. He had been an Indian who had spent some time in England, returned to India, gone back to England and then gone to Mexico to try his fortune. He was a Freddy from Fareidun not Frederick. I could now explain to myself my own skin, eyes, and hair. Carmelita would feel relieved and triumphant. I also learned from my self-proclaimed cousin Roxanne that my father had not been a Catholic like the devout Sanderses, "not any kind of Christian," but a Zoroastrian, a Parsi. This, according to her, justified my long, thin nose with the hint of a hook at the end of it, which had been a source of anxiety and embarrassment for me from the age of thirteen to sixteen. My best friend of those years, Eileen Taylor, had a TV-commercial perfect nose.

Roxanne praised my nose and warned me about it. "It's a wonderful nose. A distinctly Parsi nose. But the hook will get more pronounced as you grow older and if your eyes remain as dark and sharp as they are now, children brought up on *The Wizard of Oz* will take you for a witch. Not the good, sweet one. The other one with the monkeys and the peanut-brittle laughter."

I told Roxanne that the only Parsi I had encountered was the mysterious figure in *Moby Dick*.

Roxanne snorted in a manner that Theresa Sanders would have considered most unladylike and said, "Moby Dick-Foby Dick. I will tell you about us Parsis Jarthoshtis. Jarthoshti turned into Zoroastrian! It's all this language-fanguage thing." And then she proceeded to tell me about Zoroastrianism. "The only rule to follow is: Speak good words. Think good thoughts. Do good deeds. Fight for the right cause! That is if you can discover the best way to fight for the right cause of course. And do not hang on to dead corpses."

I pointed out that she was being redundant. She agreed with me that corpses are dead and then pointed out that "we Jarthoshtis" do not bury, do not cremate. Dead Zoroastrians were to be placed in the Towers of Silence. Until recently a dog would be brought into the room where the Zoroastrian corpse lay, in order to make sure that the corpse was really dead because dogs supposedly turn away from dead corpses. Only then was the corpse taken away to the Towers of Silence for the vultures to feed.

I decided there and then against a Zoroastrian funeral. I told Roxanne that my friend Ratna believed that the reason sex and death had become related in people's minds was due to the custom of burial and the establishment of cemeteries.

I shouldn't have been surprised when Roxanne said, "There is nothing sensible or reasonable about death, politics, or sex."

Roxanne insisted on accompanying me next day to the Cooper home where my aunt Agnes Cooper Driver resided.

A sturdy cement ramp, which started at the front door of my father's house, cut across the deteriorating garden and ended at the iron gates that opened up to the street. The gates had not been closed for many years and the iron had rusted under the assault of monsoon rains and the ground underneath had been pushed upwards, cracking under the pressure of the roots of an enormous banyan tree that grew outside on the road, a few yards from the house. That afternoon when Roxanne took me to meet Agnes Driver, crows were making a tremendous racket in the branches of the tree, stalls selling soda water, cigarettes and paans were set up between the numerous trunks of the tree. Two little girls had established their imaginary house in the safe circle of five new trunks. Plastic and crystal chandeliers for sale hung from some of the fibers that had not quite reached the ground.

The multiplying tree in front of my paternal ancestral home reminded me of a series of caves. Caves without solid walls. Some of the roots looked as if they had always been fixed into the earth while others seemed very happy to remain above ground, hanging down from branches. When I first saw the tree, I thought of Ratna's way of distinguishing stalactites from stalagmites. A stalactite, she said hung on tight, afraid to let go. Stalactite dharma, according to Ratna, was not to fall down. For the stalagmite, its dharma was to endeavor to stretch upwards so it might, if its karma so decreed, reach the top. I had always envisioned a lot of effort on the part of stalactites and stalagmites as they attempted to fulfill their dharmas. But the many-rooted tree in Devinagar carried on its business, circling back upon itself, without any effort or sound. Only the crows, the humans and the transistor radios were busy creating noise within the shelter of the tree.

Roxanne introduced me to Agnes Driver. "Agnesmai, this is your niece from America. She has a photograph of herself with Freddy and Margaret and her name is Katy Cooper. Katy, remember you are having dinner with me and my companions, Nanibai and Saleem, tomorrow night." And then she left.

Agnes Driver, sitting regally in her pink upholstered wheel chair, said, "Your name is Katayun, not Katy. I will call you Katayun. I am very, very happy to meet you at last."

"Not Katherine?" I asked.

"No, your Katy is not from Katherine with a capital K or a capital C. It isn't even Kathleen. Not with capital C's or K's, double ee's or one y or l or r. It's Katy from Katayun, Empress of Pars. You were named in honor of Katayun Cooper. She was my lovely, wonderful mother and of course, your father Fareidun's mother. Your paternal grandmother. How I envy your name! I always wanted a good Parsi name from Iran instead of my English grandmother's name. The name of your paternal great-grandmother, Agnes Mason."

According to a story I heard later, Agnes had thrown an impressive temper tantrum when she discovered the meaning of her name. Agnes was eight years old at that time. Miss Jones, her teacher, announced to her students that only one of them had a civilized, English name. And that was Agnes. A name, this Parsi child should learn to live up to. As soon as Agnes heard the meaning of her name, she asked to be taken home because she had developed a very bad ache in her stomach. When she reached home, she screamed, she jumped up and down, she even tried to pull out a few strands of her hair and demanded that her name be changed. At once. She made it clear that she wasn't a lamb, she wasn't meek, she wasn't mild and much as she wanted very curly hair, she certainly did not want white wool all over her. She was content with the sweaters her mother knitted for her every year to shield her from the two month's of Devinagar's winter. She couldn't decide between Avamai and Alamai for her new name. But she did think that it would be good to have a grown-up sounding name with a respectful "mai" at the end. Young Agnes wanted to be Avamother or Alamother. It was one of the few times in Agnes' childhood that her father didn't indulge her. She remained Agnes. She told me that being called "Agnesmai" was at least a reward for having survived into old age.

Right after she told me that I was really Katayun, my Aunt Agnes said that American women had always fascinated her. "Because they come in so many shapes, sizes, colors, and dimensions. Look at you, Katayun. You and Ella Fitzgerald and Doris Day and Eleanor Roosevelt . . . all Americans! The only other place that happens is right here in India. Look at Devinagar. You and I and Roxanne and Nanibai and my old friend Safia who died last year and of course Margaret Shriver who used to live here. Amazing!" And then she began to tell me about Eleanor Roosevelt's visit to Karachi.

Agnes Cooper's story about Eleanor Roosevelt began with, "When I was nearly thirteen years old, my father Eddie Cooper decided to send me away from Devinagar to Karachi for a few years. He said that he could no longer live in the same house or even the same small town with a daughter who never stopped running. Katayun, you should have seen me then, my dear! I used to run up and down the marble staircase, across the front lawn with the English roses, through the back vegetable garden with the peas, tomatoes, barren mango tree, lotus pond and three resident snakes and then throughout this town of Devinagar with all its Hindu temples, Christian churches, Muslim mosques and the one Zoroastrian agiari. And of course, every one knew that I collected an amazing amount of information as I moved from place to place. My father didn't like that. And so I was sent off as a boarder to the Mama Parsi Girls' High School in Karachi. Karachi had just become the capital of the newly established Pakistan. The 'Mama' had nothing to do with a mother or a maternal uncle. It was the family name of the school's benevolent founder."

It was much later, when Agnes was about seventeen, that she discovered why she had been sent off to Karachi. Margaret Shriver was pregnant. Margaret was known to be her father's, my Grandfather Eddie Cooper's mistress. It was also suspected that she was his son's, my father Freddy Cooper's lover. It was a nasty situation. Eddie Cooper was worried that with all the ground his daughter covered and all the information she collected, she would discover the current Devinagar scandal. Margaret miscarried but Agnes was sent off anyway.

There were only two events during her three years in Karachi that Aunt Agnes remembered as being significant. One was her introduction to camels and the other was Eleanor Roosevelt's visit to Karachi.

Camels, according to my aunt, were like the region east and south of San Diego, California. They were both made from the materials which were left over after the main creation of the world. Unusable rocks for the land and mismatched bones for the animals. She had seen the borderlands of southern California during her honeymoon trip to Los Angeles. She did not remember much about her husband's relatives who had emigrated from Bombay to Los Angeles and with whom she and her husband spent two weeks. But she did remember one of the daughters wanting to be a film actress and arguing with her family that learning to recite the speeches of Shakespeare's heroines, with the correct English diction and much wringing of hands, would not make her a film star. In her more ridiculous moments, my Aunt Agnes had been known to insist that she saw her aspiring actress relative-in-law years later in a Hollywood film in the role of a junior wife in a harem.

Agnes blamed her hatred of traveling by air on the twenty-two hour wait she had to endure those many years ago in the Los Angeles airport. And many years after that delay at the airport, she was still angry. She was angry because due to missed airline connections she hadn't been able to visit her older cousin Dinaz Mehta, and Dinaz Mehta's baby daughter, Kamal, in Wisconsin, USA.

She explained to me, while telling me about Karachi and San Diego and camels and Eleanor Roosevelt, that she and I and Roxanne and Dinaz Mehta Mehta, "yes, maiden name Mehta, married name Mehta, a Parsi Mehta and a Hindu Mehta" were family-connected through a Parsi man from India and a Chinese woman from Malaysia. The two had met and married in Malaysia. Our Indian ancestor had chosen to remain in Malaysia with his Chinese wife but had selected one child, their second son, to return to India. The son was initiated into the Zoroastrian religion and set up his branch of the family, which became known in Bombay and Devinagar as the "Japanwallah family."

The day after my visit with Aunt Agnes, Roxanne Japanwallah tried to show me how the Coopers and the Mehtas were connected to the Japanwallah family. The Japanwallahs seemed to have connections from India to Iran to Malaysia to China to the United States of America. But as far as anyone knew, the Japanwallahs had no connections with Japan.

I tried not to groan at Aunt Agnes's story about the Indian man, the Chinese woman, the American cousin. Theresa Sanders had taught me that groaning in public was impolite. But I must have looked dazed and stunned.

"What is it dear?" my Aunt Agnes asked me.

I said, in my most polite voice, "I didn't know I had so many relatives." What I really wanted to do was to yell, "You are quite a wonderful lady and I am glad you are my aunt. But I want to go home where all I have are my two dear friends, Ratna and Carmelita. I just want to find my mother. I don't want so many relatives! I am content with you and Roxanne."

I didn't yell even when she said, "Don't worry dear, we have just started with some of them. I don't want to overwhelm you. But Roxanne will tell you all about what she calls 'the who is who in the annals of the Japanwallah-Cooper-Mehta family-bamily.' I just want to tell you about my favorite cousin, Dinaz Mehta. She ended up in America. Just like Fareidun and you."

"I think that my father spent very little time in America. He was mainly in Mexico. He died there."

"I know that, Katayun. But it's all the same to me. North America, South

America, in-between America. All of it is so far away! Now, about our cousin, Dinaz Mehta. Of course your father was still in India or England—I can't remember—when I went to California. I wanted to see Dinaz Mehta because Dinaz had been my heroine ever since the day I found out that she and her fiancé, Ashok Mehta, had decided to fight for India's independence by making bombs to throw against our British rulers. This was before I was sent off to Karachi. The two Mehta families were heartbroken and terrified at their children's actions. The families were neighbors and satyagrahis. Followers of our Gandhiji. They wore hand-woven khadi, went on the great salt march and attended classes in passive resistance while their daughter and son, happy to wear whatever their parents gave them to wear, attended secret meetings advocating violent resistance. When the two families discovered what was going on, they married off the two young people and quickly smuggled them out of British India. Dinaz and Ashok were sent off to America with the financial assistance of Roxanne's Grandmother Meheramai and my mother, your grandmother, Katayun. Those two women were also followers of Gandhiji. Dinaz's husband, Ashok, I hear, was killed in New York while Dinaz was pregnant. When I got married some years after all that had happened, I agreed to that honeymoon in America—so far away from India—because I wanted to meet my older cousin again. And to see her daughter. And anyway, the other choice was England. Which I refused to even consider."

From the rest of her story, I surmised that my aunt, furious at not being able to see Dinaz, had survived the wait at the Los Angeles airport without driving her husband crazy because she was able to make friends with a fellow traveler, Mary Mattson. Mary Mattson and Agnes Driver talked about various matters, including viruses, politics, religion, opera and Eleanor Roosevelt.

Dr Mary Mattson was a scientist and loved opera. Operas, according to my aunt, were created from leftover sounds. But she didn't divulge that information to Mary Mattson because she wanted a conversation, not an argument or a polite silence. When Aunt Agnes discovered that Mary Mattson's mother had spent her life trying to navigate around the fact that the Virgin Mary had been known to appear, disguised as a vagrant, to test human faith and basic goodness, she told her new friend, Mary, that her mother was absolutely correct.

"Katayun dear, Mary Mattson looked a bit ashamed of what her mother believed so I told her that in Devinagar we exist quite cheerfully with the knowledge that the Goddess is constantly present among us. In and out of disguise. Of course so is God. In all His forms. But He seems a bit far away and very busy with other affairs. Our mothers, doctors, teachers, journalists and even lawyers use the Goddess, in one way or another, as their special source of secret information. Information which has been given to them in order to make life more just, more understandable or merely less boring. I told Mary Mattson that everyone in Devinagar knows that a female deity in the form of a large white bird presides over everyone's birth in Devinagar. And it will appear again at the time of death."

Dr Mattson had matched my aunt's stories about Devinagar with the highlight of her family history: The day her father Tony Mattson, tipped his hat to Eleanor Roosevelt and said "Good morning Mrs Roosevelt" when he saw her on the steps of the Capitol in Washington, DC. Aunt Agnes was absolutely delighted.

Many years after her meeting with Mary Mattson my aunt beamed at me in her living room in Devinagar and said, "You see, Katayun, I was fated to meet Mary Mattson. I have a vested interest in Eleanor Roosevelt."

Long before Agnes Cooper had gotten married and visited America and met Mary Mattson, while Agnes was still a young girl at the Mama Parsi Girls' High School in Karachi, the Government of Pakistan was informed that Eleanor Roosevelt would be visiting Karachi. The schools in Karachi were notified that the students were to line the route of Eleanor Roosevelt's motorcade from the airport to Government House. They were dressed in their school uniforms and each of them was given a small green and white Pakistani flag and a small red, white and blue American flag. They were told that they were to wave both flags with great enthusiasm and smile as Eleanor Roosevelt's car passed by. It was known that Eleanor Roosevelt was most interested in the education of girls and therefore the girls' schools were allocated the more visible places along the motorcade route. The Mama Parsi Girls' High School students were taken to their designated place on Victoria Road in front of the Bai Virbaiji Soparivala Parsi Boys' School on big flat carts pulled by camels.

The camels, according to my aunt, were the only unexcited members of the trip.

The young Agnes, in exile from her father's home in Devinagar, had found herself between Naheed Suleiman, the lone Muslim girl in her class and Roshni Behram Ghadiali who had been savagely hissed at by a camel as she crossed Bunder Road. Naheed had told Roshni that she would be safe from camels and other attacking creatures, if she would just cover herself with a burqua. My Aunt Agnes told me that she was still thinking about that. She wasn't sure that Naheed was absolutely wrong.

Their classmate, Thrity Kerawallah, was also in the vicinity. Thrity

Kerawallah, my aunt said to me, did not speak very often but when she did, she made pronouncements. She spoke in headlines. She exclaimed. She proclaimed. And she always won first prize in elocution competitions. My aunt and her friends were always quite impressed by her.

Naheed had confided to my aunt that whenever Thrity recited her Portia speech, Naheed's right arm began to twitch. It was an arm well-trained in the art of mashing and straining lentils, dried beans and split peas through a colander and that, said Naheed to Agnes, is what her arm thought it was being told to do when Thrity got under way with the quality of mercy not being strained. Agnes Cooper tried to explain to Naheed Suleiman that Portia's speech had nothing to do with cooking, mashing and straining daal. But daal and Portia's speech were stuck together in Naheed's mind. As for my aunt, she did not think of lentils and daal when she heard about the quality of mercy. She had visions of the K-Wality restaurant across from the Regal Cinema on Preedy Street, not far from Mama School.

Aunt Agnes stopped her story to say that K-Wality had blue walls and the best bright green pistachio ice cream she have ever tasted. "What is your favorite ice-cream flavor, Katayun?" she asked me.

"Pistachio." I wasn't lying. I wondered how Ratna's story about the ice cream-selling detective was progressing in San Francisco.

Aunt Agnes told me that she would get me the best pistachio ice cream in Devinagar. But on that special day of Eleanor Roosevelt's visit to Karachi, Agnes, Roshni, Naheed, and Thrity were not happy. They had been told to line up next to the younger girls. They wanted to be closer to the senior students. After all, Naheed, only a few months older than Roshni, Thrity and Agnes, had already had her first period nearly a year ago. But before the four of them could negotiate a more prestigious arrangement, they heard the motorcade.

Aunt Agnes, sitting in her pink upholstered wheelchair, talking to me about her childhood memories said, "Everything started to move faster and faster and at the same time everything seemed to have frozen into an off-focus photograph. Like a nightmare. You know the type, Katayun, when the legs are moving fast but the body remains stuck in the same place? And the monster that somehow never seems to get stuck, comes closer and closer. Just like that. The white uniforms of the school children, the flags being waved, the motorcycles thundering by, the first line of cars, all began to blur together, stood still. And then just as the car with the American lady drove towards us, we heard Thrity's voice. 'Agnes, Roshni, Naheed look! *Look*! Even camels get it!'

"The three of us followed Thrity's voice, eyes and finger pointing backwards, away from the motorcade, away from the American lady, until we found ourselves looking at the camel who had pulled our cart. She was bleeding and the camel driver was tying a rag around her nether regions. Thrity continued, 'C..c..c..camels also get p..p..periods!' The four of us were amazed and educated.

"Katayun dear, don't you see? I told you I was fated to meet Mary Mattson. Her mother believed in female deities descending and her father had looked Eleanor Roosevelt right in the eye and had tipped his hat to her. I look at the pictures of Eleanor Roosevelt whenever I get the chance. Magazines, books, old cinema news reels. And really, dear, she has the look of a camel about her. A benevolent camel. An endearing one. A most camel-like look. Don't you think so Katayun dear?"

I did not know what was expected of me. A "yes," a "no," a "how interesting," or silence. She did not wait for an answer.

"Of course, because we were looking at Thrity's bleeding camel, we didn't see Eleanor Roosevelt. She rushed by so fast. And I was staring at Thrity. I realized that she had stammered. Thrity who never stammered. But my brother Fareidun stammered whenever our father laughed at him. And sometimes to make our mother laugh, Fareidun would call her Katy and sing that ridiculous K..K..Katy song to her. Margaret, who was supposedly your mother, named you Katy. For Katayun. Most probably she did not know who your father was. My late father? My late brother? Maybe even my late husband? So she named you Katy. For the wife or the mother or the mother-in-law. She could have easily named you after me. Agnes. For the daughter, the sister or the wife. But there you are. One never quite understands these things. You are named after my mother by your mother. Or most probably, by your father."

As she continued to talk about her school friends, about Mary Mattson, about camels, pistachio ice cream and the naming of children, I remembered how my father would sing "K..K..K..Katy" to me whenever I needed comfort and solace. I saw the black butterfly fly into my aunt's living room. The old woman walked in and sat down on one side of a love seat, facing my aunt. I looked at her sitting with her bare feet tucked under her on the sofa and thought that there might have been a parrot in my father's home in Mexico who had learned to repeat the Katy song my father sang to me. I remembered the last time my father had stammered out my name. The stammering was not an act. He was not singing. He was falling down, carrying me down with him, telling me to run for safety to his employer, Mr Sanders. I was not really sure of that memory.

My aunt lifted the woolen tea cozy with maple leaves embroidered in

Kashmiri chain stitches from the English china teapot placed in front of her wheelchair. She poured herself another cup of tea, offered me a plate of Peak Freans Ginger Crisps and said, "Oh yes, this lady has appeared on and off in this room and in my bedroom ever since I got that formal letter from the Sanderses from Mexico informing me that my brother had died. They also told me that he had made them your guardians and they were leaving for the United States taking you with them. But I never could get their address in the States. Even my old friend Mary Mattson could not find them. You know, I loved your father very dearly. I wish he had sent you to me. But that is all in the past. And you have discovered me again and you will come and visit me again. Do you know who this old lady is?"

I said, "No, I don't know who she is. And you are the only one who has seen her. Besides myself. At least as far as I know. My friends Carmelita and Ratna know about her but they have never seen her."

"Of course I see her. I am your aunt. And this is Devinagar after all. Does she always follow you wherever you go?"

"Yes. Since I first saw her. I sometimes doubt my sanity. Being trailed by a barefoot old woman I don't know and no one else can see! And we can't even talk to one another. Not very sensible is it?"

"As our Roxanne would say, 'sensible-fensible.' Sensible according to whom? I can see the old woman. She seems quite sane. A bit stubborn and eccentric. Amazing, isn't she? Old, barefoot, the scar on her neck, and that lovely embroidered blouse. Clothes no self-respecting woman of her age is supposed to wear but which of course, only self-respecting old women should wear! And those ribbons in her hair! Have you checked up on that pain in your knees?"

I know how to handle segues in conversations. It is the way Carmelita talks to others, to herself, and to her angel and the Virgin of Soledad.

"According to the doctors, there is no reason for the pain. The pain is not supposed to be there."

"Nonsense! Have you tried hypnosis? Do eat one of these biscuits." She again offered the plate of Peak Freans to me. "Your father's favorite biscuits. I am sure Nanibai, Roxanne's unofficial chaperone and housemate, will see your lady tomorrow night when you go to their house. Roxanne might see her but she will not think it at all strange and so will not even comment on her. On the other hand, she might be so busy telling you all about her family and our family that she will see nothing. But Nanibai—yes, she will see her. She sees everything and knows nearly everything worth knowing. But she will most probably not say much. She doesn't always talk too much."

Agnes looked in the direction of the old woman and smiled. "Maybe she has shown herself to me because she knows that I loved my brother and I have always loved you. Even though I couldn't find you for so many years! Did you have the pain when you were in Mexico with your father?"

I told her that the pain had started after I left Mexico. But I wasn't sure. I didn't have many memories of Mexico.

"Don't worry, dear, one day you will remember. And if you don't, all of us in Devinagar will give you all our memories to fill up those vacant places. Roxanne and I will talk to you and we will write to you when you go back to California. We will tell you stories, good gup-sup gossip, rumors. And maybe one day, this lady will tell you something."

And Agnes smiled and raised her teacup in salute to the old woman. I didn't want to see if the old woman smiled back at her. I didn't want to confess to my aunt that the old woman had begun to scare me. I couldn't ignore her anymore. I didn't ask her if she also saw the black butterfly flying around the room.

# IV.

## Devinagar, India

### *The Terrifying Labyrinth of Relatives*

As my Aunt Agnes had predicted, I found out much more about my family from Roxanne Japanwallah the next evening, my third day in Devinagar.

Roxanne had cooked rice, daal and spinach for us. Her eighty-year-old companion, Nanibai, had persuaded Roxanne to cook mashed potatoes and to heat a can of American baked beans as well, in case their visitor from the USA didn't like Indian food and wasn't willing to try Roxanne's special rendition of Parsi daal—three types of lentils, lots of onions, red chilies, garlic, spicy masaala and vegetables served over fried rice carrying the aromas of cinnamon and raw brown sugar. I loved it. Roxanne's lover of many years, Saleem Ahmed, ate the daal with the mashed potatoes. He ate American baked beans only with people who couldn't eat Indian food. Saleem was the only pharmacist and bookseller of Devinagar. As we were eating, he wondered aloud if he should go to Dubai to make enough money to buy a new refrigerator and fan for his store that was also his home. Roxanne told him to forget about "Dubai-fubai" because even if he came back a rich man, he would never get a new refrigerator or fan since he always used whatever money he earned to set up scholarships for the Devinagar fishermen's children. "You can keep on doing that right here. Earning whatever you do earn in Devinagar. Maybe you can sell your books and stuff on a sliding scale instead of giving *everyone* a discount. And anyway who would join me in my detective work if you leave?"

"Nanibai will still be with you. She is our real leader," said Saleem.

Roxanne and Saleem became friends when they were nine years old and two of their teachers decided to see which child was more intelligent. They had both won according to the teachers. Roxanne because she thought and talked fast. Saleem because he took his own time to think and speak. No one in Devinagar dared to question them when fifteen years later they decided to become lovers and announced that they would not marry until they were sixty years old, and could call upon at least one grandchild to act as a witness to their marriage. Roxanne's Grandmother Meheramai had given Roxanne her small home and Saleem his two-room pharmacy-book-store-home as her pre-wedding gifts. She didn't expect to be around when Roxanne and Saleem were sixty years old but she wanted the citizens of Devinagar—especially Roxanne's father—to realize that she blessed a union in whatever form between Roxanne and Saleem.

The quiet expressions of the passion between Saleem and Roxanne were a bit unnerving for someone brought up in Theresa Sanders's home, where sex and even love had scientific explanations. Lust was a word I discovered when a friend in high school lent me her mother's copy of a historical romance. It was about a Lady Serena and the pirate Jonathan who was really a duke in disguise. My foster mother discovered the book under my mattress. I wasn't a very original child. She shook her head and tsked-tsked and told me to return it to my friend. Gregory Sanders insisted on reading the book before I returned it. For Halloween that year he dressed up as a pirate and went around town singing silly pirate songs and with a sandwich board over his pirate costume which said, "Where, oh where is Lady Serena?" Theresa Sanders and I refused to be seen with him in public for at least two weeks.

My cousin Roxanne and I were very different. From our brief acquaintance, I realized that even as a child she would have walked with my foster father around town singing the pirate songs.

Roxanne had decided to educate me about the Cooper-Japanwallah-Mehta families by preparing an annotated bibliography.

I, who knew nothing about my birth mother except that she was a beautiful and polite Englishwoman, and had forgotten anything my father might have told me about my family, found Roxanne's genealogy terrifying and bewildering. Perhaps if she had mapped it out with lines and circles and triangles and colors, I might have found it acceptable. I looked at the long sheet of paper in my hands, said thank you and gave it back to Roxanne. Nanibai laughed. Saleem, whose family consisted only of his widowed mother and her brother, glanced at the genealogy and said that Roxanne might as well have gone all the way back to Adam and Eve. Roxanne told us that for Zoroastrians the first mother was Mashyani, "ancestress of Eve and everyone else." Mashyani, according to Roxanne, had six pairs of twins. Roxanne also said that through her written genealogy she was trying to explain to me how she and I and her mother's cousin Dinaz and Dinaz's daughter Kamal,—"they are in the United States, you really should make an effort to meet them, Katy"—were related.

Nanibai said, "Very simple. You are all descended from the Parsi gentleman who went to China, married a Chinese lady, had many children, remained in China and sent back one son. Your great-great-grandparents either on your father's side or your mother's side are the Parsi gentleman and his Chinese wife. Khattum—that is all there is to it."

But of course that wasn't all that there was to it. There were stories about the different members of the family. I learned that my paternal grandfather's actual, legal name was Edward. His mother, described by Roxanne as "a high Anglican, Church of England, confessions, incense and all, English lady" had insisted that although her only child, her son, was to be initiated into his father's ancient Zoroastrian faith, he would have a European name, Edward. Edward became Eddie to his friends but remained Edward to his mother.

"Edward" said Roxanne, "was transformed into Edulji by the officiating mobeds when they included his name in the family prayers of rejoicing and thanksgiving. Good priests that they were, they refused to include an English name in the prayers. God knows what they do now with so many of our children being named Natashas and Seans and Neils and Jennifers. Ballet, *War and Peace*, Hollywood, and American soap operas have had their way with us. Anyway, according to my Grandmother Meheramai, the English "Agnes" was included in the prayers as "Arnazmai." I think that is the name they use when they pray for your Auntie Agnes."

Eddie Cooper disliked his son, my father Freddie because he was not a healthy boy child, he tended to turn to others for protection, looked like his mother and was very intelligent. Father and son agreed on one point. The British. They revered their foreign masters. My grandfather and my father also loved Agnes. She was beautiful and bright and noisy. Agnes was in awe of her gentle mother and loved her father. But she loved her quiet, studious brother Freddie the best. She always gave her brother gifts from England such as walking sticks, biscuit tins with royal portraits on them, and replicas of the Buckingham Palace, the Royal Coach and the Tower of London.

It was Agnes Cooper Driver who fascinated Roxanne and Saleem the most, but it was Nanibai who knew most of the stories about young Agnes. When Agnes was barely eighteen years old she married Rohinton Driver who had come from Bombay as a junior partner in one of her father's business ventures. Rohinton Driver loved to dance. Waltzes, fox trots, rhumbas, tangos. And of course, so did Agnes. Roxanne remembered "distinctly" that Agnes' husband always wore white shoes and that as soon as he married Agnes everyone called him Roy. Except his wife Agnes and her mother Katayun. As a young boy, Saleem was fascinated by the number of suits and ties Rohinton Driver seemed to possess. Suits and ties, said Saleem, were two of the biggest jokes the British had tried to play on India.

I began to rub my knees and bent down to rub my ankles as I sat there listening to the stories about my father's sister told by Roxanne Japanwallah, the leading lady lawyer of Devinagar, and Saleem, beloved by citizens of Devinagar who searched for books or needed medicines. Roxanne didn't seem to notice my pain but Saleem brought a blanket from Roxanne's bedroom and draped it across my legs. He also pulled a small coffee table closer to me to put up my feet. I noticed that his hands were long, slender and callused. I found out later that he also worked as a carpenter building bookcases and tables for the public library, the school library and sometimes for private homes. As Saleem went back to sit beside Roxanne, Nanibai told us that after Rohinton died, Agnes had given Rohinton's suits and ties to Saleem's uncle. To use, to share, to give away or to burn.

"Because" said Roxanne, "Your Auntie Agnes didn't like her husband very much."

Two years after her marriage, my Aunt Agnes found out that her husband had a mistress. She shrugged, bought herself a baby cheetah, walked around Devinagar with her pet on a leash and said nothing. Roxanne and Saleem loved that cheetah. It had one orange eye and one blue eye. Roxanne decided that she would get a cheetah when she was grown up and walk around Devinagar with it. When Agnes found out that Rohinton's mistress was Margaret Shriver, her father's mistress, the cause of her banishment to Karachi and the endless pain in her proud mother's eyes, she said nothing. The morning after she found out the name of her husband's mistress, she announced that she was unable to leave her bed. She refused to stand up, she refused to walk. She donated the cheetah to the zoo in Bombay. She had her bed moved to the window facing the back vegetable garden. She refused to move out of her bed. She refused to leave the house.

Saleem and Roxanne missed both the cheetah and Agnes. When Roxanne's grandmother told Agnes that the children—Roxanne and Saleem—missed seeing her and the cheetah, Agnes invited them to visit her on the second and fourth Thursday of every month. She taught Saleem to knit and Roxanne to cut wood and hammer nails during those Thursdays. Apparently, my Aunt Agnes's room had been turned into a workshop of sorts for the two children.

When her husband was killed in a car accident about eight months after she took to her bed, Agnes did not go downstairs for the funeral. When her mother, Katayun, died ten months later Agnes asked her brother to carry her downstairs for the funeral. She heard rumors about a possible affair between her brother Freddy and Margaret. She heard the arguments between her father and brother. She demanded that their arguments not be brought into her bedroom when they came to visit her every evening. She refused to even try to walk, and after some time said she didn't want to see any doctor or hakim who might have cured her. There was a Muslim pir who did visit her often. She told Roxanne's Grandmother Meheramai that she liked "this delightfully unselfrighteous, unholy holy man" to visit her because he told her wonderful stories. Her father and brother dined with her in her room at least three times a week and Freddy spent an hour with her every morning to share the newspapers he received from Bombay and Karachi.

I tried to picture my father Freddy reading newspapers in our house in Mexico. But I could not even remember the house I had lived in with him. The rooms, the furniture, the angle of the light as it entered the house. Those were lost to me. All that remained were the colors and the sounds of the landscape surrounding the house, the voice of my father, his face, and his smile.

Roxanne's Grandmother Meheramai and her friends had held their Devinagar Ladies' Reading, Sewing and Charitable Group meetings at least twice a month in the Cooper house. Depending on how Agnes was feeling, they met in her bedroom or in the living room presided over by Buckingham Palace, the Tower of London and the Royal Coach. The models of the palace, tower and coach had been presents from a quite anti-British young Agnes to her very pro-British older brother, my father Freddy. They were supposedly proofs of her love for him regardless of his political beliefs.

Political discussions and debates seemed to have been the main topic of conversation for the Devinagar Ladies' Group. The founding members had all been in favor of the Quit India movement, and any woman who didn't share their passionate resolve to send the British back to Britain was subtly but firmly excluded from the DLRSCG. Some women took it as a mark of patriotic duty to their overseas rulers to request membership and be rejected. Other women promised to mend their ways and fight for India if accepted by the group.

Ten years after the British left India, Eddie informed Agnes that he was going to England to settle down with Margaret. He invited Agnes to go with them. She refused. As soon as Eddie left India to settle down in England, Agnes took down the portrait of Queen Victoria from the dining room wall. Agnes insisted that Queen Victoria in that portrait had worn a shimmering Jell-O dislodged from its mold onto her head as a crown.

Margaret had not left India in 1947, when her parents and the other British left. A few years before independence, my father, Freddy, had gone off to some place or another. Most probably to England. But when he heard about his father's plans to go to England with Margaret, he returned to India to persuade Margaret Shriver to go off with him. She had once again announced that she was pregnant. According to Nanibai, no one believed my mother. My Aunt Agnes remained silent even when she and everyone in Devinagar saw Freddy's terrible depression because my mother insisted on going off to England with my grandfather, Eddie.

"I tell you, Katy," Roxanne felt she should console me about my mother's treatment of my father. "Your father was a deluded man, but even with all his disappointments, he remained a kind man."

I remembered my father as a kind man. I did not remember him as being deluded. But then my memories of him were incomplete. I did not want to argue with Roxanne. I wished the pain in my legs would ease up. That the old barefoot woman would just leave. That I could be back in Half Moon Bay walking through the familiar, comforting fog. The late evening heat of Devinagar had wrapped itself around me like a soggy quilt as I listened to Roxanne talking about my parents, Freddy and Margaret, my Aunt Agnes and my Grandfather Eddie.

Roxanne looked at me as I shifted in my chair, brought an extra cushion for me and continued.

"Your Auntie Agnes did not say anything when she saw your father—of course he was not your father then—suffering, but she did find out that she had truly lost the use of her legs when she tried to run to him to stop him from shooting himself. By the way, I don't know when or where Freddy and Margaret got together to conceive you but I don't think they were ever married. But somehow, somewhere, you were born and Freddy took care of you."

I got up. I wanted to leave. I didn't want to hear any more of Roxanne's stories. But the pain in my knees forced me back into the chair. Nanibai put out a hand toward me. Roxanne came over and patted me on my head.

Saleem reached over and began to massage my feet. I felt that for a brief time, I had found my real home.

"It was not a very successful attempt," said Roxanne. She wasn't very disturbed. After all, for her, it was just an old Devinagar, often repeated, Japanwallah-Cooper-Mehta family story.

When the cook, Ferdinand Pereira, shouted that Freddybaba had locked himself in the library with a gun, Agnes tried to go downstairs. She found out that she couldn't stand up when she pulled herself up from her wheelchair. She slid down from her chair, got down on her hands and knees and crawled towards the stairs. When she reached the balustrade, she held on to it and stood up. But as soon as she put her foot on the first step, she fell down the whole flight of stairs, just a second before a shot was fired. The failure of Agnes's legs and the commotion created by her fall may have saved my father's life.

As far as Roxanne was concerned, the bullet had already done some damage to my father's brain, because of what he did next. He left Devinagar with me, his baby daughter. She believed that he had first gone to England to see some of his old employers. They sent him to Mexico to work under an American boss who in turn was working for a British company.

In those pre-Independence days, many years before I was born, my father had been a spy "of sorts for the British" according to Roxanne. He had been a spy for the British at the same time as when my mother's cousin Dinaz Mehta and her husband Ashok were about to be arrested in Bombay for making bombs to throw against the British. As Roxanne said, "It takes all kinds of people to make a family."

I told Roxanne about Agnes's disappointment at not having seen Dinaz and Kamal Mehta in America. Nanibai said that Tehmurasp Mehta, Dinaz's father was a good man but didn't know what to do with his young daughter after his wife died.

"Dinaz was quite as wild and strong-willed as your Auntie Agnes. All of us women must have inherited that from our Chinese ancestress." Roxanne seemed determined to add me to the wild women list. She gave me no time to explain myself. She thought I should know something about Dinaz's father, Tehmurasp, in order to pass on her memories to his granddaughter Kamal in America, in case she never met Kamal.

"Tehmurasp lived in genteel poverty in his ancestral home in Bombay, on Malabar Hill. The house was falling down, room by room, like a set of dominoes. One room would deteriorate and the roof would fall in. Jhooong. Then another room would lose its roof. Jhooong. And so it went. When I was six years old, I saw a ghost in one of the old rooms near the kitchen. But the library—not that big a room—was always kept in excellent condition. I think that Tehmurasp slept on the aged sofa in the room. There were bookcases against three of the walls. Huge bookcases. Reaching from the floor to the ceiling. They were filled with an incredible number of books, especially about ancient Iran and China. The old gentleman lived with his daughter Dinaz and an eccentric parrot, Meethamai. Tehmurasp was a deeply religious man who recited his prayers loudly and clearly every morning and evening, sitting on the verandah where the parrot lived in her brass cage. The parrot had memorized parts of our prayers. The books on China were his dead wife, Khorshed Japanwallah's collection."

I wanted to yell, "Stop! I don't want to hear any more! Why don't you just write a letter to Kamal."

Roxanne continued as if I had always known all those people she was talking about.

"Dinaz has a legendary silk sari from China. A gaaro. Our Chinese ancestress had sent it to India with her son. It was given to my mother by her aunt-in-law Virbaiji whom you'll meet in Bombay. Since Virbaiji had no daughters and since she adopted a son quite late in life, she gave the sari to my mother because my mother was the oldest daughter-in-law in her generation. And my mother gave it to Dinaz. To protect her in America. But Virbaiji doesn't know anything about that. She is superstitious about those six yards of silk. She believes that India and China will never get down to a real, all out war as long as the sari is in Asia. So if by any chance I am with you when you go to Bombay, and Virbaiji asks about the sari—which she does every now and then—I will have to lie to her. And then you can come with me to the agiari where you and I will pray to Ahura Mazda to forgive me for lying to our great-aunt Virbaiji. My grandmother Meheramai often wonders aloud how many Parsis, during the last years of the Independence struggle, prayed for the British to stay and how many for the British to leave. Did you know that your father went to the agiari quite often? She would say that Freddy's prayers alone would weigh at least ten times more against those of us who prayed for an independent India, because he was a good man. Misguided but good. Do you know how they found out about this stupid, shameful work he was doing those years before Independence? Long before he tried to shoot himself? All because of the Margaret Shriver-Margaret Friver business? Sorry, I know she was your mother but..."

I was trying to understand the idea of my father as a spy, my relatives as bomb-throwing freedom fighters, Roxanne's seemingly unlimited store of stories about the Coopers and the existence of the DLRSC Group. I shook my head. I was sleepy.

It was Nanibai told the last story of that evening. The story about how she and Roxanne's grandmother Meheramai had saved my father from the spying business.

A few years before 1947 and Independence and Partition, Nanibai, who was still in the prime of her profession as the leading lady thief and leader of the Devinagar's organization of thieves, went to Meheramai to tell her that Freddy Cooper seemed to be recruiting some of the men Nanibai knew for some kind of secret activities. According to Nanibai they were men of definitely questionable morals. At first, Meheramai was worried that she had one more zealous, non-Gandhian, bomb-throwing freedom-fighting, family member on her hand. She told Nanibai to tell Freddy that bomb-throwing was too dangerous a profession for him. But then Meheramai realized the impossibility of it. My father, the champion of all things English, had warned everyone in Devinagar that India would "fall into chaos and anarchy and into an era of horrible lawlessness" if the British ever left India. Nanibai and Meheramai were fond of Freddy. Actually he was quite a favorite with all the citizens of Devinagar. Regardless of his politics and his insanity over Margaret Shriver, he was a gentle and a most generous man. He was known to pay for many of the Devinagar school expenses, especially picnics, theater events and annual sports events. Nanibai and Roxanne's Meheramai decided to find out why my father was recruiting the not-so-very-respectable residents of Devinagar.

They found him a few blocks from the Cooper house, in the compound behind the Irani tea shop.

He was surrounded by a group of about fifteen men. Even Nanibai's friends would not mingle with them voluntarily. My father was trying to tell them about the joys, benefits, and blessings of British rule. He was promising to pay anyone who would confide to him the names of the people who were carrying out, or even thinking about carrying out, violence against the British rulers. He was also attempting to teach them "The Charge of the Light Brigade."

I paid careful attention to the next part of Nanibai's story because I knew that Carmelita would enjoy it. Meheramai and Nanibai watched these activities from the backdoor of the Irani tea shop for about twenty minutes. When my father abandoned his plan to teach "The Charge of the Light Brigade" to the bewildered men and instead tried to teach them "God Save the King" and "It's a Long Way to Tipperary"—which were of course somehow coming out from the men, to Freddy's great disappointment, a "God Save the Tipperary"—Meheramai decided to act.

She walked up to the men and demanded that Freddy stop all the nonsense and disband his group of "thugs and goondas who are too lazy even to learn how to steal." Freddy, brought up to respect older women, especially when they were the leading citizens of Devinagar—which Meheramai was—and when they were brandishing monsoon-defying umbrellas—which Meheramai was doing—paid the men for attending the meeting and told them, "no more secret work for now."

Roxanne's grandmother told my father that although he was a good and virtuous man, he was quite ineffectual in secret dealings. Nanibai added that he should stop trying to spy for the British since their days in India were numbered anyway. She advised him not to spy for the Indians either, since he would mess it up. India didn't need any more messing up. Nanibai and Meheramai recommended that he leave Devinagar until the gossip about his strange behavior was forgotten and before he got into trouble with his fellow citizens who were anti-British.

The fragments of memories of my father that I had held onto were of a man who went out everyday to check on men and women as they worked among the fields. He was a thin man with skin that burned easily, eyes that could have been hazel or light brown, and a mustache that had to be coaxed into growing onto his long, thin, sweet face. He did not look like a spy. He was a kind man. And he had stammered my name as he had run with me in his arms from our house, across the wet, slick mud of the yard, toward the river. When he fell he had pushed me away from him and told me to leave him, to run away.

I looked at the piece of paper on which Roxanne had sketched out the Japanwallah-Cooper-Mehta genealogy and started thinking of a tree. But how could I draw life into a tree of names? Where would I fit in Gregory and Theresa Sanders? Where would Carmelita and Ratna join the tree?

I asked for a pencil and began to sketch a tree. It turned into the banyan tree in front of my father's home in Devinagar. With roots and branches growing in all kinds of directions, intertwining at odd places, remaining completely separate in other places. A rooted tree that traveled across the earth.

As I looked at the tentative branch that was my father, reaching out to meet my mother, Margaret Shriver, I felt as if I had been handed a box of jigsaw puzzle pieces. A box containing pieces from at least three different puzzles. I was being asked to put together one complete puzzle, which would be a portrait of my family. And I had to do it without leaving out one single, individual piece.

I looked at Nanibai wrapped in her shawl, and the other old woman sitting next to Nanibai, with her bare feet tucked under her, and I wondered if ghosts belonged on genealogy trees. Or was the lineage of ghosts to be seen as a flowing river spreading over the land as it fed into tributaries, flooded its banks, disappeared into oceans?

Roxanne and Saleem did not seem to be aware of the extra person in the house. Nanibai recognized the woman. She nodded at the old woman and smiled at me. At one time, it seemed as if Nanibai would take off her own shawl and cover the old woman with it. But she didn't complete the gesture.

That night, in the bedroom Agnes had allocated to me, I dreamed of my father. I heard my father's stammered words in my dream. "R-r-r-run, K-K-K-Katy! G-go to Mr Sanders. He is waiting in the truck. O-on the other s-side of the river! I l-l-love you, my dear." And the words became visible. They turned into separate lengths of ribbons. Pink, green, yellow, lilac, red, blue, white ribbons woven into the two braids wound around the head of the old barefoot woman.

# V.

## San Francisco

*How I Met Ratna Sharma
Who Was Not Virginia Woolf at San Sebastian College,
San Mateo, California*

*How I Met Carmelita and Got a Glimpse of the Dog
Monty on Highway 1, California*

I described my Devinagar dream of the word ribbons to Carmelita about a week after I returned from India. We were waiting for Ratna to return from work, the three of us having planned to go to the Asian Art Museum in the Golden Gate Park for a Bharata Natyam performance. I told Carmelita that while I was in Devinagar, I had decided that the old, barefoot woman looked just like I had always pictured Carmelita's Grandmother Luz: dark, sturdy and vibrant. Carmelita had never shown us a picture of her grandmother, but Grandmother Luz figured prominently in Carmelita's stories and philosophical announcements.

"Barefoot?" demanded Carmelita as soon as I finished naming the colours of the dream ribbons in the old woman's braids.

I said that I didn't see anything wrong with bare feet. I wished my foster mother had let me run around the house and the yard in bare feet. I had never liked shoes.

"Nothing wrong with having to go barefoot? You think that because a person is poor she likes going around with bare feet? My grandmother didn't get her first pair of new, not-hand-me-down zapatos until she was nearly fourteen. She didn't want to wear them out, so most of the time she carried them around in a basket filled with her mother's tamales. From the time she was six years old till she married Grandfather Ignacio when she was seventeen, Grandmother Luz sold those tamales around Colonia Jalatlaco, all through the old parroquias of Oaxaca, from early afternoon until late at night. She didn't look anything like your old woman."

How would Carmelita know? She had never seen the barefoot old woman. But absence of personal experience never deterred Carmelita.

"When I was a little girl and would spend the night with Grandmother Luz, she would tell me stories about the nights when she would go around shouting 't-a-a-m-a-a-a-le-e-s.' "

"OK, bare feet aren't glamorous. . ."

"You are missing the point, Katy. Poverty isn't glamorous."

"Carmelita, for heaven's sake shut up! Being reminded of your Grandmother Luz has nothing to do with feet, bare or otherwise."

Carmelita laughed nervously. I seldom lost my temper. But when I did, I ended up shouting, "Shut up!" and then shut up myself. Sometimes for weeks on end. I felt as if I had betrayed my foster mother by shouting. She had never shouted at me. Never raised her voice or her hand against me. True, she had also seldom hugged me but she had made her love for me evident in other ways. Silent, carefully ritualized ways. Reading to me, talking with me, laughing with me, taking trips with me, drawing and painting with me, keeping me warm and feeding me wholesome foods.

Carmelita trod gently around my frustration and offered to practice some new body-work techniques she was learning to ease the pain in my legs. As she began to work on my right hand, I asked her what pulling on my fingers had to do with the pain in my knees.

"Trust me," she said. "I think I know what I am doing. One of these fingers is connected to your knees."

I decided to trust her.

"Where do you think your old woman is from? Why does she remind you of my Grandmother Luz?" Carmelita's attention was focused on the bottom of my right thumb.

"I don't know. Maybe because of her clothes. The skirt and blouse she wears look Mexican, but sometimes the embroidery on her skirt sparkles, as if there are sequins sewn all over the skirt. It reminds me of Indian or even Chinese work."

"Sounds like your lady is an aged China Poblana. A woman from Puebla, Mexico not Puebla, US of A. Decked out in her traditional Poblana finery. My Grandmother Luz once told me that there was an original China Poblana. From Asia. India? China? But I don't think of la China, from Puebla or China or India, as being barefoot. My Grandmother was of course a Oaxaqueña. Born in Oaxaca. The city. Not in a village like her husband, my Grandfather Ignacio. She died in Los Angeles. That's where she learned about hippies and beach bums and such. She always wore a black and white woven shawl. And no sequins on her skirts. So why do you think your father's words ended up as the ribbons in the old woman's hair?" At this point, she was at the base of my third finger.

Early in my friendship with Carmelita, I had asked her if she felt that she was being turned into a personal dream repository by me. I telephoned her at least twice a week to tell her my latest dreams. When I asked her if she felt unduly burdened by my dreams, she was surprised. She found it odd that I would even think about our friendship in those terms. She said something like, "Burdened? Unburdened! I love dreams. Yours. Mine. The dreams of the lady who shops Safeway every Thursday afternoon. From 3.30 to 4.15. Very punctual. She always talks to herself as she goes up and down the aisles. Anyone can hear what she is saying. When I am there, I follow her and without fail, she talks about one of her dreams when she reaches the produce department. Usually in front of the avocados and the tomatoes. She tests them for ripeness quite mercilessly. And anyway, how can anything you do burden me? After all, you, Katy, did save me from an eternal hitchhike on Highway 1. From out of a yet-to-be numbered circle in hell. Or at least from Purgatory. You were my salvation. Mi salvadora. You picked me up when I was hitchhiking!"

I had met Carmelita a few years before the photograph fell out of its frame and my subsequent trip to India. I was still teaching at Sierra College in San Mateo, my foster parents were still alive and I was living in a rented house on Spruce Street in Half Moon Bay. One Saturday afternoon, I noticed a woman with wildly curling, red hair and a dog trying to catch a ride going north on Highway 1 which cuts through Half Moon Bay. The sun had burned through the fog, and the ocean, west of Highway 1, was calm. The woman and the dog were in front of the green railroad caboose at the Shoreline Station complex. Her hair seemed to become more vividly red when she saw my car turn right from Kelly Street onto Highway 1. I was going north for only about a block, for my weekly visit to the Bay Book and Tobacco Company. I would not have picked up the woman even if I had been going to San Francisco. I was not enamored of dogs. In a gesture I thought was polite, I held up the thumb and index finger of my right hand a few inches apart. I was sure the woman would get the message about the brevity of my journey. She raised her middle finger high in the air. I must have looked shocked because the woman relented and laughed. When I looked at her in the rearview window, she was waving and blowing kisses towards my car.

Returning home nearly an hour later, I saw the woman again. She was in front of Tres Amigos on the other side of Highway 1. This time she was trying to hitch a ride going south. The dog was missing. Since it was a glorious day and she recognized me and waved to me, I decided that I would drive towards Santa Cruz and give her a ride. Actually I wanted to see the her hair up close. I was wondering if I could reproduce the color and the eccentric flying angles of her hair in a painting. Eventually, I did use the image of her hair in my paintings—again and again. But the best representations of hair like Carmelita's are in Remedios Varo's paintings of cats and human beings caught within finely drawn webs of electrical currents.

After she had buckled up, the redheaded woman explained why she had been going north and then later trying to go south. "I have been working both sides of the road. It couldn't be helped. It is all the fault of that dog. He is my neighbor's dog and he always looks as if he has never had any fun in his life. Just like my neighbor. I felt sorry for the dog, so I decided to borrow him and bring him to Half Moon Bay for a run on the beach. I was trying to take him home to San Francisco when you saw us. Chasing sea gulls all afternoon had made him quite demented. Every time a car stopped in front of us and the driver leaned over to open the door, the stupid dog would bolt. He would run across the highway. Back and forth, back and forth. It's a wonder he wasn't run over. And by the time I had chased him, I too was on the other side of the highway. So I decided that I might as well go to Santa Cruz as to San Francisco. The idea was just to get that dog in a vehicle and to go on. After some time the direction—north or south—didn't seem to matter."

I told her that I wouldn't have stopped if she had the dog with her when I returned from my trip to Bay Books. I hadn't only stopped for her, I had also turned the car around and begun driving north to San Francisco when she asked wistfully if I weren't going to San Francisco eventually.

"Stupid dog. I should have just let him go. He got abducted anyway. By a woman in a baby blue convertible. As she drove out of the Tres Amigos parking lot, she smiled at Monty. That was his name, you know. He just jumped into her car and off they went."

On the way to San Francisco, I asked the woman who had introduced herself as Carmelita Gutierrez, "at your service as a nurse and beautician," if she would sit for a portrait.

She sounded delighted. "A portrait! Can I have it when it is finished? Buy it or trade it? Are you very expensive? I would like to give it to my Tía Lucía. She lives in Oaxaca, Mexico. She has just announced that she is leaving her house to me, in her will. She would like me to live with her now. But since I am not quite ready to make my life there, she wants a big photograph of me, so that her cats and her canary and her long-time companion Tía Elena and her neighbors, all of whom she is sure will outlive her, can get used to seeing me. A portrait will be better than a photograph. And I trust you. You took me into your car even after I gave you the finger."

I told her that I was not really a portrait painter. I had done only three portraits in ten years. The last one had been almost a year ago. It was of a colleague of mine, Ratna Sharma. Ratna was from India and taught in the English department at Sierra College in San Mateo. I tried to describe the portrait to Carmelita. Ratna's face was a moon and she looked like a school-girl with long black braids and knobby knees and a blue uniform. She was stuck inside a paper kite. The simple diamond type. And while encased within the kite, she herself was holding a kite. A flying dragon. She was trying to tear herself out of the diamond kite. The flying dragon in her hands was curled downwards, trying to cut the string of their kitecage. Virginia Woolf was holding the string to the diamond kite with Ratna and the dragon kite in it. I didn't know if the woman I had picked up on Highway 1 would like a nonportrait portrait of herself. I said, "So you see, maybe if I do paint a portrait of yours and you do send it to your aunt, her friend and her neighbors might not recognize you when you do show up at the house in Oaxaca."

"But the cats would! Cats are wise! Why Virginia Woolf?"

"It has to do with how Ratna and I met."

As I tried to concentrate on driving over Devil's Slide during that first conversation with Carmelita, happy that no salivating dog was in my back-seat, I remembered how my foster parents had tried to make me into a true American child by presenting me with a dog on my twelfth birthday. A little black puppy. Everyone thought he was cute and cuddly and perfect. Not I. I was terrified of him. He had tiny sharp teeth. I had enough to deal with—my father's death, my loss of memories, the sharp pain in my legs and the strange old woman—and I didn't appreciated the puppy trying out his new teeth on my ankles and hands. I hated that poor dog's dependency on me. I was glad when Gregory Sanders realized that I didn't like the dog and gave him away to his secretary's son. I don't know if the dog could see the old woman but he was always getting entangled in her skirt. She didn't seem to mind. But I did. I was scared the old woman might fall down and then I would have to pick her up. How does one pick up a ghost?

As I negotiated one of the curves on the Devil's Slide part of Highway 1, Carmelita leaned across me so that she could look down the cliff and watch the waves break around the rocks. She asked, "So, how did you meet the lady-of-the-dragon-kite-inside-the-diamond-kite?"

"Don't lean over to my side. It makes me nervous. Watch the scenery on your side. I'll tell you how I met Ratna after we reach Pacifica." I told her.

A green pick-up behind me was trying to force me into speeding up or crashing into the hill or crossing over and falling off the cliff into the Pacific Ocean.

Carmelita waited. As soon as we reached Pacifica at the bottom of the hill, she said, "So?"

The green pick-up swerved off to the surfers' beach.

I pulled over to the slower lane of the road and told Carmelita how I had met Ratna.

Ratna Sharma had walked into my office one Friday afternoon, about a year and a half before. She was carrying a coffee mug in one hand and a bag of M&M's in the other. The coffee mug had on it in bright red and yellow letters, "JOYCE. From the Latin. The Merry One. JOYCE. The name of a FAMOUS WRITER." She walked into my office and said, "Hello, Professor Cooper," and offered me the bag of M&M's. She then walked around the office looking at the art on my walls. She spent the longest time looking at the print of Remedios Varo's LA LLAMADA. She didn't seem too interested in my art museum posters of Durga on her tiger and Shiva on his mountain but she leaned forward as if she wanted to touch the large amate painting by Cecilio Sanchez of flying women and minotaurs etched in gold, red, and white on the brown whorls of tree bark.

She then turned to me and asked, "Professor Cooper do I look like Virginia Woolf to you?"

I looked at Ratna Sharma's hair. She wore her long black hair coiled at the nape of her neck.

I told Ratna that she didn't look like Virginia Woolf. Then in case that was not the right answer, and always striving to be pleasant and helpful, as I was taught by my foster parents, I added, "Maybe your hair. You know the way you wear it in a bun. . .That classic chignon. . . Please call me Katy."

My passenger Carmelita, the nurse-beautician with the wild red hair asked me. "Does your friend from India wear her hair a la V Woolf because it is comfortable or because it makes her feel comfortable with her colleagues?"

I told her that Ratna had answered that she wore her hair just the way her mother did.

After Ratna sat down and I returned the package of M&M's to her, I said, "What about Virginia Woolf. . .?"

Ratna's doubts about herself as a non-Virginia Woolf woman arose from a guest lecture she had delivered recently at the college. Professor Walker, the grand old man of the Psychology department at Sierra College, had invited Ratna to speak to his class about ancestors. He had asked that she discuss the ancestresses who had influenced her. He had also told her that she should speak from her heart and her own experiences. "None of this academic bullshit. Speak about your feelings about your ancestresses," he had instructed Ratna. "Tell us what you have learned from them."

Ratna had taken the task seriously. She had gone to the class armed with photographs of her paternal grandmother and of her maternal aunt who had been a staunch anti-British fighter. The aunt had spent so many years in jail that her own children called her "Aunty" and her more biddable sister, Ratna's mother, "Ma." Ratna read passages from her aunt's letters to her mother to the students in Professor Walker's class. They were letters from different prisons from all over India. Since Ratna actually believed that the women of Indian legends and myths were also her ancestresses, she told the class the story of valiant Queen Draupadi who refused to shut up and about Kannagi.

Somewhere around Daly City, I told Carmelita about Kannagi who avenged her husband's wrongful execution by destroying a king and his kingdom with the power of her words and of her breast which turned into a roaring fire when she tore it off her body and hurled it at her enemies.

Carmelita was mightily impressed. "¡Que milagro! Much, much better than that poor Joan of Arc. Now, if Joan would have somehow spread the fire, she could have taken some of her judges and executioners with her. All arriving together at St Peter's gate."

I had nothing to add to Carmelita's fantasy, so I continued with my story.

When I had told Ratna that I was impressed by her lineage, she said, "Well, Professor Walker was apparently not impressed. I saw him a few minutes ago and he stopped me to thank me for visiting his class and said, 'But you know you were disappointing. Most disappointing. All those stories about unknown women and those strange translations. Now you should have heard the presentation your colleague Patricia Michaels made. Brilliant. She spoke about Virginia Woolf and other women writers like Elizabeth Barrett Browning and Emily Dickinson, real women, and how she counted them as her soul-ancestresses.' And all I could say was, 'Oh, I am so sorry!' And he patted me on the head and said, 'Don't worry. You are in very good company. You will learn from Patricia. Just pay close attention to her. Let her be your mentor.' And off he went."

I assured Ratna that Patricia didn't look like Virginia Woolf either. I felt stupid as I said that to her. So I offered to paint a portrait of her.

After I told this story to Carmelita in order to explain Virginia Woolf flying a kite which contained Ratna and her dragon kite entrapped in it, Carmelita thought quietly for a few minutes and then said,

"Is this Walker man Freudie, Jungey, or Native?"

I didn't know what she was talking about.

"Is he a Freudian psychologist-person, a Jungian type, or does he go in for what he considers Native, like drumming and sweat lodges and rattles and such. No, couldn't be the Native type. He would have appreciated, maybe not understood, but appreciated, the real ancestresses."

"I think he is a Jungian."

"Tell your friend that she failed the test. Women—alive or from books—from India are not in the Dictionary of Archetypes. Obviously not in the Dictionary of Archetypes for Professor Walker."

"And Virginia Woolf is?"

"Seems to be. So, do I get a kite too?"

I hesitated. "I don't know. But it is your hair I am interested in. That red. I was thinking of red coral."

"And my eyes would be fish? Amber fish? Eyes of a dead, drowned woman turned to amber stuck in coral? Don't change them to pearls, please. I will not wear pearls. Never. How will you explain amber in the depths of the sea? Oh Holy Mother of God! Help me our Good Lady of Soledad! Did you say my red hair? Que lastima! I was thinking of letting it go au natural. Starting tomorrow. It is a good, strong Indian black. Can you start painting right away? And why don't you have dinner with me tonight?"

Later that evening as I was leaving her apartment after dinner, Carmelita told me that she would like to meet Ratna Sharma. And then she told me that she had a dream when she first arrived in San Francisco in which the Queen of England and Virginia Woolf were having tea and discussing how they could help the women of Asia and Africa. Maybe even Australia. Carmelita shook her head when she said, "Elizabeth Regina the Second says, 'We should help those poor women. After all, our men folk certainly didn't behave very well, did they, in their countries?' 'Yes,' says Virginia the Writer, 'we should become their mentors, their helpers, their role models.' No, I made that up, right here and now, about being role models. But both spoke in New York accents! What can I do? I dream a lot and I remember all of them. And I talk a lot about everything. Dreams and all. I once dreamed of Ronald and Nancy Reagan flying a few feet above the sidewalk in front of this building. Nancy had healthy, chubby cheeks and long blond Shirley Temple curls."

A few weeks later when Carmelita came to visit me, I told her about

Ratna's decision to live in San Francisco. Carmelita said that she had a spare room and if my friend Ratna didn't mind sharing a kitchen with a dedicated carnivorous but otherwise healthy and sane woman, she could stay in Carmelita's apartment until she found a place in the city. But Carmelita wanted to meet Ratna before she was ready to back up her offer of the spare room.

Within half an hour of meeting Ratna, Carmelita invited Ratna to share her apartment. When she said, "Why don't you just forget about searching for a place of your own?" Ratna turned her eyes towards Carmelita's ceiling, determined not to indulge Carmelita with laughter. "Share this apartment with me. As long as you want," said Carmelita. And that is how Ratna and Carmelita became friends and apartment mates. As they shook hands on their agreement about who would pay how much rent and such matters, it began to rain in San Francisco. That wasn't unusual. It was winter. What was unusual was that it thundered and from Carmelita's living room window, we could see lightning streaking across the Bay. Northern California rains were seldom accompanied by thunder and lightning. After the rainstorms in New Hampshire, I found the rain in San Francisco to be a sneaky kind of rain. Carmelita took the thunder and lightning as an auspicious sign. Rain, thunder and lightning had to do with fertility and good beginnings for any venture according to Carmelita's Grandmother Luz. Ratna agreed with Carmelita, shaking her head the Indian way. That was the first time I saw those hairpins of hers falling out of her chignon. She didn't pick them up from the rug on the floor.

A week after Carmelita and Ratna became apartment mates, I dreamed of yellow ostrich eggs and yellow curtains. Carmelita was also in the dream. So I called her up and told her about the yellow dream. I didn't tell her that my old woman was also in the dream, with yellow ribbons in her hair. I didn't know how Carmelita felt about ghosts. But that is how I began telling Carmelita my dreams, which she later assured me were no burden for her.

I waited a few months before I told Carmelita and Ratna about the old woman. I had not told anyone else about her. I broke my silence about the barefoot old woman and the black butterfly one evening after dinner when Carmelita was trying to explain the difference between a phantom and a ghost. She had recently seen a PBS special on haunted castles.

A phantom, according to something Carmelita had read, appears to you as you sit on the wall of a castle in Scotland or Spain. This phantom is most probably playing bagpipes or a guitar. But as you walk toward the musician or as he comes toward you, he passes right through you. Playing the bagpipes or the guitar. A ghost on the other hand, Carmelita explained to us, will stop, cease the music-making and have a conversation with you. Or at least make terrifying faces at you.

"What about women phantoms and ghosts?" Ratna asked.

"What about women ghosts who appear to you at any time, anywhere and even in dreams?" I asked.

"It's been known to happen," was Carmelita's answer to both of us.

Ratna said, "Go ahead Katy, tell us."

And so Carmelita and Ratna became acquainted not only with my ghost but also with the pain in my legs.

That is how I saved Carmelita, if not from purgatory or hell, at least from a long wait on Highway 1 in Half Moon Bay. That is how we became friends. And that is why I was sitting in her apartment, a few years later, allowing her to try her newly acquired pain-relieving techniques on me, telling her about my final Devinagar dream of words-into-ribbons, arguing with her about the resemblance or lack of it between the old woman and her grandmother and remembering that the fickle dog's name was Monty.

# VI.

## San Francisco, California—Anaheim, California— Oaxaca, Mexico

### *Why my Friend Carmelita was a Healer and a Beautician*

I had requested that we go to the Bharata Natyam recital in honor of my Aunt Agnes. She had always wanted to be a dancer. But her father disapproved of any dancing except ballroom dancing for his daughter. "And anyway, Katayun," she had said to me, "I got married and lost the use of my legs. Maybe in my next life I'll be a dancer."

As I told Carmelita my Devinagar dream about the metamorphosis of my father's words into ribbons in the old woman's hair, and we argued about feet, bare or otherwise, and I ended up shouting at Carmelita, I remembered Carmelita's old dream about Ronald and Nancy Reagan.

"Well, at least in your dream of the Reagans, Nancy didn't have braids. And Ronald's words didn't become ribbons in her hair! Strange isn't it how the words got braided into the old woman's hair?"

"Not at all," said Carmelita. "Haven't I told you that my Grandfather Ignacio, Grandmother Luz's husband, had a braided tongue?"

Carmelita invented stories to suit any occasion just so she could prove that nothing ever shocked her. I had said as much to her a few weeks before I left for India. Her answer was, "Yes, it's my form of good, strong machisma!" How could one respond to that?

Since I had spent the last few days telling Carmelita and Ratna about Roxanne's Grandmother Meheramai and what my Aunt Agnes had told me about my Grandmother Katayun, I was willing to listen to more stories about Carmelita's Grandmother Luz. But I hoped Ratna would come soon. I wanted to go to the concert, return to my house in Half Moon Bay, and go to sleep. I was still fighting jet lag.

"A year or so after my grandparents, Ignacio and Luz, were married," Carmelita said, "my Grandfather Ignacio ran into la llorona."

As far as Carmelita was concerned, la llorona hadn't killed her children because her lover had abandoned her to marry a rich woman. Carmelita believed that the woman had killed her children because she didn't have enough food to feed them. Or because she thought the alien conquerors with all their magical killing machines and snorting beasts would enslave her children and eat them. After transforming them into gold. Because it was gold they always inquired about even before they asked for food or water.

"My Grandfather Ignacio," said Carmelita to me, "knew of course how la llorona wanders all over, haunting rivers and lakes. Looking for her children—killed and drowned by her—weeping and crying and lamenting and in the process terrifying children and grownups into silliness or death or some other misfortune. My grandfather of course, knew all that. And he also knew that his wife, my Grandmother Luz, never invoked la llorona, as too many grownups do, to scare naughty children. Anyway, Sister Llorona appeared to Grandfather Luz one dark, dreary and dismal night. It must have been a dark, dreary and dismal night—she wouldn't appear otherwise. I have heard people say that she really appears only to men but my Grandmother Luz told my Mom that la llorona has been known to appear to women also. They just don't make too much about it because being women they expect disasters, with or without an appearance of the woman who weeps. And anyway, who really asks women to tell their stories of la llorona? Grandmother Luz also insisted that Our Lady of Guadalupe first appeared to a woman. To Malintzin, Doña Marina, no less."

According to Carmelita's Grandmother Luz, Malintzin told Mary that no one would really believe she had seen the Goddess of the Americas. Because she, Malintzin, had borne a son to Cortez and was then passed on to someone else and was now about to die, how would anyone believe that she could see the conquerors' Virgin? And she said that since no one seemed to be able to decide if she was the Great Mother or the Great Traitor, the Dark Lady of Beauty and Roses should appear to someone else. "Be sure it is a man you appear to if you want your message to reach the rulers, their priests. Men sometimes listen to other men. I will be grateful if you select a man of my people." According to Carmelita's Grandmother Luz that is what Malintzin said to the Virgin of Guadalupe.

When Carmelita's Grandfather Ignacio was accosted that dark, dreary and dismal night by a woman who was weeping his heart broke to see her sorrow. He recognized who she was, but he couldn't turn his back on her. He couldn't even close his eyes. He wanted to help her and asked what he could do for her. She said to him, "Whenever you see a child who has been abandoned, a child without a family or a home, take that child to your woman so that she can take care of the child."

After that, whenever Carmelita's Grandfather Ignacio found a child without a home and whenever he thought he could get away with presenting his wife with another child, he did so. And to make money for his growing family, he began traveling in search of jobs. There weren't many jobs in his village. Not too much in the city of Oaxaca either. So he went to Mexico City, then to Merida, back to Mexico City, then to Mazatlan, to Tijuana, to South Texas, to Los Angeles, to Salinas, to Anaheim to Oaxaca and then back to Los Angeles and finally back to Oaxaca where he died. And as he traveled and worked, he sent children to his wife. From all over the place, including one from Texas and two from California. "Fíjate, children from California and Texas sent to Oaxaca!" said Carmelita.

Carmelita's grandmother and mother had told her that as her Grandfather Ignacio moved further and further away from his village in search of a livelihood, he lost more and more of himself. Parts of him were absorbed, taken over by the people who gave him money for his work. He worked in the fields and ranches. Then he started working as a busboy and rose to the ranks of a brunch cook in a three star hotel in Anaheim. Many years later, after his death, Carmelita took her grandmother to Disneyland.

Grandmother Luz began to notice that whenever her husband came back for his brief visits, he was like two men. One was the man of his village. He used the language, the movements and gestures of the men of his village. He was the man she recognized. But there was less and less of that man left in him as the years went by. The second man was constructed from the few fragments left of him after he had given over parts of himself to his bosses and his work. The second man, she said, might have been recognizable by his employers and his coworkers, but neither she nor the children nor the old family dog, not even the one mirror in their house, could recognize the second man.

Carmelita was silent for a few minutes before she continued. "When my grandfather came back to Grandmother Luz after his longest absence, three years and eight months spent at that hotel in Anaheim, she noticed that his eyes had grown cataracts, grays and whites, as if trying to mute down all those different and strange sights and visions he saw while traveling. Or maybe he was trying to blind himself from his loneliness. His mind, she said, seemed to go round and round. A serpent coiling in and out and around all the things he thought about as he had to move further and further away from his home. He said he had hated cooking eggs to order every Sunday, standing behind a table covered with trays of cheese, bacon bits, mushrooms, onions, ham and three different strengths of salsa. All of these surrounded by ceramic pineapples, plastic grapes and oranges—and what he hated the most—big green leaves made of paper stuck on sharp wires. He had nightmares about those breakfasts. About putting pineapples and plastic oranges and green paper leaves in omelets. Scrambling eggs with pieces of their shells mixed in with salsa and the plastic grapes.

"Grandmother Luz observed that when her husband visited his family, he wouldn't always answer when called by his name. He said it was because his employers, the headwaiters and the people he waited upon usually called him either Juan or Jose. One of the ranchers he had worked for in the Salinas valley for a number of artichoke years had called all the workers Sam. So grandfather would answer to Juan or Jose or even Sam. But he had become uncomfortable around Ignacio.

"What really bewildered my Grandmother Luz was that her husband, who had always told the best stories, who had always been trusted to settle disputes between his neighbors with his kind and careful words, who always sang and whistled and told long, complicated jokes, could no longer be understood when he spoke—except by his wife, my Grandmother Luz, and Beto, the first child he had sent to her, from the Yucatan.

"About a week after he came home that last time, my Grandmother Luz asked him to open his mouth wide. She saw that her husband's tongue was torn into separate strips. 'Shredded and split, it had dried blood all over it,' she would say to us, her grandchildren. 'And children, I realized at once what had happened. My poor man's tongue, your grandfather's tongue, had been cut, sliced apart, different strips hanging separate from one another. One part was his mother's Zapotec language. The other was the Spanish he had learned at the Benito Juarez School in Oaxaca City. Another was the Latin that Padre Simeon had tried to teach him when he worked for the Padre in his village. And then of course, there was the English. During the first year of our marriage, I had not slept much. Because he spoke in his sleep. In all these different languages. But his words were strong then and he could speak. Now he could barely speak. So I decided I had to make his tongue become strong and healthy again. So that people could understand him again.'"

Carmelita's Grandmother Luz had known what to do about her husband's affliction.

She sang. Lullabies, love songs, sacred songs, work songs, war songs, peace songs, railroad songs, children's songs, raunchy songs, songs without words, songs she made up, songs she had sung since she was a child, songs Ignacio had taught her, songs her children had taught her, songs she heard on the radio. As she sang, she braided together the separate strands of her husband's tongue. Slowly and carefully. With great artistry. And then she told him to be silent for a few months.

But he refused to obey her. He began to speak of the things he had seen and heard and thought. He spoke of la llorona, the woman who had been betrayed, who had betrayed herself, who had killed her children and now could not rest nor let others rest. He made la llorona into a figure around whom he began to rally a group of men and boys. They were to be a group dedicated towards helping children who were abandoned, orphaned, abused, taken advantage of. They gave speeches, they acted out little dramas at street corners. They got up in churches and spoke out against abusive parents and teachers and priests. They tried to fight bosses and employers and priests and nuns and parents. "All of this, of course, did not please the police and the bosses and the employers and the parents and the priests and the nuns and the teachers," said Carmelita.

"One day Grandfather Ignacio and Beto disappeared. And the police began to harass Grandmother Luz and the family that was still left with her. She got a message from her husband to go away with his brother to Los Angeles. He would follow her if he could, but only if he thought that his work would be carried on. His brother and Beto arrived at her house three weeks later. They said that her husband had died in the jail. Ignacio was singing and telling stories and talking about the horrors that God has in store for those who don't take care of children. He wouldn't stop talking even when the prison guard told him to be silent. The story which has been going around in the family is that my Grandfather Ignacio refused to die quietly and was buried in some unknown prison yard by a jailer he drove to murder with his words. The story also says that we will find where he is buried only when we find a place where the earth speaks. His brother brought Grandmother Luz and my mother and two other children to Los Angeles where he worked for a landscape business. But you know all that.

"And now you know why I am a nurse and a beautician. Because of my Grandmother Luz. They say that not only was my grandfather's tongue stronger and healthier after she healed him but that the perfect weave of the tongue also made his words more beautiful than ever before. But Katy, I don't think that the different parts of his braided tongue had bright ribbons woven through. Nothing like your old woman's braid."

Ratna came home soon after Carmelita ended the story about her grandparents and the three of us left for the Bharata Natyam performance. I didn't want to think anymore about Freddy's words and the ribbons in the old woman's braids. I knew that the old woman would follow us to the Brundage Museum. Not because of the Asian art there but because she seemed to love watching people dance.

During the reception after the dance recital, Ratna told us that she had taken Bharata Natyam classes as a very little girl. But when she had announced to her parents that she would be a dancer when she grew up, the classes had stopped.

"Katy," Carmelita said, "I keep on telling you that there is a pattern to your meetings. Your Aunt Agnes and your ex-colleague, our friend, this Ratna Sharma. Both frustrated dancers."

She asked Ratna, "Ever thought of walking through San Francisco with a cheetah?"

Ratna showed no surprise. "No, it's tough enough walking here in a sari."

"Even in San Francisco?" Carmelita was surprised.

"Yes. Even in San Francisco. Especially if people realize that I am wearing a sari as a part of my everyday clothing and not as a costume."

Carmelita said that after living in Texas, San Francisco seemed like the epitome of a liberal, tolerant society. Ratna had been made to believe that Berkeley had that distinction.

At the mention of Berkeley, a woman with a friendly face came to join the three of us. She said, "Hi! I am Tracy Robertson. I live in Berkeley. Wasn't that a lovely performance! I wish I could wear such a lovely costume every day."

# VII.

## Berkeley, California—Oaxaca, Mexico

*Ratna defends her honor at Tracy Robertson's Party and Carmelita Finds the "Lady's Support" at the Same Party*

*I Encounter Customs Officers in Mexico City and in San Francisco*

Tracy Robertson insisted that I tell her my real name. She understood Carmelita's and Ratna's names. But as far as she was concerned, the name Katy Cooper did not suit my physical form or color. Carmelita explained that the name "Katy" was really from Katayun, a good, solid Zoroastrian name, that "Cooper" was not an uncommon name among the Parsis of India and that I was born in Devinagar, India. Tracy had never heard of Devinagar and was unaware about the contemporary existence of Parsis or Zoroastrians.

"Parsi? Like that strange guy in *Moby Dick?* There aren't any Zoroastrians left in the world. My comparative religions teacher told us that."

Carmelita said, "Then we should present Katy to your teacher. As a fossil."

Tracy assured Carmelita that her teacher had studied under Joseph Campbell so he couldn't be wrong and then she looked at the three of us very carefully, nodded her head as if she approved of what she saw and invited us to her next party.

Foreigners, or as she had been heard to say, "foreign Americans," fascinated Tracy. Tracy's zeal was neither nastily patronizing nor overly depressing. She genuinely liked people. As soon as we stepped into her house, we could smell the spices which had barely been cooked before being mixed into the casserole of refried beans, blue corn tortilla chips, chunks of non-pork sausages and melted cheese. Bright yellow turmeric powder was sprinkled with festive abandon on top of the casserole that put forward a brave front, masking the ineptness of the cook and the fragmentation of ingredients.

As far as I could see, there was nothing fragmentary about the elegant lady sitting next to the table. Everyone who entered the house had to pass by her. Tracy Robertson announced, "And this is my dear friend, Mrs Chou. She is seventy-eight years old. Can you believe it? Look at that porcelain skin! And that hair! I could kill for such hair and skin! Poor dear, lives alone, next block. I keep an eye on her." And as the guests bowed or smirked or shuffled restlessly and put out a hand, she would say, "Oh dear! Don't bother. She doesn't really speak English. I make do with sign language with her." She would smile and bow at the lady and the lady would smile and bow to her. As the evening progressed, Tracy Robertson's smile became a bit blurred, her bow became deeper and sometimes she even patted Mrs Chou on her head. The depth of Mrs Chou's bow and the angle of her smile remained the same. She sat in the seat of honor bestowed upon her by Tracy, back straight, legs neatly crossed at the ankles.

I heard Ratna's sari being extravagantly praised by many of the guests. Before we left the Carmelita-Ratna apartment, Ratna had confided to us that it was a synthetic wash-and-wear sari. About half an hour into the party, one of the male guests decided to test the silkiness of Ratna's sari as well as her skin. "But isn't that why Indian women have bare midriffs?" he asked, when Ratna told him to go away and to keep his hands to himself. He tried to make Ratna understand him. "You must get with it. This is Berkeley, California. We are in the midst of enormous changes. Berkeley is the home of free speech, peace, and the sexual revolution. Try it! You will like it!" He leaned over to gaze into Ratna's eyes with great earnestness. As his hand moved forward to touch Ratna, this time on her cheek, Ratna stopped his advance with a few clearly articulated words and a quick, sharp kick aimed towards his shin. She threatened him with a higher kick if he didn't move away at once. Ratna was definitely a descendant of strong women.

I sat down next to Mrs Chou and asked her if I could bring her some-thing to eat. I was sure that Mrs Chou was not completely unacquainted with English. She bowed her head in assent. But just as she was about to speak, Tracy brought over a late arrival. "Mrs Chou this is my dear and wonderful friend, Robert Brentano." Bow. "Robert, this is my dear neighbor, Mrs Chou." Bow. Robert, who seemed to be a friendly sort said, "Hello Mrs Chou! You know I had a chance to go to China last summer." Tracy broke in, "No, Robert. Don't worry. She doesn't speak English. Do you think she was one of those picture brides? Isn't she quite lovely? So delicate. And just look at her tiny feet! Wonder how it feels to wear those expensive pumps on feet which must have been bound!"

At this point, Mrs Chou leaned over, picked up the napkin from my lap, wiped her mouth and said, "I was born in San Francisco. So were my parents. And I have been known as Dr Ellen Chou ever since I got my medical degree as a young woman. I have practiced medicine in Hong Kong and in the United States. I am now retired. My feet were never bound. Nor were my mother's, nor my grandmother's. My feet are naturally small and I am rather proud of them. I wear only Italian shoes. I do not dye my hair but I do use a special cream for my complexion." She grinned. "A Chinese secret lotion. Thank you for the party." She got up, bowed, and left. Tracy offered Robert a glass of "authentic sangria."

Carmelita, Ratna and I left Tracy's party soon after Mrs Chou's exit.

Ratna opened the back door to Carmelita's car, since the passenger seat in the front was always covered with books, magazines, and health and beauty supplies. But as soon as she started to get into the car, she backed out and slammed the door shut, giving a gasp. When I bent over to look in, I too pulled back at once. A woman sat stiffly in the backseat. She was a strange figure, shrouded in what looked like a large sheet.

Carmelita urged us into the car.

"It's all right. It's all right. No one will hurt you. Get into the car. Just get in!"

Ratna and I got into the back seat, next to the woman. As Carmelita pulled away from the curb, Ratna began to laugh.

"She is. . . It is . . . She's not a person. She's not a woman."

Carmelita announced, "I've found her at last."

"Not a person. Not even half a person!" Ratna continued to laugh.

Carmelita was serious, "Don't touch her. Just let's go home and I'll show you."

Carmelita carried the covered figure into the apartment. As she silently set the figure on the floor and unwrapped it, Ratna wondered aloud about the presence of the bottom half of a female mannequin. Carmelita explained that this was not the bottom half of a female mannequin. This was the bottom half of the image of Nuestra Señora de Soledad, La Soledad herself.

Ratna and I looked at one another; we then looked at Carmelita and waited for her to tell us what was going on.

Carmelita told us that she had always been looking for the bottom half of the Virgin of Soledad. Whenever she went to Oaxaca, she visited the Church of La Soledad in Oaxaca with her madrina Glafira. She remembered one of those visits very well. On the way to the church, near her madrina's house, they had passed a boy with the face of a fierce toreador. He was about Carmelita's age, thirteen. He was barefoot and sitting in the middle of some kind of a circle he had made around himself with beautifully painted rocks and stones and sticks. He was making strange looking balloons and piñatas from newspapers. Carmelita was completely fascinated by the boy and his creations. She smiled at him. He smiled at her madrina but glared at Carmelita when her madrina Glafira introduced her to him as "my goddaughter Carmelita. And Carmelita, this is my good friend, Rogelio. He comes to help me in my garden." Carmelita was very grumpy all the way to the church because the boy had been so unfriendly towards her. Rogelio followed Carmelita and her godmother to the enclosed garden of the La Soledad church. He apologized for his rudeness to Carmelita saying that he was Señora Glafira's friend and he didn't want to be discourteous to her goddaughter. When Señora Glafira told him that Carmelita was visiting from the United States, he smiled at Carmelita and asked her about the United States. He wanted to travel all over the world when he grew up, even to the moon and the stars. He then hugged Señora Glafira, gave her a beautiful stone he had found in the mountains and ran off.

After the boy had gone, Carmelita's madrina took her to the enclosed garden of the Soledad church where a group of ceramic donkeys and their ceramic masters were placed on a small stretch of grass. All of the statues— donkeys and masters—were life-sized. They stood on the very spot where some donkey-train men had discovered an unattended, unclaimed extra donkey. The masterless donkey carried a wooden chest containing the bust of a middle-aged woman. The event was promptly hailed as a miracle by the priests and the bust was claimed as the Virgin of Soledad sent to protect the city and valley of Oaxaca.

"She was then properly clothed and pedestalled." That is how Carmelita ended that story about the boy with the stones and newspapers, the donkey train and the discovery of the Virgin of La Soledad.

Ratna had already begun a close inspection of the wooden diaphragm, belly, buttocks and legs of the figure Carmelita had placed in the middle of their living room. Neither Carmelita nor I thought it strange when Ratna bent down to touch and count the toes and then looked up the legs, with odd reverence, to check out if the torso was anatomically correct.

Ratna's unsolicited statement after her examination was, "As far as possible. After all, she is wood. Nice paint job. Pedastelled?"

"Since Madrina Glafira had mentioned only a bust and not a complete body, I asked if that particular Virgin had legs. Madrina didn't know. She just nodded when I said that they had most probably built the lovely, miraculous lady a solid block of wood and set her up on it. I have always been looking for legs for her. She deserves them. It was she of course, who showed me my own angel. I hope both of you get to meet her one day."

Carmelita had found the half-woman in Tracy's bedroom. Carmelita had tried so hard to swallow her laughter at Mrs Chou's announcement that she was Dr Chou, and Tracy's calm acceptance of this news, that she choked. Tracy had taken her to the bedroom in search of Kleenex and that's when Carmelita saw the figure. Tracy had explained to Carmelita, with great pride, that she had found and bought the "half statue" at the flea market in Sebastopol. The guy who sold it to her told her that it was part of a column to a porch in Nepal. When Tracy left the room to allow Carmelita to blow her nose in peace, Carmelita wrapped up those wooden legs in Tracy's counterpane and carried them out through the back door and into her car.

Carmelita promised us that she would call Tracy the very next morning to tell her all about the legs, the Virgin of Oaxaca and the counterpane. Carmelita had snuck out of the house like a thief with her "miraculous find" because she didn't want Tracy to substitute her for Ellen Chou as the topic of conversation for the rest of her party.

I asked how she was so sure the legs were part of the Virgin of Soledad.

"Right color, right size, right shape, right aura."

She looked at me for a long time and said, "You are the one, Katy. You have to take this part of the statue to Oaxaca and join it to the top half."

"What? Why?" This was absolutely outrageous, even for Carmelita.

Carmelita could be very persuasive. She knew what bothered me the most in life. "I know that if anyone can cure you of that pain in your knees and legs, Nuestra Señora de Soledad will. She might also explain the old woman to you. I don't know about the before-you-were-eleven- memory part though."

I told her to stop being ridiculous.

Ratna looked on with interest.

Being called ridiculous didn't stop Carmelita. "When you get to Oaxaca, you can dress up as a nun. A foreign one, since I think, Mexican nuns are still not allowed to wear holy clothes on the streets. You can tell the bishop or priest or even another nun, someone in charge there, that you had a vision and found this part which belongs to the Virgin."

When I tried to remonstrate again, Carmelita pleaded, "Katy, you must go to Oaxaca with the legs of the Virgin. Please do this for me. I can't go because as you know, my favorite patient may die any day now and I have promised her that I will do her hair and face for her funeral."

Ratna nodded her head in affirmation, and the expected number of hair pins fell out of her hair. As I helped her retrieve them, I remembered Roxanne's description of Zoroastrian funerals. "The dead corpse--I know, I know, Katy, that is redundant-is laid on the ground, wrapped in a simple white shroud. No one has to make-believe that the body is alive."

Two days later, Ratna dressed up what was by now being referred to as the "Lady's Support" in a long skirt from Rajasthan. Carmelita went out and bought me a nonrefundable ticket. Ratna offered to go with me but Carmelita was adamant: I had to do this alone. She had dreamed of a meeting between La Soledad and myself; no one else was with us. I told myself that it would be interesting to find new landscapes for my paintings. Mountains and valleys instead of the Pacific Ocean and California coastal hills. But I refused to impersonate a nun.

I was able to enter Mexico by assuring the custom's officer at the Benito Juarez Airport in Mexico City that the partial body in my large suitcase made of wood and dressed up was no, not a statue, it was a mannequin, actually a tailor's dummy. I told him that my friend in Oaxaca, a seamstress, had asked for this particular half-mannequin because she was going to specialize in skirts, mini, midi, long, for the tourists. No, I did not know why my friend had asked for a mannequin made of wood, but I did know that my friend's sister was going to embroider the skirts. He looked sceptical. "Señorita, I am sure there are half bodies made of wood to be found all over Mexico." He shrugged and let me go. As I walked down the long hallway, towards the gate from where the Oaxaca flight was to leave, I heard a strings rendering of "The Song of India" over the sound system. I felt guilty. I thought that I should be in England looking for my mother, Margaret Shriver. But I didn't want to go to England.

The pain in my legs intensified as soon as I stepped off the plane in Oaxaca. The old woman sat so close to me in the plane that I hoped no one else could see her-an old woman curved into the lap of a younger woman, absorbing the space and the shadows allocated to a live human being.

Once in Oaxaca, I panicked. To approach Catholic priests, trying to explain half a wooden body without the aid of a genuine, acceptable miracle, seemed ludicrous. When I did visit the Church of La Soledad to look at the Virgin, I was so distressed by the appearance of the barefoot old woman, who seemed to have grown into a terrifying presence at the entrance to the church, and the butterfly, which flew straight towards me, that I left without entering the church. But I saw enough pictures of La

Soledad all over Oaxaca to assure myself that this particular Virgin, Mother of God, seemed content to be resting on whatever legs she had been allocated by her devotees.

I returned to San Francisco within a week, the "Lady's Support" never having left my suitcase.

Neither the "Lady's Support" nor I were as fortunate with the San Francisco airport officials as we had been with the Mexico City customs official. My explanations of having found the half wooden statue in an antique store in the arcades in Zona Rosa in Mexico City and my offer to pay the correct amount of duty for bringing in an antique did not raise any shrugs. My suitcase and I were taken into a private room and a dog was brought in to sniff at the suitcase. My comment on a dog being brought in to view the corpse at Zoroastrian funerals went unacknowledged by the two officials with flat, expressionless eyes as they proceeded to break open the diaphragm and the belly and to slice through the legs of the wooden half woman with single-minded thoroughness. I wanted to weep with frustration and anger as they destroyed the "Lady's Support." But Theresa Sanders had taught me not to cry in public. When they found nothing legal or illegal hidden within the wooden woman, they politely confiscated the pieces of wood and escorted me to the exit of the custom's room, handing me my passport and my suitcase.

Ratna tried to get back the broken pieces of the "Lady's Support" from the US Customs and Immigration office but quickly gave up the idea when faced with the paperwork. No one blamed me for bringing back the legs and then losing them to the customs officials.

Carmelita had already taken the counterpane back to Tracy and explained the whole situation. Tracy found the whole episode wonderful, refused to be financially compensated for the abrupt abduction of the legs, and was suitably furious at the San Francisco customs officials when Carmelita called her to update her on the legs. We lost sight of Tracy after a couple of months. She had said something about going off to New Mexico to work with a shaman.

# VIII.

## Half Moon Bay

### *The Woman who had Saved Washington DC Everyday during World War II*

Crossing rivers and borders, going to Zoroastrian funerals and to Mass with the Sanderses started to take over my dreams a few weeks after I got back from Mexico. I began to brood on the pain in my legs and the old woman. Carmelita was worried about my depression. She said I should just accept the ghost-phantom. "She is tied to you, Katy. A part of you. She is your vocation. She is a part of your life, even a part of your family in Devinagar. Remember, she has appeared to your Auntie Agnes. And Nanibai. Maybe they have seen the old woman again and have ideas about her. Ask Auntie Agnes the next time you write to her."

I wrote to Aunt Agnes about the party in Berkeley and my trip to Mexico. I mentioned neither the persistence of the pain nor the old woman.

I received a reply a month later.

"Dear Katayun," she wrote. "Sorry about the officials at the San Francisco airport. But what can one do with such people? Our Roxanne might have tried to fight with them but you know that even she probably wouldn't have won. And Sarosh, who is the son of my Aunt Virbaiji, your great-aunt of course, will envy you when I tell him about your trip to Mexico. He thinks that the "New Age" will arise in Mexico and Peru. I don't know why he says that and I have never wanted to find out. And every time he talks about this New Age, our Roxanne says, 'What new age-pew age?'

"And now to the most important reason for this letter! Thank you so very much dear, for the painting. I always thought that rivers rather than trees stood for borders, but that lovely stand of trees makes sense. So many,

many trees! With the 'No Trespassing' signs and that terrible dark orange fire (is that what it is?) on the other side of the trees-! Lovely. But quite frightening too, I must confess. I have hung it up above my bed! My friend Sister Annie, who has visited me ever since I stopped walking, once brought me a small wooden cross to hang in my room. She said it would help me. But I really couldn't do it, not even to please the dear woman. When she saw your painting she nodded and said, 'Yes, it looks right there, over your bed. It is such an Indian picture.' She said that the trees reminded her of 'those ladies the Hindus pray to. You know, those ladies with many arms.' I told her that they were Goddesses. She just nodded in that patient, not-really-listening-to-you manner so many nuns seem to have. Roxanne said that the trees in the painting are real trees, except one. She says it is a stylized version of our Zoroastrian winged Asho Farohar. Maybe it is your guardian angel. And she said that the trees are a wall a determined person can walk through. She said that that is why you called the painting, 'The Border Patrol.' I am sorry dear, but all I see are the wonderful trees, all those greens and browns, and what I think are the flames behind them. I like it very much and ever since I hung it up-actually Roxanne's unofficial husband, that wonderful Saleem hung it up for me-I have had many dreams of us. You, Freddy, and I, walking all over Devinagar and Half Moon Bay. Yes, even I am walking! Imagine! After all those years!

"By the way, Roxanne's Grandmother, Meheramai, said that in the last letter she received, about two years ago, from our relative Dinaz Mehta, Dinaz said that she and her daughter are now living in San Francisco or in Los Angeles-Meheramai couldn't remember. But they are in California. They are the relatives I couldn't visit when I was in America. My dear, it seems that that happened at least a century ago! Please do try and contact them. They are family and I think Kamal must be just a few years older than you. Maybe you can see if they have a phone. Roxanne assures me that Americans are very efficient about phone directories and such things.

"Roxanne is quite upset these days. Her sixteen-year-old niece has announced that she is in love, has found the right man and wants to get married. Roxanne apparently sat her down and told her that it wasn't love, but 'just a case of healthy, raging hormones-formones,' and that she should concentrate on using all that energy to study instead of thinking of getting married at this age. You know how Roxanne is. Actually Meheramai and I agree with Roxanne but we also think that she is being too harsh on her niece. I hear that in America unmarried young women can go to a doctor and get birth control pills so that they can act upon the urgings of their 'raging hormones-formones.' A very sensible idea. But Roxanne's sister and brother-in-law will most probably just marry their daughter off to the young man she has decided to fall in love with. One unmarried woman living with a lover is usually enough for one family. And maybe you can come for the wedding. Everyone sends you greetings. Nanibai is getting old but remembers you every time she comes to visit me or when I see her at Roxanne's house. She said that maybe your legs hurt because you live in that cold, damp climate. But then we remembered that you were in pain even when you were here when it was relatively warm. I am sure one day the pain will go away.

"And now I have to write something that will disappoint you my dear. All my inquiries about Margaret Shriver have been useless. I wrote to my father's old office in England and to some of his English friends who are now in England or America, and the woman seems to have disappeared. No one knows where she went after my father died about five years after he left Devinagar with her. I never did see him again and she did write me a nice short letter after he died, telling me that he had always loved me and all those kinds of things. But I can't find her. The woman who was *always* around when I was growing up is now gone! When I was a child I hated her because her frocks were always so clean and well starched and pretty and because her bright nail polish gave me nightmares of a woman with blood dripping from her fingers! Those were the days of very bright, very red, nail polish colors. I am too old to be bothered with anger and all that. But I must tell you Katayun that after my husband died, I couldn't be angry with her. Not on that count. I realized that he must have been very stupid to get involved with her. Dreadfully stupid. Unfortunately, I never felt the same about my father and your father and couldn't quite forgive them for their madness about this daughter of their British business part-ner. I am sorry, I know she is your mother and should not write bad things about her to you. I will let you know if I hear anything. I am sorry, my dear, that you never knew your mother. My mother, your Grandmother Katayun, was an absolutely wonderful mother. But you did tell me that Theresa Sanders took good and loving care of you. I now add her name in my prayers. I add both the Sanders in my prayers. I also add their names to the list I give the mobedjis when I ask them to perform special prayers and rituals. But since some of them may not want to add non-Parsi names in their prayers, I put down Theresa as Tehmina and Gregory as Godrej.

"Please do convey my greetings to your friends, Carmelita and Ratna. I always forget to ask you! Is Ratna from the Bombay Sharma family? The family that lives next to the Tilak Bridge in Dadar? I send you my love and hugs. And I look forward to another painting from you. I feel as if Freddy is with me when I look at your painting. Your loving aunt, Agnes."

I decided to track down my cousins, many times removed, Dinaz Mehta and her daughter Kamal. I found a K Mehta in the San Francisco phone book but when I called, the number was disconnected with no forwarding number. I found numerous Mehtas in Los Angeles but no Dinaz or Kamal Mehta. Since I was in the midst of starting a new painting in order to dispel my general state of depression about my pain and since I thought that my aunt and Roxanne and her Grandmother Meheramai were sufficient relatives, I didn't pursue my quest for my Mehta relatives, with great diligence.

Ratna said that her family did live in Bombay but not in Dadar.

Carmelita declared that my stories about aunts and grandmothers and great-great-grandmothers had made her long for her own Grandmother Luz who had died many years ago in Los Angeles, before Carmelita decided to come to San Francisco. In order to deal with her need for a grandmother, Carmelita took a job in a senior citizen complex which had a medical clinic attached to it. She worked as a nurse during the mornings and then three afternoons a week she manicured nails, cut hair, gave perms and tried to teach Spanish to the elderly women who needed such services.

She was entranced by one particular woman who told everyone that she had been an airforce pilot in World War II and had saved Washington, DC from a bomb attack. Apparently, in real life, she had been the wife of a minor functionary in Washington DC for many years. Her daughter who visited her every day encouraged her to expand her story as extravagantly as she pleased. The daughter told Carmelita, "Before she dies, I want my mother to live her own life. When I was four years old, I thought Mom's first name was 'h-o-n-e-y why is my best shirt not clean?' and her last name was 'h-o-n-e-y, can you please get me something to drink?' When I was about five years old, I asked her why her name wasn't 'Mary Smith' or 'Tina Brown' or some such normal name. Why was she called, 'Honey Get Me?' She laughed and said, 'It's OK dear. To you, I am Mom.' When I was taking her to the hospital after she broke her arm last year, I asked her if she was in terrible pain and she said, 'I hated Washington DC.' She has saved Washington DC ever since that day."

When Carmelita told us about the woman who saved Washington DC everyday, I told them that I missed my Aunt Agnes and Roxanne and her Grandmother Meheramai. Carmelita suggested that I try once again, to paint a portrait of the old woman with the ribbons in her hair and no shoes on her feet. I had of course, tried to paint the old woman many times in the past but the only things I had been able to put on paper were bare feet and a black butterfly. Carmelita remembered my failed attempts and said,

"This time paint glass slippers on the feet." And then she went on to tell us about what the lady who would be a pilot had dreamed the night before. She had added a lover to her stories, a lover who called her "Amapola." Amapola, and her lover had motorcycles they rode throughout the countryside of England, in between saving Washington DC and London.

Instead of the old lady, I painted a motorcycle rider for Carmelita. Carmelita said that even in her wildest dreams she wouldn't have seen such a motorcycle rider. She insisted that the white haired woman motorcyclist's face was a pink hibiscus flower. All I had painted was a circle with an abundance of wrinkles. The woman's black leather motorcycle jacket was open displaying her breasts, which had obviously nourished more than one child. At my age, old breasts seemed stronger and safer. I had tried to paint Carmelita's guardian angel's breasts, with Mary and the Mixtec warrior. But the motorcycle rider had other ideas. One of her breasts had a tattoo of a butterfly and the other had a tattoo of two bare feet.

When I completed the painting, I signed up as a Hospice volunteer at the South San Francisco Kaiser Hospital.

# IX.

## Half Moon Bay, California

### *Putlibai*

### *Heaven and Hell, Mermaids and Reincarnation*

While working for Hospice, I met a patient named Putlibai. A month later she came to live with me in Half Moon Bay. And two months later, I dreamed of glass jars. Jars filled with preserved fruits, pickled vegetables, dried lentils, Basmati rice and seeds from a patch of California poppies. A haze of kitchen grease covered the surfaces of the containers. I took the jars down from the old wooden shelves, arranged them in my kitchen sink and began to wash them. As I traced the raised glass lettering under the full stream of water, I remembered in my dream that there was a drought in California. Too many Northern California winters had passed without rain. The nights were cold and clear and the days were temperate. Water in Half Moon Bay was strictly rationed. The fog had spread with spectacularly vicious beauty over the cemetery across from my house early in the mornings and at twilight. The trees on the bluffs at Poplar Beach seemed to thrive, draped in thick gray fog. I had painted them as rows of curved, hooded women in mourning. Shrouded women dancing steadily towards the ocean, in isolated, solitary grief.

The drought and the water rationing made me feel guilty about washing those glass jars. I turned off the faucet, left the jars and bottles in the sink and went to the kitchen window to see if any of my neighbours were watching me wasting water. In my dream even the window was coated with dirt and grease. I tried not to look at the thickening veins in my hand as I wiped circles of grime from the window pane. Most of my neighbors' lawns had been converted to rock and pebble fantasies. But in the dream, when I looked out, I saw a stretch of bright green grass, luxurious and neatly trimmed. On the edge of the grass was a chubby elderly gentleman in a fishing hat and not much else, sitting on a small tractor, a fishing pole in his hand. He was smiling and waving at me as the old woman's butterfly hovered above the fishing pole. The old woman herself was nowhere to be seen.

I woke up to the sound of rain and recognized the unexpected late October downpour as signaling the end of the drought and the beginning of our normal wet winter. When I went to the guest bedroom to check the windows, I knew that the woman on the bed, Putlibai, my new friend, was dead.

The next afternoon I had a lunch appointment with Carmelita and Ratna and went off to the Italian restaurant in Colma. Carmelita explained that she had invited us to lunch in Colma because it was the end of October. According to her it was an excellent restaurant for us to celebrate the upcoming Day of the Dead. "No sugar skulls, no yellow and gold flowers. But there are at least some candles on our tables. After all, it is an Italian restaurant. But just think about it! We are in a restaurant that serves food in the middle of acres of cemeteries and car lots. Here in Colma the dead even outnumber car salesmen. There is a bumper sticker that says, 'I am Glad to be Alive in Colma.' Do you two know that Wyatt Earp is buried in Colma?"

I said, "I have a dead body in my freezer."

"Putlibai?"

Ratna and Carmelita weren't surprised. It was an expected death.

I told them how I had awakened to the sound of rain in the middle of the night and found Putlibai dead. It had taken me an hour and a half to drag her to the garage and into the big chest freezer. I hadn't wanted to insult Putlibai by dragging her to the garage but I had to put her in that freezer. My friends knew of my promise to Putlibai. Her death was not to be certified by a doctor. As far as her doctors and nurses were concerned, Putlibai had gone to India to die.

It had been a long night. Carmelita and Ratna reached over and touched me. "Katy," said Ratna, "You should have called us right away. We would have come over to help you. But don't worry, Putlibai wouldn't have thought of your dragging her to the freezer as insulting. She would have laughed."

I wondered where my connection with Putlibai would have appeared on that banyan tree of relationships I had attempted to draw in Devinagar, involving the Coopers, the Japanwallahs, the Mehtas.

I met Putlibai when we were allocated to one another at the South San Francisco Kaiser Hospital. Putlibai's nurses and doctors had felt uncomfortable with the fact that only they and Putlibai knew that she was dying. There was no one in Putlibai's life, no family, no friends to share with her this fact of imminent death. It wasn't as if the medical staff hadn't come across a friendless, familyless dying patient. It was just that they felt that the old woman from India who always listened to their instructions with careful courtesy and spoke to them as if her mouth was constantly surprised at the English words that emerged out of it, should have some-one else besides her medical attendants to share the last months of her life. During one of my visits to the hospital, I saw that my name had been entered on a form as "Katherine Cooper." I explained to the woman in charge of the Hospice volunteers that I was Katayun not Katherine. That led to the discovery of my Indian connection and the woman remembered the request for a Hospice worker for Putlibai.

She took me to Putlibai's bed and said, "Hello Putlibai, I have a surprise for you! A friend from India!" and left the two of us to stare at one another.

I said, "I am sorry. I am not. . .well I was born in India. My father and I were born in Devinagar." And then more firmly, "I have only visited India, once. Not lived there. I don't speak Hindi. Only a few words of Gujarati."

"Hello!" said Putlibai. "Don't worry. Now I speak Hindi only in my dreams. I was born in Sindhu, the village near Devinagar."

I smiled, because I remembered that Roxanne and Saleem gone to Sindhu one day during my visit to Devinagar, for what Roxanne called, "One of our fact-finding detective-fetective missions. They make wonder-ful almond halwa there."

I said, "My cousin Roxanne who lives in Devinagar said that the almond halwa from Sindhu is very good."

"Even now? It is still good? I am glad to hear it. It used to be good when I lived there. Very, very long time ago," said Putlibai. "I have been to Devinagar. A long time ago. It is also at the edge of the ocean. Just like Sindhu. I love the sound of the ocean. Before I got sick, I worked in Pescadero in the fields. We could hear the ocean. We couldn't see the water but you know, always the sound of the ocean was there."

I was surprised. "I live in Half Moon Bay. North of Pescadero."

"Nice town."

I agreed with her and told her that I would like to visit her while she was in the hospital.

"That would be very nice!" said Putlibai. "You come when you have the time." I noticed that she was beginning to doze off and started to move away. She reached out and grabbed my hand. "How do you say 'baari' in English?"

"Bury? Put in the ground? Do you want to be buried, in the ground? Not cremated?"

Putlibai dismissed my questions. "In the end, I want to be in the ground. Near the ocean. What do they call 'baari' in English? I forget some words now."

The next time I visited Putlibai, she was lying on her bed, with her face turned towards the wall. "Baari" she told me, as she sent me a shy smile over her shoulder, "is window." She pointed at the window across the room. "This," she said, with her hand stretched across until it touched the wall next to her bed, "is deewal, a wall." She needed to connect words with their tangible counterparts. She began to trace the progress of a fine crack in the wall. "Made by earthquake. Earthquakes come, earthquakes go," she said philosophically as she carefully followed the crack with the little finger of her right hand. "My first earthquake in California went bang, crash, bang, crash, all the cans fell down. And I got married."

"You got married during an earthquake?" I wondered why no one had bothered to tell me that Putlibai had a husband. Alive or dead. I found out later from Putlibai that she never mentioned that she had been married until she was sure she was talking to a friend. Putlibai always indicated "single" on legal forms and questionnaires.

Putlibai shook her head. She told me that long before that earthquake in California, many long years before she checked herself into the hospital and met me, a long time ago, while she was still a child in Sindhu, her nose had hurt her terribly. She had run into the wall in front of her house, during Divali celebrations. Her mother had lit small oil lamps made of clay all over their courtyard and taught Putlibai how to light sparklers and whirl them around. Putlibai ran into the wall because her brother Mohan had chased her around shouting, 'I am a twelve-headed monster. I am a gigantic rakshas. I am a fourteen-headed rakshas. I have to wipe out all little girls with two braids from the face of this earth. My master Ravanna has ordered me!' Putlibai believed him because she had seen the Ram Lila performance and because she usually believed her older brother. After she crashed against the wall, she began to rub her nose. She told her mother that her nose had become a Divali firecracker. Two sparklers. Zrrrr, zrrrr, zrrrr, round and round. There were stars on her nose. All around her nose. Her mother had laughed because Putlibai was trying to cross her eyes and turn her head to see those sparklers around her nose. It was now nearly sixty-five years later when Putlibai told me her story about running into the mud wall of her house in Sindhu.

Putlibai was still tracing the crack in the hospital room wall when to my complete bewilderment, she said, "My brother Mohan took very good care of me, after that day. He was sorry he hurt me."

"I am glad he took care of you," I said, as I stood there looking at Putlibai's back.

Putlibai turned away from the wall, laughe,d and said, "Please sit down, Katy. Bring the chair closer to me so I can see you better."

When I was close enough, Putlibai began to clap her hands very softly, with gentle, slow rhythm, as if she were listening to music. I tried not to look too surprised.

She said, "You are thinking, 'What's this funny old woman doing, sitting here in this hospital bed, clapping her hand?' You know, Katy, I was remembering the time when I was a very little girl, so many years ago, in Sindhu. My brother Mohan chased me, and I banged into the mud wall in front of our house and I thought that the gulmohor tree near the wall had become three, four, five gulmohor trees. All bright and gold and green. Even though at that time there were no flowers on the tree. And my brother cried because he had hurt me. But he always took care of us. My mother and me."

"Is your brother in India?" I asked.

"Oh no. He is dead. We came to America together." Putlibai continued to clap her hands and began to sing a song. "My mother taught me this song. My father was dead. 'Mitti me mil jaega . . . mitti me mil jaega . . .' Do you understand, Katy?"

I told Putlibai that I was trying to learn Gujarati. I didn't tell her that I was trying to learn my father's language from a book Carmelita had found in a bookstore in Berkeley, called *Learn Gujarati in Thirty Days*.

"The song says that in the end we all fall back into our natural element. All creatures to dust. Dust to dust. Mud to mud. Everything falls down and becomes what we really are."

I thought of a human wall of bones and gristle and blood come tumbling down into a pile of fine ashes embellished with small, bright crystals, white, gray and black.

I wanted to draw Putlibai's hands. Large palms with long, strong fingers and neatly trimmed nails, the deep brown skin covered with black hair, the veins and delicate bones showing through the skin. Putlibai's hands were like a contour map. Hills, mountains, valleys, rivers, lakes and oceans standing out in relief against the flat earth. I sat in that hospital room looking at a dying woman's hands clapping in slow rhythm to her mother's song.

"Yes, my brother Mohan took very good care of us. Very good care. Always. Because we had no father, you know. So my brother took care of us. When he was fifteen years old he took us to Karachi. You know Karachi? It is that port north of Devinagar."

I said, "Yes my aunt told me about it. She lives in Devinagar but went to school there. Just for a few years. But I haven't been there."

"Mohan took us there because he found out that there was more work there than in Sindhu or Devinagar. He worked on the Kemari docks. He told me that he liked to watch the fishing boats pulling in with their nets filled with sparkling fish while the big steam ships sailed off with men dressed in stiff white uniforms on the decks.

"When we were in Karachi I worked in many homes as a servant. I woke up in the middle of the night, at four o'clock, and started sweeping, dusting, mopping floors, washing clothes, scrubbing pots. All that work you know, all in other people's houses. I worked till eight o'clock at night. I washed their clothes with big yellow soap or soft, white Lux Flakes. The soap depended on how rich the family was or how delicate the clothes were. I worked for many families. Some of them were very rich and others not so rich. I scrubbed dishes with dried coconut fibers and ash. Not like here where we have all the easy liquid soaps and powder soaps and detergents. Quite nice. I like all the soaps here. I swept floors bending over a broom, no vacuum cleaners there, and mopped the floors squatting over a wet piece of gunny sack, pushing it across the floor. Do they have wet mops there, in India, now?"

I shook my head, "I don't think so. My friend Roxanne sweeps the floors of her small house and mops the floors just like you did."

"No servant?" asked Putlibai. "Poor?"

"No, not at all poor. But she says that she likes to clean her own house after her work in the office. Her friend Nanibai, who lives with her, cooks."

"What does she do with all her money? Saves it all? Big house? Yes, yes. She must buy lots of jewelry. It's the only way to save. We know that in India."

"No, she buys lots of books and I think she pays for many children's education and also helps the hospital. That is what my Aunt Agnes told me about Roxanne."

"That too is good. My mother began to have high fever every night after we went to Karachi and we admitted her to the hospital. A charity case. She died six months after we moved to Karachi and then Mohan decided to become a sailor. He sailed to Africa and Japan and New York as a deck hand. During one of his stops in Karachi, I told him that I was lonely. I wanted to join him on ship, disguised as his brother. I wanted to go either to Africa or to America. I liked the sounds of both those names, you know. My brother just laughed at me and sailed off to Japan. When he returned, he found me dressed as a young man."

"Really!"

"Yes. I cut my hair, bound my breasts and put on the clothes of a young man. I stole the clothes from where the dhobhis dried the clothes they washed for other people. It was near the Gandhi Gardens Zoo. I went there often because I liked to talk to the lions. They were always lonely or hungry and they roared. They didn't make just one loud noise. They made up and down noises. Hohf-hohf-Hohf-hohf-Hohf-hohf. Like that, you know. Sort of sad."

The only lion I was familiar with was the MGM one. And that one usually looked like an irritated cat trying to grab an invisible dangling cord by moving his head sideways, his mouth wide open. I had never paid much attention to his roaring.

"I suppose I shouldn't have stolen the clothes but what could I do? And you know, it was fun putting on those pants and the shirt." Putlibai laughed. "Mohan was of course very angry but he saw that I was very, very serious. So the next time he went, I sailed with him to America. I became his younger brother, Prem. I sailed off as a deck-swabber and latrine cleaner. I think Mohan took me on that ship not only because he was afraid I would run away when he was gone but also because he was scared. He knew that India would become free and then most probably it would become two different countries. And so he took me on that ship."

As she lay in that hospital bed, Putlibai looked quite proud of herself and her brother.

"My brother Mohan was very clever. He decided that we needed to find a new place to live. India would be divided up and we had no family to return to anyway. We left the ship when it arrived in New York and disappeared into the city. Mohan found work in an Indian restaurant run by an Irani man. I found work sewing clothes in a small room. There were no windows and no fan, no heat, in that room and we were twenty women. The room was on the twelfth floor of a tall building in New York. We did not talk to one another very often. We all didn't have the same language, you know. We were told what to do, and we did it. Work was completed and each of us was paid. Not very much. Late at night, Mohan tried to teach me English. He had learned some on the ship. And now he gave a few dollars every month to his boss's chauffeur to teach him English. That chauffeur always wore a shiny black jacket and two-toned shoes. It was exciting, living in New York and all that, but I missed the land."

Putlibai told her brother that in America there was no earth. Only cemented land. Even trees grew in cement pots. Mohan decided that they had to leave the city and find some land to cultivate. Putlibai had laughed at him. She felt that his years on the sea, his work in the kitchen of the restaurant and her work in Karachi and New York had made them unfit to work on the land. She had said to him, "We have forgotten that onions grow under the soil. We just pick them up from containers in the markets here." But when an Indian man, a friend of the cook in Mohan's restaurant, offered to take Mohan and Putlibai to his home in California, they left New York for the farmlands of California. Mohan and Putlibai were sure they had heard an offer of marriage from him but they found out when they got to California that he was already married to a Mexican woman, Rosario, sometimes known as Rosario the Brave.

Putlibai patted my hand. "Rosario, she became my friend. My sister. They called her 'the Brave' because she had once killed a snake. And she was never afraid of our bosses. Her husband had brought us to California to help him in the fields because he said he liked us and saw the wish for land in our eyes. And because Rosario had mentioned at one time that she would like to have an Indian sister-in-law. To know what it felt like to be a woman from India. She was lucky. I became her sister-in-law. You would have liked Rosario, Katy. Everyone liked Rosario. Even the people she yelled at.

"Rosario and I became very, very good friends and she also taught me to speak more English. I could speak some English you know. I had to speak because nearly everyone around me, since I had come to New York, spoke English. So I learned to speak. But for the reading and writing part, Rosario found some of her niece's schoolbooks and decided that we would teach ourselves how to read and write. She said to me, 'It can't be too hard, Putlibai. After all, lots of people know how to read. Even stupid people. And we are not stupid. We will learn fast.' I agreed and we began to teach ourselves how to read English. Her niece who was all grown up by then, helped us. And I taught Rosario whatever I learned at the grocery store. About English."

"You worked in a grocery store?" I pictured Putlibai at Cunha's Country Store, clapping her hands in time to the music permeating the store.

Putlibai shook her head. She explained that every Saturday night when Mohan went to the Indian grocery store to gossip and gamble with other Indian bachelors, he took her with him. He had apparently forbidden her to talk to, or even to look at, any of the men. And so Putlibai sat Saturday night after Saturday night, in her one good pink lotus sari, primly facing the longest wall of Mohan's friend's grocery store. The wall was lined with rows of cans carefully arranged on narrow shelves. Metal containers enclosing fruits and vegetables and fish and meat and juices and even prepared foods. That wall was Putlibai's schoolroom.

Putlibai described how she had learned English, and at the same time sharpened her eyesight, by trying to decipher and identify the substances within the cans as described on their labels. Of course, she told me, there were some confusions. How was she to know that "Dole" did not describe the bright yellow fruit that Putlibai knew as "annanas" pictured on the label? She wondered about the word she read, "pineapple." The fruit she knew as "annanas" and the picture on the can were nowhere near being an apple, and the only pine she knew was on cleaning bottles. According to Rosario's niece, it described the fresh smell of a tree. "But when I learned about pineapple upside-down cake from Rosario," Putlibai said to me, "I connected the picture with p-i-n-e-ap-p-l-e. Peaches, pears, and tomato juice were easy but I still don't know why anyone wants to put chicken and fish in cans. Even cooked spaghetti. The spaghetti, the sauce. Meat and everything."

One evening, she was sitting in front of that grocery store wall, looking at the cans, trying to learn the spelling of "tomato sauce" and "tomato paste" and trying to remember about the difference between sauce and paste. Which one was thinner and flowed easily into the pans from the cans when she was cooking and which was the one she had to scrape out of the can and into the pan. Which one was better for curry and which one for Rosario's Mexican-Italian spaghetti sauce when fresh tomatoes were expensive. And as she was thinking about curry and spaghetti and her friend Rosario, the floor under her feet rose up and rolled. The wall in front of her swayed and cracked and began to fall down. Putlibai screamed, the others screamed, but the earthquake noise was very loud. The cans made a terrific sound as they fell off the shelves. When the sound subsided and the earth stopped moving, Putlibai opened her eyes. One of the men from her brother's gossip-gamble group was lying next to her. She didn't know his name. She didn't even know if she had seen him before. She had followed Mohan's order not to raise her eyes and look at any of the men. But she had to look at the man lying next to her because she knew that she had to pull him out from under the cans and away from further disaster. A few months after the earthquake she had to marry him.

Putlibai laughed at the look on my face when she came to that part of the story. "You are surprised. This man was called Vikram and he really did not want to marry me. Poor man. He did not want to marry anyone. He was always sad and also I think, he was always an angry man. He said that people had lied to him. America had not given him riches, only hard work, very little money, people who hated him, and he had to pay taxes. He missed his family in India very much. He lived in Berkeley. He worked in the evenings as a janitor in an office building while studying to be an accountant. He had been visiting his friend, the grocery-store owner, the night of the earthquake. He did not want to marry an American woman. Not even a woman like me, an Indian woman who lived in America. But my brother Mohan who had been searching for me, in all the wrong places of the fallen down grocery store, at last found me as I came out from under a wall. I was dragging a man, my arms around his shoulders, his head against my breasts. Other men and women had also seen this sight. Mohan insisted that the man should marry me. After all I had saved his life."

Putlibai said that she had been quite excited about this next chapter of her life in America. But even now, so many years later, as she was dying in a hospital room, she did not know what her feelings were about her husband, except that somewhere at the back of her mind, he was still a man she was not supposed to look at directly.

While Vikram had worked or studied, Putlibai went to a series of jobs. She was once again in small windowless rooms behind sewing machines. She sewed in sweatshops run by Irish immigrants, Chinese immigrants, Indian immigrants and others whose immigrant ancestors had taken over the land a couple of centuries earlier. Putlibai had walked all over Berkeley. In an attempt to protect herself from the stares and voices of people, she went from job to job dressed in pants and tunics, long skirts and blouses instead of the saris she preferred. What she wore did not matter. Some people looked away from her, passed their words through her, made her transparent, insubstantial. Others deliberately, cruelly shot glances and their words against her. Their resentment of her, this dark, foreign woman, was reflected in their cold eyes and sharp words. She was also aware of the others who patronized her with their controlled smiles and loud voices. Her body ached as she moved through Berkeley after spending many hours hunched over a sewing machine under a bare light bulb.

The wall under which she had found her husband haunted Putlibai's marriage. And years later, in that South San Francisco hospital room, Putlibai still thought about how walls seemed to have followed her around the world.

"You know, Katy, I sometimes wonder what would have happened if I had not pulled that poor man out from under that wall. I don't think he would have died or anything like that and he certainly would not have had to marry me."

"Wasn't he a good husband?" I asked her.

78

"He was an OK husband, I guess. He didn't drink or anything like that. He didn't ever hurt me or anything like that. He didn't waste money and gave me money when I needed it. But he punished me whenever I was late coming home. Because I had to work late or because I had taken a longer road. I often did that so I didn't have to pass the man with the dog who always shook his finger at me and said, 'Take your filthy self back to where you came from.'"

"He beat you."

Putlibai should have left Vikram under the wall.

"Nah! As I told you, nothing like that. What he did, you know, was he made me stand with my face turned towards the wall. For many hours without food, no water. He said that he was actually being good to me. He was trying to teach me to be punctual. Everything and everyone in America had to be punctual. His boss had told him that. Otherwise we would never be successful. He kept on saying, 'Time is Money.' He made me stand like that, my face to that wall, because that is how his teachers in India had punished him. He said that is how he had learned and that is how he was going to teach me. I told him he was crazy, but if I didn't stand like that, he got very angry and yelled, 'I will send you back to my family in India. I will tell them you are a bad woman. You now belong to me, my family.' So I stood there, my face against the wall. I didn't tell Mohan. He would have worried and been angry. But I was already married, you know. What could he do? That is what I thought."

Putlibai looked at me and smiled her shy, sweet smile.

"I'll tell you something, Katy. Because I know you won't laugh at me. To pass the time while I was facing that wall, to make it easy to stand without moving for so long, to make myself not to think of my muscles which used to tremble and then after some time become stiff, I used to imagine that I was flying over the whole world, that I was visiting places I knew— Sindhu, Devinagar, Karachi, New York, Rosario's house. And also places I wish I could go to. You know, the places Rosario and I used to talk about. So I flew from Berkeley to Sindhu to Karachi to New York to Marysville to London to Moscow to Rio with that big statue and the mountain and to Tokyo and even to Machu Pichu and the North Pole. Rosario had told me about that place in Peru and Mohan always wanted to know everything about the North Pole. Even when we were living in Karachi he told me stories about the North Pole. You should have seen me Katy, I flew over houses and through forests. I held out my arms like this, as I flew over land."

Putlibai stretched out her arms, sitting up in her bed, supported by numerous pillows, her white braids meager and long against the starched pillowcases. I could see Putlibai on her journeys. A sea creature moving through air. Over lakes as large as the Mediterranean, rivers as wide as the Mississippi. Looking down on mountains and hills and cities with wonder.

I said, "My friend Carmelita knows all about these things. I know she and my other friend Ratna would like to meet you. I will bring them to visit you. But only if you want to meet them, Putlibai."

"Katy, isn't it good to have friends! Carmelita is from Mexico, yes? And Ratna is from India? Of course I would love to meet them. It gets a bit lonely here. Do you know that one day Rosario actually saw me land in the watermelon field she was working in? That evening she phoned me all the way from her home in Marysville to my home in Berkeley to tell me that I had appeared out of nowhere and that I had told her about a Chinese way of healing. Acupuncture. I must tell you, Katy, I was quite surprised."

Women flying around the world on their own power, landing in watermelon fields to visit with friends wasn't all that different from my own ability to see a strange, unexplained woman with a butterfly. I nodded at Putlibai, silently acknowledging my own familiarity with dislocations of time and space. In one of her discussions on "the other-worldly," Carmelita had told us that her Grandmother Luz had explained to her that the ability to bilocate in time and space was a power reserved strictly for extraordinary beings. Santos, santas, or the Devil himself. I knew that Putlibai was aligned with the former beings, creatures, whatever way Carmelita would classify them.

Putlibai explained the real cause of her surprise when she received the call from Rosario. "A few days before Rosario saw me, a Chinese woman who sat next to me at one of my jobs—we both sewed fancy buttons on blouses—had told me about acupuncture. The next day, I was late coming home. I tried hard but I never was good about time and all that, and I was more afraid of that man with the dog than of standing facing the wall. So while I was standing, looking at the wall, I flew to China. I thought I would fly over that long wall that Rosario and I had read about in one of her niece's books, but instead I flew over a very long, very narrow river. There were houses with balconies hanging over the water and boats with rooms with roofs made of big, dried leaves sailing on that river. And I said to myself that I would tell Rosario about this place in China and acupuncture. And I didn't even have to phone her to tell her! I just flew over and told her. And I didn't even know I had done that! Pretty good if we could do that all the time. Save on telephone bills!"

I said, "My friends Ratna and Carmelita say that we can teach ourselves to do it."

"The phone company would not like that, you know!" Putlibai laughed. "Rosario reminded me about that surprise visit two years later when I left my husband and went to her. Rosario was a widow by then. Her husband had died one year after the earthquake. I went to Rosario the day after she phoned me to say that my brother Mohan had died in an accident. He was driving a friend to the airport when a car tried to pass them and crashed into the car Mohan was driving. He died at once."

Putlibai wiped her eyes with the corner of her bed sheet and for the next few minutes clapped her hands quietly, singing her mother's song softly to herself.

I sat by Putlibai's bed and remembered how I had danced that strange circular dance in my room in Lakewood, trying to recapture my memories of my childhood home, my father, my friends of those lost years. I wondered if clapping my hands would have helped. I didn't know if my mother had ever taught me any songs.

"You know what I did when I heard about Mohan's death?" Putlibai asked. "I told Vikram that I was going to Rosario's farm to bury my brother or to cremate him. Whatever I could do. And then I would work for Rosario until I had enough money to buy a little house next to the sea. I missed the sound of the ocean. Vikram looked at me as if I had become completely crazy. He didn't even shout his usual, 'Go! Go! Face to that wall. Quickly.' He pointed to the wall. His hand was shaking. That was the time that I saw that the wall was watery green. Ugly. I had never noticed that before. This time I couldn't fly. Not in the air, not over the waters. I just stood at the wall, crying for my brother. I loved him so much. And then when I turned around, I saw that my husband was also crying. That is the first time that we hugged. You know—outside the bedroom and all that. And he told me that I should do what I wanted and he would tear up our marriage certificate and would return to India. He told me to take whatever money I wanted from the cabinet under the table. Next morning before he went to work he left the key to the cabinet on top of the television.

"I didn't go to any of my jobs the next morning. I opened the door of the small cabinet and found a manila envelope with five hundred and sixty dollars, an Indian movie magazine with pictures of Madhubala. She used to be very pretty in those days. Long time ago. There was also a small wooden elephant with ivory and a green velvet howdah, a small brightly colored metal statue of Ganesha and a notebook with blue lines and red margins with a picture of Gandhiji on the cover. The note book was filled with words and sayings from political speeches of leaders from all over the world. I removed two hundred and fifty dollars from the manila envelope, closed the cabinet door carefully, placed the two hundred and fifty dollars in my bag, boarded a bus to San Francisco and then another bus that took me from San Francisco to Rosario. She sent me off to Pescadero in her cousin's truck. I liked Pescadero very, very much. It has fields and the ocean."

I found out about Putlibai's life in Pescadero during my next three visits to the hospital.

Putlibai had worked in the artichoke, brussel sprout and pumpkin fields of Pescadero. Sometimes she helped Rosario's cousin's family run their small roadside stand. She learned to drive a truck when she was fifty years old. And she covered the walls of the small house she rented with pictures cut out of magazines. Pictures of actors, actresses, models, gardens, dogs, cats, cows, butterflies, cars, houses, flowers and even politicians had brightened her walls. She told me that her neighbors' children loved to visit her so they could either identify the pictures for her or listen to the stories she made up about the pictures.

A few years after Putlibai had set up her little house in Pescadero, Rosario had come to live with her.

Rosario died seven years later, absolutely convinced that her husband from India was waiting for her in whichever part of heaven God had set aside for them.

Putlibai and Rosario had many arguments about reincarnation. Putlibai had wanted assurances from Rosario that she would be her blood-sister in their next shared life. The choice of the earthly location was left up to Rosario. Rosario, a devout but relaxed Catholic who had felt no need to convert Putlibai, had tried to explain the permanence of heaven and hell to a rather confused Putlibai.

"You burn forever, and forever and forever? Why?" Putlibai had asked.

"Because of sin. Bad things you have done. For not loving God. Sometimes not forever. Sometimes you can go to heaven after some time spent in an in-between place. Not hell, not heaven."

"Heaven sounds better. Isn't that where you hear angels sing all the time and there are no troubles?"

"Can you think of anything better?"

"Not really except maybe if I get to sing sometimes!"

"Not with your voice!"

"Why not? I'll sing the songs my mother taught me. I'll sing my mother's songs in this Christian heaven."

Rosario told Putlibai that she would have to learn to translate those songs better. Even she, Rosario, had trouble understanding Putlibai's English-Spanish renditions of her mother's songs. And that just wouldn't do for the angels in heaven.

Putlibai was never quite convinced about the permanence of hell or heaven. She had another idea.

"What if after we both die, we become those fish women? Like the ones you have on the shelf in the living room. Not made of clay or ceramic like the ones you have but real flesh-and-blood fish women. They swim and sing all day long. And take care of babies. And get married only if they want to. You told me that yourself."

Rosario refused to even consider that idea. "If I come back, I come back as a human being. A human woman. With legs and all that."

I sketched a mermaid for Putlibai on the back of the photograph of Rosario that Putlibai had propped up against her water pitcher on the table next to her bed.

As I was wondering what kind of a frame I should buy for the photograph of Rosario, Putlibai said, "After Rosario died, I would look very carefully at all my neighbors' new babies to see if Rosario had at last decided on coming back to this earth but had messed up the timing, you know, and been reborn while I was still alive but was already on my way to death. She would be here and I would die soon and be there. Very messed-up timing!"

When Putlibai said that, the old barefoot woman entered Putlibai's room for the first time. She was always next to me whenever I drove to the hospital but disappeared as soon as I entered the hospital lobby. I leaned over to rub my knees and my ankles when I saw the old woman. The pain was horrible and I didn't want Putlibai to see the old woman. To distract myself from my pain and the entrance of the old woman, I asked Putlibai how she had come to the hospital.

She said that when she realized that she was getting old but was still healthy, she took out medical insurance. When she knew that the pain in her stomach was going to lead to her death, she bid a cheerful farewell to her friends and neighbors in Pescadero. She invented a niece who had just come from India to Berkeley and told them that she was going to live with her and then go off to India. She said that she wanted to die in India. She explained to me that she had lived independently for so long that she didn't want to burden them with her death. But Putlibai was determined to die in America. That was the only way she knew how to acknowledge the land in which she had lived for so long, where Mohan had been buried, where she had found her friend Rosario and rediscovered the sound of the sea.

Her illness took her to the Kaiser Hospital in South San Francisco. She ended her story with, "Here I met you. My new friend. From Devinagar. You know Katy, you could have been my daughter. You look so much like my mother and a bit like me." I didn't tell her that my mother was an Englishwoman.

A few weeks after Putlibai told me about Rosario's death and her fears that Rosario would miss her timing and come to earth right when she herself was dying, Putlibai started having nightmares about dying in her hospital room, her face turned towards the wall with the crack. She dreamed that she was being pulled into the wall, absorbed by it, as she was dying. She told me about her nightmares, and she asked me to find out if there was a home outside the hospital where she could die.

I talked to Carmelita and Ratna about Putlibai's fear of dying in the hospital.

Carmelita said, "For heaven's sake, Katy, take her in. You have an extra room. You know how to take care of invalids. And you said you missed the company of older women now that you have been to India. And at least this one will talk with you. Not like your barefoot, butterfly lady with ribbons in her hair."

Putlibai discharged herself and came to live with me. I watched her as she sat hour after hour in the backyard which is surrounded by ragged, staunch hedges. She remained in the yard even when the fog moved into the street and over the cemetery like layers of starched muslin, even when the sun had set and the fog horns could be heard from across the highway and the bluffs. She looked at the flowers and the vegetables. She caressed and sniffed the small rocks bordering the marigolds and the petunias. And every morning the first thing she did was pick up a handful of the earth. She kept the dirt in her left hand until she decided to go to bed. At that point she slowly walked over to the vegetable plot, knelt down and patted her fistful of earth over the soil which was kept aside for tomatoes, beans, peas, pumpkins, lettuce, sage and cilantro. As the weeks went by, I found myself having to walk out into the backyard every evening to help Putlibai get up from her task of placing the earth back on to the land.

One evening, after dinner, Putlibai asked me about her family. I told her about Agnes and the Sanders. I tried to explain that I had no distinct memory of my life before the age of eleven. I spoke of my hazy memories of Freddy and green places and the song "K-K-K-Katy."

"And your mother?" asked Putlibai.

"I don't know where she is. She was an Englishwoman named Margaret

Shriver Cooper. My Aunt Agnes is trying to find out where she is."

Putlibai smiled. "Never mind. Now you have a mother. An old mother you are helping to die happily. Too bad we didn't meet earlier. I would have taught you how to sew properly and how to make your nice long black hair in a better style than this bundle you wear and I would have protected you so that you would have many memories, many happy memories. And if you would have allowed, I would have come to listen to you when you taught at the big university. I would have prayed for the Sanderses when they left you all the money so that you could live in this house, and paint and grow flowers and vegetables."

And then she laughed, "If I had been your mother, there would have been no Sanderses! But we would have done alright, the two of us. Maybe in our next life, I can take care of you."

I who had not cried in grief, anger, or pain in such a long time that I had completely forgotten the mechanics of the eyes, nose, throat and ears as they become involved with tears, found myself sobbing, blowing my nose, wiping my eyes and getting a terrible headache.

One day, Putlibai said, "Katy, I want to be buried in your backyard. Near the vegetables."

"I don't think it is possible."

"Why not? I am an old woman. Quite thin and light now, you know. I am sure Carmelita and Ratna will help you. If you want, you can burn me first and then bury the leftovers."

"Putlibai, people can't bury people in the backyard. There are zoning laws and death certificates."

"Why the death certificate? I don't have any papers, certificates. Why now the death certificate?"

"We will tell everyone a few days before I die, that I have gone away to India, to die. I will know when it is time to tell our story. I will then remain hidden in the house and yard. Very careful, you know. And then you can bury me in the backyard."

"And what will happen if I move away, go to another house?"

"Nothing. I will be dead. And the tomatoes will grow much better."

"And you will haunt the yard?" I laughed nervously.

"Nah. Have you seen any ghosts in the cemetery across from us?"

I said nothing and began to rub my knees.

"You have! How interesting. But don't worry, I will not haunt you or anyone. I know what I will do! I will become one of those women with fish tails and live in the sea. Just like I talked to my friend Rosario."

"A mermaid. And how will we then meet in our next life? I don't want to be a mermaid."

"Mermaids don't have legs and knees to hurt!"

I told Putlibai that only fish should have fish tails. And if reincarnation really did happen, then people should be reincarnated as people. I wished I could believe that the dead remained dead.

"Putlibai," I said, "Please tell me what I should do with you when you die. I really can't bury you here. Too risky."

"I'll think," said Putlibai and went off to her bed.

I thought Putlibai had forgotten about the burial in the backyard idea until she brought up the subject when Ratna and Carmelita were visiting us one Friday night.

"You will please help Katy bury me in her backyard," she told them very politely.

Carmelita nodded. Ratna said, "Not cremate?"

I tried to argue. Putlibai once again outlined her plan. She would supposedly return to India but in truth she would die in my house and be buried in my backyard. Carmelita said that she thought that not only was this a good and feasible idea, it was the only place where Putlibai should be buried.

"What kind of a coffin do you want?" she asked.

Putlibai thought for a moment. "No coffin. Just a big white bag. Put me in it. Make a very deep hole and then cover me up."

Ratna said, "But Putlibai you are a Hindu. Don't you want to be cremated? We can then scatter your ashes in the ocean."

Putlibai was tempted but then realized the difficulties. "Nah. Just bury me. How will you burn me here, in Katy's garden? Too messy and all that. Just bury me."

Ratna helped Carmelita sew a heavy white bag of parachute material. Putlibai inspected it and approved of it. I realized that events were being taken out of my control. Just like the time Carmelita had sent me off to Oaxaca with the "Lady's Support."

A few weeks later, as Ratna, Carmelita and I sat in the Italian restaurant in Colma, and I announced Putlibai's death. I described how I had slipped the white parachute bag over Putlibai after giving her a sponge bath scented with her favorite lavender water, placed her on a rug, carefully dragged the rug to the garage and then put her in the big chest freezer.

The three of us had already dug a hole five days after Putlibai's request. The hole was deep and secure. Ratna and Carmelita had lined it with dried sage, cedar shavings and sandalwood incense sticks and then covered it with a piece of wood. I had transplanted some flowers from five small, tough green plastic containers on to the mound of earth, which we had piled up out of the hole we had dug. It was while she was overseeing this digging of the earth and the transplanting of the flowers that Putlibai told me that she didn't want to have anything more to do with doctors. I phoned Putlibai's doctor and left a message for him saying that the old lady had turned stubborn and left for India.

We buried Putlibai very early in the morning of the day after our lunch in Colma. I, who had not followed the Sanderses' religious teachings and any of the Catholic rituals since I had left high school, was surprised at the ease with which I could join Carmelita as she recited the rosary over Putlibai's grave. Ratna quietly recited a hymn her grandmother had composed in Sanskrit when her grandmother's older sister had died. She didn't translate it.

# X.

## Half Moon Bay, California

### *Ratna Returns to India*

As we sat in my living room after Putlibai's burial ceremony, I looked at the graves across the street rising like islands from the streams of water flowing through the cemetery. Carmelita was restless. She wandered into the kitchen, got herself a glass of water, fiddled with the radio, and walked back into the living room. She said, "People keep on telling me that association with death makes human beings want to create new life. I read all those novels, when people jump into bed and have great sex after having been at funerals or after having escaped death themselves. I don't think of beds and sex, or even of creation, after funerals and accidents. Ever since I saw my Grandmother Luz's face at my Mom's funeral, I have been turned off from the idea of giving birth."

Carmelita told us that her Grandmother Luz hadn't cried when her daughter, Carmelita's mother, died but her face had caved into itself, collapsed into her skull. All the parts that made up her face—the cheeks, the forehead, the chin, the nose—retreated from the outside world. Only her eyes continued to look the same. She didn't lament her loss as personal or unique. She kept saying, "No woman should see her child die. No woman should have to attend her own child's funeral. God should not let it happen. It proves that He is cruel." Carmelita's grandmother never smiled afterwards and the only picture of the Virgin she allowed in her house after her daughter's funeral was that of La Soledad. And the only story she would tell her grandchildren was about la llorona, the woman who had appeared to her husband, Carmelita's Grandfather Ignacio, so many years ago. She told the story again and again and again, always look-ing for an explanation for the woman's act. She would say, "Maybe she didn't kill her children. The real murderers told the world she had." Then later she would ask, "Who made her so crazy that she killed her own children? I tell you she killed them because she had no food to feed them." The last time she told the story to Carmelita, she said, "The reason why she killed her children was because that was the only way she knew how to kill herself. To kill her soul. The children went to heaven but she didn't go no nowhere. Not really. Just wandering around, with nowhere to go. Just scaring people with her screams and her tears." Grandmother Luz died the morning after she told Carmelita this version of la llorona's story, five weeks after Carmelita's mother's funeral.

I pulled my sketch book towards myself, leaned over to pick the pencil which was stuck in Ratna's chignon and, of course, dislodged numerous hairpins from her hair. I began to draw the rain falling through the eucalyptus trees. Sharp, liquid knives, filling up the creek across the road. One of the trees formed the outlines of a woman's bloated body. The woman's tears were thick streams of blood that flowed onto the small creatures with hungry, open mouths crouching at her feet. I knew that I would use oranges, reds, and grays for the painting. No hint of blue. I passed a Kleenex to Ratna, who was crying as she got up from her chair to put her arms around Carmelita.

Carmelita thanked Ratna and said, "So here we are, three middle-aged women who know something about death, who have buried an old woman in a garden, defied, I suppose, some kind of man-made law. But none of us have given birth. To a human child."

Ratna came back to her chair, "I have."

We stared at her.

"You have?" Carmelita forgot her grief. She was angry. "And you never told us about it? We who are your friends? Or did you think that Katy and I would not be interested in your child? Do you think we are selfish spinsters? Self-centred? Why do you tell us now? Now, after we have just faced death?"

"Shut up, Carmelita." I was also shouting.

Ratna was not shouting. "Because the time wasn't right. One tells the different parts of one's life when and if the time is right. Just as you never told us about your Grandmother Luz's obsession with la llorona after your mother's death. Just as you never talked about why you yourself had no children."

"Why now?" Carmelita was still angry.

"Because you brought up the subject of children and because I gave birth to a child and I saw her die."

"Oh Mother of God!" Carmelita crossed herself. "Forgive me."

Ratna and I knew that Carmelita in her own way was begging for forgiveness from both Ratna and the Mother of God.

"Don't worry, Carmelita." And then Ratna began to speak. Ratna who always listened to Carmelita's memories and my search for my memories with great seriousness, laughing or shaking her head in bemusement or sympathy at the appropriate times, shedding her hair pins all over the floor, Ratna who always spoke about herself in terms of her political aunt, her learned grandmother, and her ancestresses from mythology and legends; now she spoke about herself.

"My father and mother fled Karachi just a few months before the 1947 partition of India."

I looked at her with surprise.

"Yes Katy, my father's family was from Karachi and I think my paternal aunt went to the same school as your Aunt Agnes. But your aunt went to the Mama Parsi Girls' School right after Partition while my aunt had already matriculated and left Karachi with my parents. It was July 1947. Right before Independence and Partition. A Muslim friend smuggled them out of Karachi. He got them onto a ship bound for Bombay and told them to contact a Hindu business partner of his in Bombay. And of course my maternal family, my grandparents and my aunt, were living in Bombay.

"My father hid the little bit of money he had in the false bottom of a bucket—without telling my mother about it. She thought he was carrying the money in his personal bag. When they at last arrived at the docks in Bombay, the man they had hired to carry their luggage, walked off with their bags and that bucket which my mother had filled with some odds and ends from her kitchen in Karachi. She actually saw the man take out all that kitchen stuff and then toss the bucket into the sea. But since she didn't know what her husband had hidden within that bucket, she didn't tell him about it. It didn't seem as important to her as losing all their other bags and bundles with their clothes and household linens and pots and pans."

"One more reason for husbands to take their wives into their confidence." Our friend Carmelita stated the obvious.

"What would they have done if she had told her husband? Jumped into the Arabian Sea?" I asked.

"It really wasn't all that big a calamity. My parents and my father's sister arrived in safety when so many, on both sides, never arrived or arrived with nothing but hatred and bitterness, with unending grief. My father kept in touch with his Muslim friend for many years, until his friend died. And now he corresponds with his friend's son in Karachi. He even attended the son's wedding a few years ago because he said that he was the young man's paternal uncle and therefore shouldn't be absent at his wedding."

Until I went to India and met Roxanne and my Aunt Agnes and Roxanne's Grandmother Meheramai and my Great-aunt Virbaiji, I would never have understood about this family thing. Family by blood, family by duty, family by kindnesses. The Sanderses always made a very clear distinction between who was family and who was not family but merely a friend. Not that either of them had a large family. One sibling each. I mentioned this to Carmelita and Ratna, and Carmelita who had not met my foster parents said, "Katy, just think of their idea of the All American Family. But since the Sanderses had only you, Katy, they didn't quite qualify. They needed one and a half more children to be an All American Family." Carmelita was precise.

"And a dog," said Ratna. "My father said that he couldn't continue to live with my mother's family in Bombay because there were always animals in the family compound and they somehow managed to wander into the house. He was particularly allergic to one of the dogs. But of course, the real reason was that he wanted to have his own home and support his own sister and wife. And children, when they came along."

"And once again, they had only you. One child. Not very Indian."

"Carmelita," said Ratna, "I'll tell you a secret. But please promise not to tell it to anyone, any non-Indian, who specializes in studying India."

Carmelita crossed her eyes and turned them toward the ceiling. A portrait of a saint looking at heaven with demented ecstasy.

"Many Indians have only one child. And some Indians don't have even one child."

"Well your parents had you, and you have just informed us that you too had a child. I would like to know more." Carmelita looked very serious.

"My father went to his Muslim friend's Hindu business partner in Bombay and he, Mr Sharma, helped my father and did a lot for our family. He himself had no family and my mother and aunt began to treat him as a part of our family. I was born six years later and grew up thinking of him as my uncle. He fell in love with my father's sister but she had already fallen in love with someone else and when my mother kept on lecturing her about gratitude and the basic stupidity of confusing love with marriage, my aunt eloped."

"Mother of God, Ratna, and you never told us about that either! Women in my family, even good Catholics as we are, have separated from their husbands or have had affairs. Sordid, glorious, or otherwise. But no one has eloped!"

"A few years later, when I was about sixteen," Ratna was looking out at the rain, "Mr Sharma asked my father for my hand in marriage."

"He must have been at least thirty years older." Carmelita didn't seem very disturbed.

"No, nearly forty years older. He wanted to have a family. He wanted a child. He had wanted to marry my aunt and now he wanted to marry me. Because he said he wanted real ties with our family. My father wasn't too happy about the request but my mother was pleased. She felt that we owed Mr Sharma a double debt. First, because he had helped us when we came with nothing in our hands to Bombay. He gave my father a job and befriended us. And second, because my aunt had eloped rather than accept his offer of marriage. So I married him."

Ratna looked at us.

"You should see yourselves! You are acting as if you are paying me a condolence visit! Yes, he was nearly forty years older and yes, I had just turned sixteen when I got married. But no, it was not at all terrible. He was very kind and gentle and loving. And when one day I told him that the only thing I regretted was not being able to go to college, he said, 'Ratna, I promise you that once you have had our baby, I will see to it that you go to the best college we can find. You won't even have to take care of the baby. If you want to go abroad, I will send you. I promise you.' And then he began to bring home books on all kinds of subjects so that I could prepare myself for college. He even hired tutors to teach me science and math."

"Did you love him?" I wanted to know.

"Yes. And I still do."

Carmelita began to build a fire. The end of the drought also meant the beginning of the traditional Half Moon Bay chill.

"A year after we were married, I gave birth to a baby. A girl. My husband was delighted. I asked if he wanted me to wait for my college education until we had a boy. He said, 'Ratna, I wanted a baby. You have given me a baby. A beautiful, intelligent little daughter. Just look at her eyes! I tell you, she will be strong and intelligent and courageous. And we will let her do whatever she wants to do with her life.' But the baby died within two weeks. One of my friends told me it was my fault. According to her, the baby had sensed my impatience to exchange marriage and motherhood for college and so had decided to die and go away from me. I became very depressed and my mother told me that I should be ashamed. No woman had the right to go mad. Women had to be strong. My husband was furious at both my friend and my mother. He told me that he saw the baby's birth and the baby's death as a lesson in humility. A lesson, he told me, not to ask for so much. Not to put such a burden on a young girl such as I. He insisted that I be present when the baby was cremated because he wanted me to start a new life. He sent off all the tutors and spent a month teaching me how to take care of finances. He then sold his business, turned over all his money to me, after paying my tuition and other expenses for an education at Columbia University, and then went off to Varanasi. He had often said that he considered that city not a city of death and mourning but of music, miracles, and learning. 'The Lord Shiva dances there, every single moment, every single second, every breath we take,' he used to say. I myself took a job at Sierra College after I got my degree because it is in California. My husband had seen some pictures of San Francisco and at one time had said that that was the only city in the United States that he wanted to see."

I told them how Roxanne had told me that if she could not live in Devinagar, the only other city she would live in was Varanasi. She liked it, she said, because it was like a living portrait of India.

"I must meet Roxanne one day, Katy. A poet lawyer! A lawyer poet?" And then Carmelita turned to Ratna, "Is your husband still there?"

"Yes. In Varanasi. I have nothing but good memories of him. And Carmelita, you may laugh as much as you want to, but I have had no lover as wonderful and as caring as he was. I miss him."

Carmelita shook her head, "I am not laughing, Ratna."

I put down the paper and pencil and began the familiar motion of rubbing my right knee with my left hand, my left knee with my right hand. Carmelita took the afghan from the back of the sofa and placed it across my knees.

Ratna looked at the two of us and said, "It is strange, but my husband's face and his voice are the only face and voice I remember from India. When I think of India now, I think of the landscape. The way the sun makes the earth smell. Sort of the dull, burned, baked smell before the rains come and then after the rains, the smell of wet soil and dripping trees. A smell that enters right into your skin. And the jasmine here does not look as seductive and secretive as in India. And I long to hear the koyal's cry before the rain. And I haven't yet found a flower in America that has the satin of the champak. No, not even the magnolia. And the roses here are so completely desexed. And I don't think there is any place in America where the light at twilight becomes mixed up with the yellow from the outdoor fires and from the low voltage bare bulbs shining through open windows. And no one in America really welcomes the dawn or the night so publicly. With

Hindu temple bells and calls of the Muslim aazan and with people cleaning their teeth and clearing their throats. Loudly."

Carmelita laughed, "Try Oaxaca. I don't know about the bird you mentioned and the temple bells and the calls to prayers. But there are church bells and all the rest you mentioned. Including sexy roses."

Ratna said, "One day when Putlibai and I were standing on the beach, looking at the ocean, she said, 'Yes, this is the sound of the ocean which connects me to my mother's home in Sindhu and the home we had in Karachi. It is always there, this sound. Sometimes it sounds like the lions I used to hear in Karachi.' I must have looked surprised because she laughed and said, 'In the distance. They were in the zoo and whenever they were hungry, or in the middle of the night maybe because they couldn't sleep, they would make loud sounds that went up and down like the sound of these waves. And sometimes the ocean sounds like very big music. One sound which goes on and on in the back while the other sounds come and go.' I have been thinking of Putlibai and the lions and the ocean and the sound of my husband's voice and have decided to go back to India. Soon. Maybe at the end of this semester. Even if it is just for a few months. I would like to see my husband again. If I can find him. When he left, he broke all ties-with me, my family, his friends. Before he sent me off to study in America, he said, 'Ratna, consider yourself free now. Do what you want to do with your life.' And I have done what I want with my life. But I do miss the land there and I would like to see him again, if I can find him."

I looked across at the old woman sitting with her bare feet tucked under her, the butterfly sitting motionless on her head. Carmelita and Ratna recognized what I was doing but they were startled at what I did next. I spoke to the old woman they couldn't see but knew was there. As far as they knew, I had never spoken to the old woman. Not directly.

"Well!" I yelled at the old woman. "And what do you think of all this? What can you tell me of my father? My mother? The landscape of my early life?"

The old woman opened her mouth and spoke. And Freddy's voice came out of the old woman's voice. "K-K-K-Katy, run. Run my dear to Mr Sanders." And I turned to my friends and said, "What is that smell? Is it the rain on the hedges in the back yard? Smells more like blood to me."

Carmelita was gentle, "It may be both. Did the woman answer?"

I shook my head. "No, just the same old thing. Freddy telling me to run to Mr Sanders. I wish Aunt Agnes had found out something about my mother. Even if she is dead or alive."

"Why don't you try again to find those relatives of yours? The Mehta mother and daughter. They may have been in touch with your mother

Margaret and your late Grandfather Eddie. They could tell you something about your mother."

"Carmelita," said Ratna, "You need to understand. Katy's grandfather, Eddie Cooper, was pro-British. He was an Empirewallah. He was traveling around with his English mistress. On the opposite end of the scale, Katy's cousin, Dinaz Mehta, was sent off to America because she and her husband made bombs to blow the British out of India! They would not keep in touch."

"I'll try some more to find them," I said.

I was very tired. I missed Putlibai. Listening to the rain, I wondered if the end of the drought meant the beginning of floods. Mud slides across 92 West and arguments, debates, discussions, letters in the *Half Moon Bay Review* about what could be done about Devil's Slide on Highway 1 falling into the Pacific Ocean.

I tried once again, to find my relatives in California. But the K Mehta phone was still disconnected and there was no D or Dinaz Mehta listed. I wrote to Roxanne asking her to see if she could get the Mehta address from our Great-aunt Virbaiji in Bombay. I had met Virbaiji very briefly during my trip to India. If a face with large, intelligent eyes and a good strong nose set in softly rounded, somewhat chubby cheeks could be called patrician, then Virbaiji had a patrician face. She certainly had a patrician bearing. And a very infectious giggle. Virbaiji had struck me as a woman who would carefully preserve all addresses, all memories of all her family members and friends.

I didn't know that the K Mehta phone was disconnected because K—Kamal—Mehta had closed up her apartment in San Francisco and disconnected her phone. She had taken leave from her job and was in temporary lodgings in a one-room apartment in South San Francisco, to be closer to her mother who was at the hospital. Since I had stopped my Hospice work at the South San Francisco Kaiser Hospital to take care of Putlibai, I didn't know that Dinaz Mehta was admitted to the same hospital soon after Putlibai left. And while I was waiting to hear from Roxanne about the Mehta address, Dinaz Mehta was dying in the hospital, a half an hour drive from my house.

# XI.

## Half Moon Bay, California

### *My Cousin Roxanne Involves Me in Her Quest*

Lucia di Lammermoor was going stark raving mad on Public Television when my phone rang. It was Roxanne Japanwallah. She was calling from the San Francisco Airport, yelling into the pay phone.

"Hello Katayun! This is your cousin Roxanne. Roxanne Japanwallah. I am at the San Francisco Airport."

I pulled my phone away from my ear and said, "Hello Roxanne. What a nice surprise!"

Roxanne continued to shout into the phone, "I am calling to invite myself to stay with you for a few days. Sorry I didn't give you any notice but I didn't have time to write to you. I tried to call you from Devinagar but you don't seem to have one of those answering machine things."

I did have an answering machine, but it was broken. I had been painting and getting used to the absence of Putlibai and had not bothered about getting a new machine. Ratna had gone to India in search of her husband, and Carmelita knew that the best time to call me was late at night

"Hello Katayun! Hello? Hello? What bus do I take to get to you? I have only one small bag. I am on a quest."

Roxanne didn't elaborate and I didn't ask.

"I have landed in San Francisco via Bombay, Toulouse, France, and New York."

"Toulouse?" I asked her.

"Yes, Languedoc, Cathars and all that."

"My friend Ratna Sharma was nearly kidnapped by gypsies in Toulouse."

"Kidnapped? Who kidnapped her? When?"

"Nearly." I wondered how the conversation had sidetracked into the subject of gypsies in Toulouse.

"I was told that the gypsies arrive in that part of France seasonally. Some of them from India. But I didn't go there for the gypsies. I went there because of our Great-aunt Virbaiji, the one who lives in Bombay, and her adopted son Sarosh. Did you ever meet Sarosh? He is a doctor."

I said that I hadn't met him.

"Anyway," Roxanne continued, "they asked me to visit a scholar in Toulouse. He studies the Cathars and has traced them to the Zoroastrians. Virbaiji and Sarosh wanted me to take some books and letters and photographs to him. I wish I could have sneaked out of India . . . but you know the family! Virbaiji doesn't know I am in America on a quest. She thinks I am on a regular vacation. She told me to go to France first. So I went there. But Katy-Katayun. I have some serious business to do in America. What bus do I take to get to Half Moon Bay?"

I told her that I would pick her up at the airport in forty minutes.

I turned off the operatic suicides, murders, and general mayhem being carried on all across my television screen, left a message on Carmelita's phone machine informing her of Roxanne's arrival, and drove off to the airport.

As Roxanne and I merged into the late evening traffic on Highway 92, going west towards Half Moon Bay, Roxanne pointed at Crystal Lake. "A lake split into two by a road!" She began counting the number of shades of green on the trees we passed. When she saw the California poppies, she said, "Yellow poppies! Yellow, golden poppies! Do people make opium or some such things out of these?"

I started to laugh. Roxanne joined in, "Of course not! We are now in the United States of America. Where is the ocean?"

And so I drove Roxanne to the Poplar Beach bluffs. Roxanne got out of the car. She looked at the ocean, one hand holding back her thick hair as the wind drove into her face, the other hand shading her eyes, straining to look beyond the horizon.

"The Pacific. I am looking at the Pacific." There was an unusual quietness in her voice. "What a luminous, gray-green. I have never seen that color in an ocean." I told Roxanne that when I met our Great-aunt Virbaiji in Bombay, she was wearing a chiffon sari the color of the ocean.

"Chiffon! At her age! I was just imagining my Grandmother Meheramai or our Great-aunt Virbaiji right here, right now. They would insist on praying to the ocean. With the entire kusti ritual, untying the sacred thread, prayers, flicking the thread, bringing it to the forehead, tying it back on to the waist. Three times around. Wonder what all these joggers and surfers and dogs and horses would make out of it? But it is quite awe-inspiring. This Pacific Ocean of yours, Katayun."

I agreed.

As we drove into my driveway, Roxanne laughed, "Katy, you never stop surprising me! You didn't tell me how grand the Pacific Ocean is and that you live across from a cemetery. Quite an exotic view for a Parsi! No Zoroastrian Tower of Silence. No vultures. Just a cemetery where bodies are buried under the earth. So very tidy!"

As soon as we entered the house, she said, "Show me your kitchen. I have brought my own box of tea. I will make the tea. Here take this. It's a letter from Agnesmai. I think it's an important letter."

Carmelita phoned just as I slit open the envelope. "You are back. Is that your cousin Roxanne, leading lady lawyer of Devinagar and poet singing in the background? She is wonderfully out of tune. What *is* she singing? Why is she here?"

"She is singing some Indian song with shoes and hats and something to do with made in England and in Japan and she is interlacing it with 'She Wore Blue Velvet,' and she is making tea and I am about to read a letter from Aunt Agnes. Roxanne is here on a quest."

"A quest? I am coming over for dinner to your place. Tell her to hold her story until I get there. What shall I bring? 'She Wore Blue Velvet,' is that what she's singing? She'll like Cunha's Country Store."

I told her not to bring anything, hung up, and pulled out the long letter from my aunt.

Dear Katayun,

Hope you are well and happy. I have to give you some important news. I have at last received news about Margaret Shriver. She is dead. I wonder how she will cope with her lovers—my father, my brother, my husband— when they all meet on "the other side" as they say. Maybe they won't meet. Who knows. But I pray for her soul as I pray for everyone's soul. *But* Katayun dear, you needn't mourn Margaret Shriver. After all, you never met her. She never tried to reach you. She didn't even care if Freddy was alive or dead. And here is the *important* news! Margaret Shriver was not your mother!! She was never your mother!

That old curmudgeon Nanibai who knows all the secrets of Devinagar (most probably of all of India), who has visited me and enlivened my life with Devinagar gossip all these years, since the day my legs stopped working, has now, just a few days ago deigned to tell me that Margaret Shriver wasn't your mother!

What happened is this. I had just received a letter from Margaret Shriver's solicitor informing me that she was dead and asking me if I knew where you were. That woman has left some money, as well as all the jewelry the men of our family gave her, to you. Ill-gotten gains, I would say. And I advise you to take all of it. The solicitor's letter is enclosed. When I told Nanibai that I would have to write to you to tell you of your mother's death, she just said, "Don't be silly, Agnesmai. Margaret Shriver was not that girl's mother. She was no one's mother. Our Katayun's mother was a woman named Maala." Katayun dear, you can imagine my surprise. And anger. I said to Nanibai that she was cruel. She knew you were looking for your mother. 'Where is this Maala?' I asked her. 'Dead. A long time ago. A month or so after Katayun was born.' And then she refused to tell me anything more! Nothing more about your mother, how Freddy met her, etc. But she did tell me that Freddy took you, his baby, to Margaret Shriver because she wanted to really trap my father into marriage. Your father had given up on her marrying him so he thought he would help her marry his father! She had of course once again announced her pregnancy, hoping she would get pregnant so that my father would marry her. She didn't get pregnant but supposedly went off to a hospital in Switzerland to have a baby and came back trying to pass you off as her baby. Hers and my father's. My father wouldn't believe her, so she gave you back to your father, Freddy, and he took you off to America and Mexico and all those places. That's all she would tell me. Stubborn old woman.

But Katayun dear, don't let all this bother you. I really don't believe that we love only those of our own blood, etc. This 'blood-flood' thing as Roxanne would say. Freddy loved you, I have always wanted to meet you and now you are an important and precious part of my life. You are my family. My niece. Regardless of your parentage. I love you and that's that.

    Your loving aunt,

        Agnes

PS Come and see me again soon. I am not getting any younger, you know. And don't worry about that mother bit.

I put the letter back in the envelope, glanced at the solicitor's letter, and placed the envelope and the formal letter carefully on top of my dining table. Roxanne was sitting at one end of the table, watching me. She had taken off her traveling pants and sweater and was now wearing a sari.

She had started to sing, then stopped and said, "Katayun, Agnesmai told me the news. And I also spoke to Nanibai. I too was angry. But she said that the time to tell you the story about your mother was not when you were in Devinagar. Not at a time when you were discovering all of us, your family. I am sorry to have brought you this bad news." She thought a bit, then added, "Not bad. Just strange."

"I should have tried harder to find Margaret. I would have then known that she was not my mother earlier. And then, I could have searched for my real mother."

Roxanne didn't say anything. She acted as if she hadn't heard me. I said to her, " I need to go to the store downtown. Do you want to come with me, or do you want to stay here and rest? I won't be gone long."

"I would love to go with you," she said.

As we drove to Cunha's country store, Roxanne said, "Even if you had found Margaret, I don't know if she would have told you the truth. And even if she had, I don't think she knew who your real mother was. Only Nanibai and your father knew. One is, alas, dead and the other is a woman who doesn't always tell what she knows. She says that it is about the right time. Timing-fiming and such nonsense, things I don't really understand. But I trust Nanibai. Completely."

I smiled at Roxanne as we got out of the car. "I am in a bit of a shock. But it will wear off. And if anyone can help that, you and Carmelita can. I wish Ratna were still here. But as you know, she left for India a couple of months ago. Carmelita wants you to wait till she's here before you talk about your quest. I hope you don't mind."

"Not at all. She has been like a sister to you. And Agnesmai and I once discussed how your friends Carmelita and Ratna have been your family and therefore part of our family. Like a marriage you know."

I didn't know.

When Carmelita arrived, the three of us cooked and set the table, and I told Carmelita about my Aunt Agnes's letter. Carmelita asked if she could see the English solicitor's letter. "Different you know. Sort of exotic. Right out of an English novel. A PBS BBC special. I am glad that Margaret Shriver wasn't your mother, Katy. I never did like the sound of her. Who knows, one day you might find out more about your real mother. Maala. Strange name."

Roxanne began to say something and then stopped.

"Does Maala mean anything bad in Hindi? Gujarati?" asked Carmelita. Roxanne said that it meant a necklace or a garland. She went on to tell us about a visitor from Florida who had fallen in love with the jasmine and marigold garlands sold in the flower market in Devinagar and had changed her name from Mary to Maala.

Carmelita laughed and talked about the craze for changing names that had swept among the younger generations in the United States in the sixties and seventies. "Names from everywhere. Other countries. Other cultures. Other species. . . plants mainly. Drove some of their families crazy."

"Good," said Roxanne. "The older generations seem to think that they never drive the younger generations crazy. Case in point is Virbaiji. She is so filled with ideas of correct ways to do things that it is a wonder she hasn't driven her son Sarosh crazy. Especially since what she thinks is correct is completely arbitrary. Nothing to do with the usual ideas about family, community, religion, nationality, etc. No wonder poor Sarosh is more interested in ancient traditions of healing than in modern medicine. He is a regular doctor, trained in England and all that. The two of them, Virbaiji and Sarosh, spend more time discussing healing plants and astral planes-fastral planes and the role of our Asho Farohars during times of war than normal topics. Of course, who knows what's normal-formal! I think that Virbaiji has an eye on you, Katayun, as a possible daughter-in-law."

"Roxanne, I barely spent half a day with her and I never did meet Sarosh."

"Sarosh is a wonderful man. He really is a good Parsi. Speaks no evil, does no evil, thinks no evil. Virbaiji has taught him well. That old, wonderful, nasty bully. She rules us! And here I am on a quest all because of her. A quest she must never know about."

"OK. It's time. What is this quest?" asked Carmelita

"To find a sari."

"In America?" I could see Carmelita's visions of visiting one sari store after another on Telegraph Avenue in Berkeley. "Can't she find good sari stores in India?"

"Not to buy a sari. To find a sari. A particular sari. An heirloom. A gaaro. I told Katy about this special sari when she was in Devinagar. A sari that has traveled from China to India to somewhere in America. This gaaro being one that our ancestress, our Chinese great-great-grandmother sent with her son, from Malaysia to India. To be passed on to the eldest daughter or daughter-in-law of the family. Virbaiji inherited it. And since she had no daughter and since Katy's Auntie Agnes had become bedridden, Virbaiji gave the sari to my Grandmother Meheramai, her sister-in-law—with the strict instructions that she should give it to my mother, who in turn should give it to my elder sister Gulnar when she turned twenty-one. But my Grandmother Meheramai and my mother gave the sari to our cousin Dinaz Mehta when she left India to come to America. It was to be a tangible remembrance of our Chinese ancestress. The sari is said to protect anyone who owns it—no matter how far they travel."

"And now Virbaiji wants it back because she wants a daughter-in-law?"

"No. I wish it were that simple. What is happening is that my niece is getting married and she and her husband-to-be are going to Tokyo. He has a job there. Virbaiji is insisting that my sister Gulnar, the mother of the bride, wear the sari. Virbaiji is not at all happy that my niece is getting married so young. Nor am I. But to avert any disasters in this marriage— Virbaiji doesn't really like my niece's fiancé—he seems like good sort to me—she is insisting that my sister Gulnar wear the gaaro at the wedding. And my sister Gulnar believes Virbaiji when she says, 'It will be a doomed marriage for your daughter—whom you should have brought up right, so that she doesn't think of marriage at the age of seventeen. If you wear the gaaro the marriage will not be doomed.' My grandmother and mother are too terrified of Virbaiji to tell her that they disobeyed her orders. They didn't keep it for my sister Gulnar. They refuse to tell her that the sari is no longer in Devinagar or even in India, that it is in America with Dinaz Mehta. So, here I am. I have been sent by my Grandmother Meheramai. Only she, my mother, my sister Gulnar, and Katy's Aunt Agnes know why I am here. Of course Nanibai and Saleem too. I am to find Dinaz, get the sari from her, borrow it if she doesn't want to part with it permanently, and return to India before my sister completely succumbs to Virbaiji's stories about doomed-foomed marriages and blurts out that the sari is no longer in India. I have to return in time for Gulnar to appear in that gaaro for her daughter's wedding. So, it will be a short trip. And all because of superstitious nonsense and a stubborn, bullying woman."

I told Roxanne that it would be a short trip, if we could find Dinaz Mehta. "I have been trying to find her," I said. "There's no phone number for her. There is a K Mehta, who could be her daughter Kamal, in San Francisco, but her phone has been disconnected."

"Don't underestimate Grandmother Meheramai and Agnesmai. They went through boxes and boxes of their correspondence. Do you know, Katayun, that your Aunt Agnes keeps your letters in a sandalwood box next to her bed? They found an address for Dinaz Mehta from about a year and a half ago. She writes to my Grandmother at least once every two years.

But just in case we needed more, they also gave me an address of Dinaz's one-time landlady and good friend, a Mrs Mary Crawford. Both the addresses are in San Francisco. And I do have to give Agnesmai's regards to her old friend, Professor Mary Mattson. She lives in Charlottesville, Virginia."

Carmelita pointed out that Charlottesville wasn't all that close to California, but Roxanne knew about the distances in America and had already decided that she would phone Mary Mattson and give her my Aunt Agnes's greetings. In the end it was the phone call to Mary Mattson that led us to our cousin Kamal and the sari in Oaxaca.

But before that phone call, Carmelita drove us to the address that Roxanne had for Dinaz Mehta. We found the apartment inhabited by an old man who tried to be helpful and kept on saying, "Maita? Don't know any Maitas. Now there was a nice old lady who used to live here before I moved in, a few months ago. I met her once. But I don't know where she is. I don't know where she went."

We asked the neighbors. Yes, they knew Dinaz Mehta but she had fallen ill about six months ago and her daughter, yes, some of them knew that nice young woman, she was an architect, had taken her away to live with her. No, they didn't know where the daughter lived.

We then tried the landlady Mary Crawford's apartment. It was closed. There was no sign of life. One of her neighbors was of some help, though. She told us that Mary Crawford had become a follower of a nice, spiritual lady, "Not one of those foreign types, you know, even though she called herself Divine Sister Magda Dolores. She was American and even wore a cross all the time. I saw her once when she visited Mary. A very nice, Christian white lady. Just like Mary Crawford," said the neighbor into our unsmiling faces. She then noticed Roxanne's bright yellow sari under the bright blue parka and closed her door.

I went off to "Oneisha's," Half Moon Bay's newly opened metaphysical store, to see if they knew about a Divine Sister Magda Dolores and to buy sandalwood incense. Roxanne had mentioned in Devinagar that every time she left India she missed Saleem, Nanibai, her family, and the clean, sacred smell of sandalwood at dawn and twilight. In the meantime Roxanne called Mary Mattson.

Roxanne was still on the phone when I returned with the sandalwood but no news about the Divine Sister.

From what Carmelita and I could hear from Roxanne's side of the conversation, Mary Mattson sounded as friendly and interesting and funny and wise as my aunt had made her out to be. Roxanne was saying, "I would love to come and see you but not this time. But I do have a letter for you from Agnesmai. . .Yes, I'll mail it off to you. . . Yes, I do assure you that she is well. She gets around wonderfully in her wheelchair. And she reads all those magazines on science that you send her. . . Yes, that's correct. She sends them to the local library. . .Yes, I didn't like her husband either. I didn't know you had met him. Tried to make a move on you? What does that mean?" And Roxanne began to laugh and shake her head. "Yes, I promise to visit you next time I come to America. But this time I am in search of a woman called Divine Sister Magda Dolores."

Carmelita and I were alerted by Roxanne's "Really! Her name is Divine Sister Magda AND Mataji Dolores? Her followers have an office and . . . what? Next to your friend's home? Right there in Charlottesville? A soup kitchen. That's nice . . . Yes, anyone who feeds the hungry can't be all that bad. Do you have her address? Her number?" I pointed to the pad and pen on the wall next to the phone. Roxanne wrote down the number, thanked Mary Mattson and hung up.

"I would like to meet that woman. Before you came, she asked me all kinds of questions about me, my family and about detectives and homicide and the courts in India. She is writing a detective novel. Apparently Agnesmai wrote to her last year and suggested that she write a detective novel. With two detective friends. One a scientist and another in a wheelchair. Agnesmai is going to provide some of the gory details. They are negotiating about who writes which obligatory sex scenes. And you know the rest about Divine Sister Mataji Magda Dolores. So, let's be detective-fetectives and call up this number in Charlottesville, Virginia."

She did, and we found out that the last known address for Mary Crawford was in Oaxaca, Mexico, and wasn't it strange that two women within a few days had asked for her. And the other woman also had a foreign sounding name. It didn't have anything to do with Japan but it was something like "Meita" and she too was on her way to Oaxaca to meet Mary Crawford. And then the woman gave Roxanne Mary Crawford's address in Oaxaca.

We looked at one another. Even Roxanne and Carmelita were silent for a couple of minutes.

"Do not underestimate the power of coincidence," intoned Roxanne.

"She's a Jungey," announced Carmelita.

"No," said Roxanne "I am a detective. And Katy you better sit down. Your legs are hurting you very much."

I sat down and stared at the old woman who seemed to be smiling at me. It was not the most joyous of smiles. It held the kind of comfort one tries to offer someone who has experienced great sorrow. Just as I turned away from the old woman, Roxanne said, "Mexico! My God and all our blessed Asho Farohars! I hope I get that sari in time. I hope that the Mehta-Maita-Meita woman has the sari easily available. No one can put a sari in a safe deposit box or some such place. After all, a sari is a sari. And this one, I am told, is the regulation six yards long. Mexico!"

Carmelita's eyes lit up and her face took on the "life is full of surprises. . . there is a pattern to it all . . . it's just that we don't know what it is . . . yet" look. I began rubbing my knees. Carmelita came over, bent down, took off my shoes and started pulling my toes and rubbing different parts of my feet.

"Hold still, Katy. Every part of your foot is connected to some part or another of your body. I'll find the leg connection and rub it and the pain will get better."

"The feet are said to be connected to the legs. And the legs to the feet." Roxanne said that just to remind everyone that she was a lawyer.

"And I," said Carmelita "am connected to Oaxaca and Katy is connected to Mexico, even though she doesn't remember much except her father's voice and green trees. But she does see the old woman, who is of course Mexican. And we all love Mexican food. Let's go to Oaxaca."

"What old lady?" asked Roxanne.

When Carmelita explained the situation about the phantom-ghost, Roxanne wasn't overly surprised. "Good," she said. "Sounds like an interesting ghost."

"I am going to call up that Sarosh. I think he suspects that this is no vacation and that it has something to do with Virbaiji. If we involve him in this search, he will never tell Virbaiji that my Grandmother Meheramai and my mother gave away the sari. And if I go to Mexico and don't invite him along, he will be very unhappy."

Roxanne called Bombay. Sarosh answered the phone.

"Arré Sarosh," she yelled into the phone. "This is Roxanne. No, no! Don't wake up Virbaiji. Yes, I am well. Yes, I am in America. In Katayun Cooper's home. Yes, I know you didn't meet her. Yes, I will give her your greetings. Listen, don't waste time. This is a business call. Get to Mexico. Yes, Mexico City. In three days."

Roxanne raised her eyebrow in Carmelita's direction. Carmelita nodded enthusiastically. Roxanne continued, "Arré Parsi don't give me these kai-fai, why-by questions now. Just meet us there. Tell her that an important conference has come up, tell her you just found out about it. Tell her it is about Zoroastrians in Mexico. Yes, yes, I know you never tell a lie, but creative thaa. . . What's the matter, can't you be creative? Just make up whatever you think will work. Tell her you will be meeting Katayun. That will please her. Don't ask kai-why, just get there in three days. Yes, Monday. The Monday of the western hemisphere. We will meet you at the Mexico City airport."

Even Carmelita was impressed.

Two days later, on Monday, we found Sarosh looking at a book on Remedios Varo in a bookstore in Mexico City's Benito Juarez airport. He held up the book to show us the title, *Unexpected Journeys* and said, "Hello, you must be Katy. I am your cousin Sarosh. You are an artist. Do you know Remedios Varo's works?"

"Yes," said Carmelita and I.

"Fantastic!" said Sarosh and then he was introduced to Carmelita. She looked at him closely and said, "You don't look at all like Katy or Roxanne. You look very much like one of my cousins. He lives in Texas and is studying to be a doctor."

"How interesting," said Sarosh. "I am a doctor and I lived in Mexico in one of my past lives, I am sure. Or I will live in Mexico in my next life. Stop laughing, Roxanne."

# XII.

## Oaxaca, Mexico

### *We Meet Kamal Mehta and Find the Sari*

As we waited at the airport in Mexico City to board our flight to Oaxaca, Carmelita bought a rose from a young woman selling roses and chocolates from a cart. The rose was so dark it could be the purple of royalty or the black of mourning, wrapped tightly within a transparent cone of plastic.

Carmelita presented it to me. "Try to smile, Katy. There is nothing to fear. We are with you this time. No 'Lady's Support' in any of our bags. You, of course, are what I always expected. A child of miracles. The father's lineage seems to be known but the mother continues to be elusive."

I didn't feel like smiling. I wanted to take the first flight out of Mexico, to go back to the safety of my house in Half Moon Bay; I wanted to return to the familiarity of those years before I knew anything about my family in India, when all I had to contend with were the eleven years of lost memories and a woman with bare feet and a butterfly. Carmelita's assurances that this time around my legs and feet would be definitely healed in Mexico did not comfort me, as I looked at the dark rose, pristine and inflexible within the plastic.

Roxanne corrected Carmelita. "Katy is definitely a woman of known family. No miracle there. Very straightforward. Aunts, uncles, great aunts, great uncles, cousins, grandparents. Of blood or by choice. Foster parents. Friends. Ghosts. Can't have one's own ghost if one has no family. And of course, our Chinese ancestress whose sari is taking us all to Oaxaca."

Sarosh smiled at me, pointed at the rose in my hand and said, "The patience of the rose close to a thorn keeps her fragrant."

I was not comforted. And when I did reach Oaxaca with Carmelita,

Roxanne and Sarosh, I was sure that my legs would collapse completely under me.

As I stepped off the plane, I understood why Carmelita always insisted that the old woman was from Oaxaca. I watched as she walked slowly from the airplane and straight towards the women standing on the viewing balcony, holding the black butterfly in the palm of her right hand. The women showed no surprise at the way she appeared among them out of nowhere. They made room for her on the balcony as they waited for their sons and daughters, husbands and sisters, their brothers, their fathers, their grandfathers and grandsons returning home for Semana Santa. The old woman and the butterfly seemed to be completely at ease.

The only place I wanted to see during this visit to Oaxaca was Monte Alban. The ruins of Monte Alban had loomed without any warning outside my window as the plane descended, sitting on top of a hill, brooding like some large, uneasy cat watching the valleys encircling its sanctuary.

I wanted to paint the pyramids of Monte Alban for Carmelita, because she had once told me that Monte Alban was the only place on earth where she had achieved a sense of peace. It had happened many years ago, when she was still in her thirties. As for the ruins at Mitla, Carmelita said that she had found no great peace there, only tourists. Carmelita planned to go to Mitla during our sari-quest trip only to check out the market. She wanted to send a jaguar mask, "all green and gold," to Ratna in Bombay.

We had received our first communication from Ratna the day we left California with Roxanne. It was a card with the portrait of the Goddess Sarasvati playing a veena painted onto a large, desiccated peepul-tree leaf. The card had been mailed from Devinagar. Ratna had written that she had landed safely in Bombay, and that she had stopped in Devinagar to visit Agnes Cooper Driver before beginning her search for her husband in Varanasi.

With the help of Carmelita's madrina, Glafira Vazquez de Leon, we tracked down Mary Crawford's house within three days of our arrival in Oaxaca. That Wednesday, as soon as we arrived at the gate of the house at the edge of Colonia Jalatlaco, we found ourselves drawn right into the center of the world of two strangers, Señora Florencia and Kamal Mehta. There was a newspaper piñata outside the gate that seemed in rather bad taste.

An old woman with steel-rimmed glasses and a bright red apron over her blue, polyester, polka-dotted dress opened the gate when Carmelita rang the bell. The bell was set inside a hand-painted ceramic niche.

Something that looked like a dragon in full flight was painted on the tiles. Roxanne was trying to stifle her urge to shout the familiar Gujarati greeting, "koi cche?" to the house. Her grandfather, who had loved to travel all around the world, had supposedly shouted out the greeting in his literal English translation, "Anyone is?" to every house he visited in Devinagar, and elsewhere. Sarosh turned out to be a ritualist. He murmured "Blessings on the house" as he stared at the woman standing behind the old woman who had opened the door. The woman was slender with transparent brown eyes and a cap of hair that was the same color as mine and a nose that reminded me of my own nose, which according to Roxanne would, in my old age, scare the children of America. The woman with my hair color and nose was nodding her head as the older woman was saying, "Yes. This is a good place to stop." She was also adjusting the weight of a heavy-looking bag on her shoulder

Carmelita's explanations to the two women about who we were and why we had come to the house were cut short by Roxanne's statement. It was directed at the woman with the bag.

"You must be a Parsi. A Japanwallah. You look just like my sister Gulnar. A bit like Katayun too." She pointed at me.

Before anyone could answer, Roxanne turned to me, "Katy, I don't know about Mary Crawford and that Sister-Mother Divine Person. But this woman, behind this older lady, dresses and stands like an American but she is one of us. Just look at her! A Parsi in Oaxaca!"

Sarosh said quietly, "Roxanne, she doesn't look at all like your sister Gulnar. But she does look very much like my mother Virbaiji. She of course was born a Japanwallah. A very beautiful lady, my mother," he smiled at the woman.

She in turn smiled at him and said, "I am Kamal Mehta. My grandmother was Khorshed Japanwallah. Married to Tehmurasp Mehta of Bombay. Mary Crawford is dead. This is Señora Florencia, who took care of Mary Crawford."

Señora Florencia looked at the assortment of women and the lone man at her gate. She shook her head at all the English being spun around her and ushered us into her house.

Roxanne faced Kamal with her determined, courtroom stare.

"Glad to meet you Kamal Mehta. I presume you are Dinaz and Ashok Mehta's daughter. We are related. You and I and this Katayun and this Sarosh. But why are you here, in Oaxaca, in this particular house?"

She didn't sound very friendly. Sarosh remonstrated at her tone of voice and her question, "Roxanne, anyone can be anywhere they want to be. Within reason and good sense."

Carmelita introduced all of us to Señora Florencia and tried to translate what was going on. Señora Florencia had already begun to put together the story.

Instead of inviting us to sit down in the living room with the newspaper flowers and the large TV, she ushered us into a bedroom.

We all stood in the room staring at a sari-draped table.

Dinaz Mehta had taught her daughter well. Kamal was not particularly distressed by the melodrama unfolding around her or the legalistic, unfriendly tone of her self-announced cousin. "Yes," she said. "I am the daughter of Ashok and Dinaz Mehta. They are both dead. I came here for this sari. It's the family gaaro given to my mother when she left India. But I am leaving it here in Oaxaca. With Señora Florencia."

"No, you can't do that," said Roxanne. "I am sorry to hear that your mother is dead. But this gaaro is supposed to belong to my sister. And she needs it. She has to wear it at her daughter's wedding or our common relative, yours and mine, Virbaiji Japanwallah Dubash—she is this Sarosh's mother—will be very, very angry. She will persuade my sister Gulnar that by not wearing this spider-patterned sari she will have doomed-foomed her daughter's marriage forever. My sister is very impressionable. She will believe all this superstitious-foopertitious rubbish Virbaiji will give her and make all of us miserable for the rest of our lives."

"Well, Roxanne Japanwallah, impressionable or not, your grandmother and your mother gave this sari to my mother in order to protect her in America. My mother died last month and left it to me. To protect me in America. And I am going to leave it here, in Oaxaca. Together with this Asho Farohar etched on marble. It was my mother's favorite image of the Asho Farohar and I will leave this angelito as Señora Florencia calls him to take care of the sari."

Roxanne changed her tone. Kamal didn't seem like the type who would succumb to a courtroom voice.

"Look Kamal, let me take this sari back to India for a short time. I'll return it as soon as the wedding is over and after Virbaiji goes back to Bombay. After she has seen Gulnar wear it."

"She can't wear it."

"May every single holy, angelic Asho Farohar protect me! Not another superstitious relative! Please don't behave like my sister! I try to overlook her superstitions. Around her I avoid anything thirteen, I don't wear black,

I try to remember that knives and scissors are never to be handed from one person to another, hair brushes and combs are to be cleaned of every tiny strand of hair every day, no houses where three roads meet are to be entered, and more of such nonsense just because she is my sister and I love her. Now, let me tell you, all these superstitions-fooperstitions are in your mind. Nothing to them."

"I agree. But she won't be able to wear it. Physically. There isn't much sari left for her to wear. After my mother made a jhabloo for me from a part of this sari for a school pageant when I was a very little girl, and Señora Florencia made a wrap-around-the-neck-three-times scarf out of another piece of the sari for her nephew Rogelio, the sari is less than even five yards. And if your sister resembles me in height as well as face, she needs all six yards of a sari."

Señora Florencia heard her nephew's name and told Carmelita that Rogelio was in Peru, in search of UFOs. Carmelita decided that the part of the sari the señora had given to her nephew was most probably in the hands of an alien, on a space ship flying at that very minute into outer space. I told her to stop being fanciful. I didn't care about the sari and UFOs and aliens. I wanted to paint Señora Florencia. Her bright clothes, her sparse steel-gray hair, the steel-rimmed glasses and eyes that looked as if she could understand whatever was said in whatever language. She reminded me of Putlibai.

"UFOs? Where is this Rogelio? I would like to meet him." Sarosh was delighted.

"In Peru."

Sarosh turned to Roxanne. "Roxanne, now that you have forced me to come to Mexico, let's go to Peru!"

"Peru!" Roxanne yelled. "I did you a favor. You always wanted to come to Mexico. Leave alone this Peru-Feru business for now. We have to get this gaaro to Gulnar, before next month, the fourteenth of May."

Kamal seemed to like us, her new relatives. "Roxanne, we are related! My mother would have said Peru-Feru. But she would have also said 'dry cleaners-fry cleaners.'"

Sarosh grinned at Kamal, at which point Kamal decided to reciprocate his feelings. I realized that they were in love. I had seen those looks and had to deal with the phenomenon every spring semester at San Sebastian College in San Matteo. Not very conducive to learning. No, not even for art classes. Kamal grinned back at Sarosh. She seemed to be showing her teeth to Sarosh!

Sarosh was dazzled and said, "It isn't just a Japanwallah trait. It is a rather common practice of Gujarati speakers. For example . . ."

"UFOs! Gujarati! Peru-feru! We have to do something about this sari mess. Right now!" Roxanne was not the leading lawyer of Devinagar without cause. She too had seen the smiles. She told Carmelita and me later that night that she was delighted at this "love-fove business starting off between those two." Sarosh had been trying to persuade Roxanne for the last two years to have sex with him, to teach him what it was all about. And she had been telling him to find someone else to teach him. She and Saleem were lovers, but just because they weren't married didn't mean she was available to give lessons. And anyway, Sarosh was the brother she and her sister Gulnar had always wanted.

Roxanne was also an excellent detective. She knew how to focus on important details. She continued with the sari question.

"Kamal, if you will let me take the sari back to India, my Grandmother Meheramai will think of something so that my sister can wear it. And I will send it back to you, to Señora Florencia, to Rogelio. Whoever you say. But there aren't any space aliens. So let's leave them out of the picture."

Carmelita was translating. Señora Florencia was laughing. And I was staring at the table, the embroidered "spiders" on the sari, the candle, the postcard portrait of the Virgin of Soledad propped against the candle and the Asho Farohar. I could not stand up. The pain was excruciating. I sat down on the floor.

Carmelita, Roxanne, Kamal and Sarosh ran to me and knelt beside me, all trying to lift me up.

"No," said Señora Florencia. "Let her rest there. The floor will not hurt her. I will try and find something for her legs. They are hurting you, aren't they, Señorita?"

"My knees and yes, my legs. But mostly my knees." And as I rubbed my right hand over my left knee and my left over my right knee, I knew that Señora Florencia had seen the woman with the ribbons in her braids and the black butterfly on her right shoulder staring at us through the window with a rose vine growing across it.

After a few minutes of watching Roxanne and Kamal bickering about the sari, I said, "It's easy. Just get a yard or so of some other suitable material and stitch it to the end of the sari. Gulnar can then wear it with the added material hidden in the first go-around of the sari draping, and Virbaiji will not feel constrained to warn her about doomed marriages."

Kamal laughed. "Of course! I didn't even think of it. And I, a daughter of an excellent seamstress. But I hate sewing!"

Roxanne nodded her head. "My Grandmother Meheramai and my mother and my sister are marvelous at it. I see a needle and I get nausea or an allergic reaction. Sores all over my palms. I hate sewing!"

Carmelita began to massage my knees while Señora Florencia picked up different bottles from the table and peered at the labels through her steel-rimmed glasses. I continued to stare at the white silk patterns on the sari. I had known neither a mother nor a grandmother nor a sister. Theresa Sanders had been an indifferent seamstress. I wondered how my Aunt Agnes felt about sewing. As I looked at the barefoot old woman staring at us through the window, I could hear my father telling me to run to safety, to go to his employer Mr Sanders. And then I remembered the screech of the parrot we used to call "Mr Green." The parrot lived on the verandah and would eat only when my father fed him. I remembered that I had heard the parrot scream as my father fell down, blood flowing from him. Then Mr Green and all the other birds were silent. I had never tried to paint that. The silence of those birds. Not even when I was young and the memories of those birds and insects and their noise were still within me.

Señora Florencia slapped a piece of cloth on my right knee and another on my left knee. I nearly jumped off the floor from the heat. Steam was rising from the two squares of cloth. They had been steeped in a basin of boiling hot water with twigs and leaves floating around. But within a few minutes the worst of the pain was sucked up into the cloth and I was able to stand up and walk to the living room. I sat down on the sofa and began to examine the flowers. Roses, tulips, orchids, birds of paradise and calla lilies, all made out of newspapers, were placed with care in the five black clay vases.

"My nephew Rogelio made them, and the piñatas outside. I like real flowers. They have colors and smells. But I like my nephew. And this is my home now. It belonged to his father who left his two sons in the care of their grandmother when their mother died at the finca he used to work at. Rogelio's father went off to Canada. All the way to Canada. I don't know what he did but he made money. He sent the money to buy this house for his sons but only Rogelio lived here. The other one. . .well, who knows. Why bring up such sad stories? Rogelio's father was my brother-in-law. I think he is still in Canada. Or he is dead."

She addressed herself to Carmelita in Spanish. I, a long-time resident of California and friend of Carmelita, was able to follow the conversation but I wasn't willing to participate in Spanish. I told Carmelita, "Don't tell this nice, old lady, but these flowers and the piñatas outside look like the work of a demented artist who has left himself hanging between the real world and his own particular hell. Piñatas on poles. Empty. Blown up like balloons. Never to be brought down to earth. Flowers made up of stale news."

Carmelita agreed that my words need not be translated for Señora Florencia but she invited the señora and Kamal, who had returned to the living room accompanied by Roxanne and Sarosh, for dinner the next evening, at her Tía Lucía's house where the four of us, Carmelita, Roxanne, Sarosh and I were staying. Señora Florencia accepted the invitation. Kamal said that she would love to have dinner with us but her flight was leaving the next morning.

Roxanne was still not very sure about this long-lost-recently-found cousin. She didn't know if Kamal would change her mind about the sari. So she asked Kamal to postpone her flight and join us for dinner. She also tried to tempt Kamal with a trip to Monte Alban we had planned to take two days later, on Friday. "Come with us to Monte Alban. You and Katy and Sarosh and I are cousins and who knows when we will all meet again. And maybe you and I can supervise this addition to the sari before I take it back." Roxanne could be very persuasive when she smiled and spoke in a voice that sounded as if she wanted to sing a song to you. She nodded her head up and down with great seriousness and her badly bobbed hair bounced up and down as she begged Kamal to spend more time with us.

Kamal thought for no longer than a few minutes before agreeing to post-pone her flight. She emptied her big bag on the sofa to look for her ticket. She found it and then proceeded to put everything she had dumped back into her bag. Among the items was a zip-lock plastic bag with what looked like ash and crystals in it. Señora Florencia put her hand into the bag, pulled out the plastic pouch, and said, "It is time to empty the rest of your mother's ashes with my Té Malabar. Maybe you can leave it on Monte Alban."

Carmelita, Sarosh, and I were quite puzzled by the señora's statement. Carmelita repeated it in English for Roxanne. And she of course demanded an explanation of why a good Zoroastrian woman was carrying a dead person's ashes with her. Kamal pointed out that she was both a Zoroastrian and a Hindu. Roxanne agreed readily but she still demanded an explanation for the comment about Dinaz Mehta's ashes mixed with tea from Malabar.

Kamal turned out to be a true descendant of the Japanwallah-Mehta-Cooper family complex. Instead of giving us a brief explanation of why she was carrying her mother's ashes in a zip-lock bag, she told us her life story.

# XIII.

## Oaxaca

*Across the United States of America and to Oaxaca,*
*Mexico*

*Kamal Mehta and the Sari Embroidered by*
*Our Ancestress*

While Putlibai was spending the last days of her life in my backyard, my cousin Kamal Mehta was spending as much time as possible with her mother Dinaz, who had been admitted to the South San Francisco Kaiser Hospital with terminal cancer. And while I was retelling the stories I had heard from Roxanne and Aunt Agnes and Putlibai to Ratna and Carmelita, my cousin Kamal was remembering the stories of her childhood as she sat in her mother's hospital room.

From her hospital bed, Dinaz Mehta had demanded to know if her daughter Kamal was a convinced American, a loyal, practicing citizen of the USA.

The question had startled Kamal. What she had expected was her mother's on-going explanations about a headache she had been suffering for seventeen days. The doctors refused to attribute the headache to the cancer that had laid siege to her bones. Dinaz agreed with her doctors, her headache had nothing to do with the cancer. It was a death-bed revival of her childhood premonsoon headache which had kept pace with the suffocating heat and the heavy clouds pushing down upon the land as the ceiling fans and the flies circled around in the haunted Mehta house on Malabar Hill without any enthusiasm.

Dinaz had of course experienced neither her pre-monsoon headache nor the monsoons in the past fifty odd years which she had spent rooting herself into an unfamiliar land, living her life on the continent of North

America. She complained she was not happy about spending eternity with her premonsoon headache. "A headache," Dinaz said to anyone who would listen, "that does not arise out of any noble reason like being beheaded for rebelling against a king or a tyrant, but because of my impatience for the rains. Seems shameful. How will I explain myself to my fellow-dead?"

Kamal had found her mother's unexpected question about her loyalty to America rather unfair, especially since it came on the day she had decided that she would offer to take her mother home to India to die without a headache. But instead of unrelenting headaches, heavy monsoons, rain-drenched fragrant earth and eternity, Dinaz had asked about Kamal and America. She was insistent.

When Dinaz asked, "Really Kamal dear, tell me! Are you a practicing, convinced American? After all, remember, you were born here. . .", Kamal was reminded of the time when she was twelve years old. Dinaz had been just as insistent at that time. She had kept on asking Kamal, month after month, for one whole year, "Kamal dear, do you know who you are? Do you know how you want to earn your living in a few years? Where do you want to go? What do you want to do? Kamal dear, you must think about these things, otherwise other people will take over your life!" And in that hospital room while her mother was dying, late in February, Kamal thought about the Thanksgiving of the year when she was exactly twelve years and one month old. She hadn't been watching singing-dancing turkeys or pumpkins. Dinaz Mehta had not been able to afford a television set. They had been living in Oakland, California, where Dinaz had rented a one-bedroom apartment with cracks in two of the five windows and a perpetually leaking toilet. Five weeks earlier, a disturbing amount of green paint from the kitchen ceiling had peeled off and dropped into the pot of lentils Dinaz had left uncovered on the stove. A couple, Philip and Ginny Johnson, had called while Dinaz was trying to decide if the paint would make them sick. Dinaz had invited the Johnsons for a Thanksgiving meal because they had been friends of her father many years ago.

Dinaz's father, Kamal's grandfather, was the Tehmurasp Mehta of gentile poverty and the constantly crumbling house with a well-stocked library and the Zend Avesta-quoting parrot.

Tehmurasp Mehta had met Ginny and Philip Johnson on a bus in Bombay in the 1940's. The Americans had recognized him as a Parsi because of his prayer cap and the fringes of his kusti escaping from under his shirt and hanging out on the back of his trousers. When the Johnsons told Tehmurasp that they knew about his community, he was delighted and

invited them to visit him and his daughter Dinaz in their rapidly deteriorating house on Malabar Hill. When the Johnsons came to the Mehta
house one afternoon and asked intelligent questions about the Parsis,
Tehmurasp was very pleased. He took them to his library and showed them
his valuable collection of books on the Parsis. Books by Parsis, Hindus,
Muslims, Christians, Sikhs, Buddhists, Jains, Indians, Australians,
Germans, Italians, Iranis, Japanese, French, Americans, British and one
which he claimed was by a Peruvian. It was in Spanish. The first twenty-
two pages that might have included the author's name and other pertinent
data were missing.

The Johnsons had gained Tehmurasp's approval by their sympathies for
the Quit India movement. He was grateful to them. "You are true friends
of India. No, no. You will soon be pukka Indians. Look at Ginny. She wears
a sari at all your embassy functions. You understand us."

Ginny tried to inspire him. "Yes! You must fight on, Tehmurasp. Just as
my ancestors did. Throw off the yoke of British rule! Only then will we,
America and India, be true and equal friends!" And Meethamai, the parrot,
sang, "Door hatho, door hatho, dunyawallo, Hindustan hamara hai." A
song Dinaz had taught him. Warning everyone to stay away from India,
India was for Indians.

Ginny had tried to explain the DAR and her family's role in the
American Revolution to Dinaz. Dinaz was not interested. "Stale propa-
ganda," she said to her father as she went off to be with her future husband
Ashok to persuade him to find a group that believed in getting rid of the
British quickly and by any possible means. As my Aunt Agnes and Roxanne
had told me, satygraha was not a concept that had appealed to my father
or to my father's cousin Dinaz Mehta. For different reasons, of course.

Tehmurasp Mehta had been known to lock himself in his room and talk
at length to the portrait of his wife Khorshed, who had died when Dinaz
was ten. Dinaz had spied on her father, and many years later she told her
daughter Kamal what she had heard. Tehmurasp had a set, ritualized
monologue that he addressed to his wife. It went something like this: "I
don't understand our Dinaz. Where did she get this stubbornness? This
determination? Not from us Mehtas! Otherwise I would be rich and most
of this house would not be in ruins. The last monsoons brought down the
roof over the back bedrooms and half of the dining room. And no money
for repairs. But of course, you must have seen all that from *up there*. I tell
you, Dinaz must have inherited all that noise and hot-headedness from
your grandfather, Dorabji Japanwallah. Have you met him *up there* and has
he explained why he insisted on marrying a Chinese woman when he was

in Malaysia? When I met your mother's uncle at our wedding he told me that Dorabji had written a letter saying, 'I don't care about all these bans and taboos against mixed marriages. Mixed marriages or fixed marriages, I will do what I know is right. If you will not accept my wife, I will remain with her. Right here in Malaysia.' Dinaz sounds just like him. Your side of the family. I wish you were still with me down here in Bombay. And now our Dinaz is mixed up with some other mischief. Just tell me what to do with her. Please." The description of the type of mischief changed every few years until it culminated in her involvement with political violence.

That Thanksgiving day when Kamal was twelve years and one month old, her mother had been very hot and frustrated because the turkey had managed to expand monstrously while it was cooking. It was impossible to baste it while it was in the small oven. Dinaz had to pull out the heavy roaster every twenty-five minutes and balance it on the stove top cluttered with the pots and pans she had used to cook the vegetables for the sweet-sour-spicy Parsi wedding stew and the sweet-sour-spicy shrimp, baste the miraculously expanding turkey and then bend down to push it back into the oven.

Philip Johnson had walked into the apartment with a package of papadums, a jar of pickled mango achaar and the news that Ginny unfortunately could not come because she had to go to Massachusetts. "A family emergency. Sorry we didn't call. Lost your number. But to make up, here's genuine papadums and authentic mango achaar from our last trip to India."

Kamal's "We had to disconnect our phone two weeks ago" was stopped by the expression on Philip's face. He was staring at Dinaz while she was in the process of carefully putting the turkey into the oven after her final bout of basting it. Philip was frowning.

"What Dinaz! What is this? A turkey! Have you forgotten to cook Parsi food? I came here for real, pukka Parsi food. And what do I see? A turkey! What do you think you are? An American!"

Kamal wondered if she should say, "But she has also made Parsi stew and Parsi shrimp." Instead she said, "But it is Thanksgiving!"

Dinaz carefully shut the oven door, stood up and said, "You are damned right I am an American!"

Later that night Kamal asked her mother how one could dam right. Right wasn't water. Her mother hadn't bothered with explanations. "You can use the word when you understand it."

To Philip, Dinaz Mehta said, "I have lived here for many, many years. I have borne my one and only child here. I have buried my husband here in America, while I was seven months pregnant. My husband, my Ashok, shot by a drunken idiot who wanted to clean America out. Get rid of all us heathen Asians. Shot because the man was insulted by my husband's accent! My husband is buried somewhere in New York. Not even cremated. There was no one I knew who could have arranged a cremation and taken the ashes to our beloved India. Oh yes. Pukka or not, I am an American. I breathe here. I speak here. I sing here. I laugh and cry here. I have left parts of my body all over this place. Nail clipping and hair trimmings across the country. My uterus in North Carolina. Both ovaries in Milwaukee. Wisdom teeth in Los Angeles and rotted teeth right here in Oakland. I have eaten the food of this land and made friends with the people of this land. And I have worked here. I have given my service to this land. Look. Look at these hands!" And she had waved her hands stained with turkey-basting and smelling of onions, garlic, green chilies, cilantro, vinegar and shrimp right in front of Philip's face. The man had retreated into a petulant silence.

"I have cut cloth. Yards and yards and yards and yards of cloth. I have sewn garments. Skirts-phirts. Frocks-brocks. Blouses-flouses. Embroidered table cloths and altar cloths and God knows what other cloths. Look. Do you see my fingers? Always swollen and cut all over. Scratched. I have nightmares. At least two every night. Those sewing machines in those small rooms with those bare bulbs burning around the clock and the tired, tired women. Women ordered to work quickly. All the time. Told to shut up and work."

"And," Dinaz continued her one-sided argument with Philip, "I have always paid my taxes. My enemies are here. My friends are here. My only family, my daughter, is here. God and the beautiful Asho Farohars, our guardian angels, are of course everywhere. You are damned right I am an American. And I am an Indian Chinese Asian. Who are you to tell me that I can't love two places? No one, no one can cut boundaries into my heart! Do you want this authentic American turkey? It will most probably taste quite good with the authentic Indian achaar. Better than with cranberry sauce." She had then horrified Kamal, who didn't much care for very spicy food, by adding, "Let's eat the red chilies in the achaar in honor of the first people of this land who gave us chilies and turkeys and a place to live and eat and love and die."

Dinaz seemed to have inherited her father's gift for the dramatic monologue.

That Thanksgiving dinner was the shortest celebration-with-a-meal Kamal had ever attended. Her mother did not serve the stew or the shrimp. That Thanksgiving was memorable for Kamal because her mother's words to Philip had seemed to be an extension of her year-long, "Kamal dear, do you know who you are? What you want to do?" It was memorable also

119

because of the glorious leftovers they ate for at least two weeks. Kamal was sure that she and her mother and their landlady, Mary Crawford, who liked rich, hot, food, were the only people in the whole world who had eaten turkey dhaan-saak for eight days straight.

When her mother was dying and asked her about "American," Kamal thought about that Thanksgiving in Oakland and the Johnsons and her mother's life in America. Since Kamal didn't known quite what to say, she asked, "Mamma, do you want me to take you back to Bombay? I will ask your doctor?"

"No. Just bury me here. Your father is a part of this earth now. It will be my gift to this land. . .swollen fingers, failed eyesight and all. After all I have eaten the food from this land and breathed the air here for most of my life. But remember. No coffin. I want to disintegrate quickly. Maybe my bones and flesh and blood will wipe out the blood spilled all over here. So much blood. Ever since that Columbus got lost."

Kamal smiled and told her mother that she sounded just like a martyr. Her Bombay convent school training was beginning to show in her old age.

Dinaz shook her finger at her daughter. "Martyr-tamartyr! Just because you are a hot-shot architect, you think you know about dead, decaying bodies and the earth. And the worms. Now, those worms . . . they do bother me, Kamal dear. And don't forget that it was after all, Mother Hilda at the convent who forced me to learn how to sew and embroider. And that is what put food on our table for many, many, many, many years!'

When Kamal reminded her that it was the same Mother Hilda who had told the young Dinaz that it was a pity she wasn't a Christian because she would burn forever in hell, Dinaz said, "Oh, she said much more than that! She said that I was a lost soul because I was a heathen and also because I was shameless. I laughed too much! 'If you must smile, Dinaz Mehta, smile with your mouth closed. Chaste, virtuous ladies must not show their teeth!' That is what Mother Hilda used to say to me. Kamal dear, here is my last advice to you. When and if you decide to look seriously for a man, show your teeth!"

Kamal was delighted. This was not the woman who had worried about carrying a headache in to the realm of death. Her mother would live.

"And," her mother said, "remember to track down our old landlady Mary Crawford and get back our Chinese silk sari, the Parsi gaaro, from her."

The sari that Roxanne's mother had given to Dinaz Mehta had then been given by Dinaz to her landlad, Mary Crawford to pay the rent. When Kamal reminded her mother that it was a fair exchange, her mother said, "I gave it to her because she had always lusted after that sari and because we liked her. She was a good woman. Of course I remember. I am not losing my mind. I am only dying. We gave her that sari and a shawl in exchange for a month's rent and money to buy those Louisa May Alcott books. And you didn't even have the decency to cry when Beth died! I cried and all you said was, 'Thank God, she's dead. At last!' Pay Mary Crawford, build her a house if you want to, but get back the gaaro. That gaaro is important. You know that it is the only thing we have from your Chinese great-great-grandmother. My mother's grandmother. It was given to me before I left India by my cousin who had inherited the sari. To keep me safe in America. My Mamma was told that the Chinese lady embroidered that sari herself. All those hand-embroidered, white spider patterns all over the sari, especially for the wife and the daughter and the granddaughter and so on and so forth of the one child, their eldest son, the one your great-great-grandfather Dorabji Japanwallah sent back to India. To be a pukka Parsi and marry a Parsi woman, etc."

Kamal explained that she wasn't all that interested in the gaaro. But Dinaz was adamant. "Your ancestress sent it to the land she would never see. As long as you have it, you will be blessed. You will remember Asia. You will remember the men and women who stayed and the ones who traveled away. I always meant to get it back." She then closed her eyes, turned her back to her daughter and fell asleep.

Dinaz Mehta woke up half an hour later and demanded that Kamal open the window. "I want to look at the air!" she said. "It smells just like the earth in the garden on Malabar Hill when the rains begin to fall. I want to look at the air."

Kamal began to argue that one couldn't look at the air. But Dinaz had closed her eyes and died. The only things she had asked Kamal to do were to bury her without a coffin and to get back from Mary Crawford the maroon gaaro, with the spider pattern embroidered in white silk. One spider in each square inch of the six-yard sari.

Kamal's voice was unsteady as she told us that when she was a young girl her mother would show her the sari every few months or so. Kamal would imagine that the yards and yards of soft maroon silk was a large communal web woven by all of the small white silk spiders spread across the silk. Spiders from China, India, America. Or she would see the "spiders" as small, silk stars covering a maroon sky. The kind of sky she had seen when her mother had taken her for a weekend away from San Francisco, to walk along the beaches and the bluffs of Half Moon Bay, Santa Cruz, Monterey, and Carmel. Kamal had not seen the sari since it had been bartered away to Mary Crawford, until she found it draped over Señora Florencia's table.

Everytime Kamal had looked at the sari she had thought of her father who was killed before she was born. Her mother had told her that her father was a gentle, kind man. A man with the softest voice she had ever heard. Kamal would rub the sari against her cheek and imagine that it was the kiss of her soft-spoken father. She never told her mother about the sari and the web and the stars and her father's kiss.

Kamal pushed Dinaz's last question to her at the back of her mind as she busied herself with arranging the memorial service. She knew she would have to go through her mother's address book to find the names and addresses of her numerous friends all across the US, to inform them of her death. She wondered if the Johnsons were still in the book and how long it would take for her letter to reach her mother's family in Devinagar and Bombay. The family that Kamal knew only through her mother's stories, a few photographs and some letters from Meheramai Japanwallah and Virbaiji Dubash.

Instead of leaving her mother's body to the mercy of worms, my cousin Kamal decided to cremate her mother. Her mother had never bothered to tell her that in the absence of a Tower of Silence, many Zoroastrians preferred to be buried rather than cremated. Kamal cremated her mother because she did remember her saying that fire purified all that it ate. Dinaz had forgotten to tell her daughter that that was a Hindu not a Zoroastrian belief. But then Kamal Mehta had a Zoroastrian parent and a Hindu parent, both of them dead in the United States of America.

In honor of Dinaz's Thanksgiving litany of what part of her body she had left in which parts of the United States, Kamal decided that her mother's final gift to the land would be best given by scattering her ashes across the continent instead of interring her in one, limited burial space.

Before we met Kamal in Mexico she had been traveling across the United States. She left small amounts of her mother's ashes in various places. She began by surreptitiously placing the fine ash mixed with tiny gray and white crystals under a tree root that had pushed through the earth in the Golden Gate Park. She then dropped some of the contents of what she called her "mother bag" into Lake Michigan in Chicago, some in the Mississippi in Wisconsin and some on a mountain trail behind a souvenir shop along the Blue Ridge Parkway. Remembering her mother's fascination with witches, Kamal set afloat some of the ashes onto the Atlantic from Salem. When her travels took her to New Mexico, she scattered ashes in a ravine on a mountain road between Santa Fe and Taos. A silent raven and a very old man with a straw hat watched her as she put her hand in the draw-string bag, pulled out some of the ashes and let them fly into the ravine. The man took off his hat and bowed to Kamal. The raven flew off, diving after the ashes, as they floated down the ravine.

Kamal's general route across the United States was preselected by her search for Mary Crawford.

Mary Crawford had apparently also been on a quest. She had left her two-story home on Santiago Avenue in San Francisco and gone to Chicago, Illinois then Boston, Massachusetts then Charlottesville, Virginia, then Taos, New Mexico and then to San Antonio, Texas. Mary Crawford had begun her quest in the company of the followers of a lady with eclectic spiritual teachings, great charisma, and a genuine urge to help people overcome their ennui and despair. The lady called herself Divine Sister Magda and sometimes Mataji Dolores.

Kamal lost track of Mary Crawford for a short time in Texas. Mary had turned herself into Mirabehen in Massachusetts and then into Zuleikha in Virginia. But by the time she reached Texas, she was back to being Mary. The name changes didn't bother Kamal. Dinaz had raised her believing that very few people knew their own real, deep-down name. And almost never another's name. "We are always named by others. And here in the grand old U S of A they rename us again and again. It's the Adam complex. Look how they insist on calling me 'Dina' and even 'Diana' and you into different pronunciations of 'camel'! Should have just named you 'Lotus' and be done with it. When your father was driving that cab in New York, his boss had renamed him 'George.' And the man who shot your father was just as incensed at your father for 'stealing a good, Christian American name' as he was at your father's accent and skin color."

Kamal wasn't overly worried or disturbed about Mary Crawford's name changes but she did wonder where she would end up next as she followed Divine Sister Magda's route, helpfully charted out for her by the spiritual leader's main office in Charlottesville, Virginia. She also hoped that her family bereavement leave plus her three weeks of annual vacation would not run out before she found Mary Crawford. She wanted to request the return of the sari and explain the reason for that request personally to her former landlady whom she remembered as a woman of great love and laughter. When she called the Divine Sister Magda's office in Charlottesville from her motel in Texas, the office computer informed her that Mary Crawford had extended her quest into Mexico. She had become interested in healing and healers and had decided to find a true curandera. The secretary at the office was generous with her time and help. She called Kamal back within a couple of hours and told her that according to her informants on the Internet, Oaxaca was currently the targeted place for those in search of curanderas. She gave her Mary Crawford's last known address in Oaxaca.

Kamal Mehta found herself in front of the small house in the city of Oaxaca. The house on the fringes of the cobblestoned Colonia Jalatlaco with a whitewashed adobe wall protecting it from the traffic on the street. A mobile made of geometrical shaped newspaper piñatas was hanging from a pole on the sidewalk in front of the entrance gate and a small statue of Nuestra Señora de La Soledad, the Virgin of Oaxaca, guarded the entrance to the yard. It was a beautiful spring day. The sun was bright and yet there was no hint of the hot weather that would descend upon the city in a few weeks.

Kamal's knock was answered by an old woman no more than five feet tall. She had two gray braids tied together at their ends with day-glo pink yarn, an apron over her polyester blue dress and a pair of steel-rimmed round spectacles firmly anchored onto her nose. She identified herself as Señora Florencia Nunez, at the lady's service, and informed Kamal that yes, Señora Mary Crawford had lived in this house but unfortunately the señora had died three months ago. She had died in the house. Her body had been sent off to San Diego to her son in an airplane. She had died peacefully.

The house, Señora Nunez told Kamal, did not belong to Señora Mary. "And please call me Florencia. Any friend of Señora Mary is a friend of mine."

The house belonged to Señora Florencia's nephew Rogelio. She had taken care of him when he was a very young boy and was left without a family. And now he took care of her. He was an artist and had asked her to share his home with him, to live with him. But at present he was not in Oaxaca. A few months before Mary Crawford's arrival, he had retreated, first to the mountains of Oaxaca and then to Peru, in pursuit of his art and to look for UFOs. Señora Florencia smiled. "Art or aliens, Rogelio always sends me money. Always sees that I am comfortable and well. But when he goes off, he doesn't often write to me. My only worry about him is that he will be ill or die somewhere, far from his home, and no one will let me know that the most important and loving person in my life needs me or my special prayers! But I know that if anything happened to me, he would be here at once."

Neither Señora Florencia nor Kamal even entertained the idea of Rogelio being abducted by aliens as he looked for UFOs. Carmelita of course discussed the possibility quite seriously.

Mary Crawford had rented two rooms in the house and Señora Florencia had been her cook, her Spanish teacher, and her nurse. And what could she, asked Señora Florencia, do for the señorita who had arrived at her door? But first the señorita should get out of the noise and fumes of the traffic and come into the house. Yes, the piñatas were her nephew Rogelio's work. He had left them there, together with the Virgin, to guard his aunt and their home.

As Kamal accompanied Señora Florencia across the yard with its fruit trees, flowers on vines, flowers in clay pots, herbs in tin cans, two sleeping parrots and the overpowering smell of jasmines, she wondered if her mother's garden on Malabar Hill had resembled this yard. Sitting in Señora Florencia's small living room, with bright pictures of the Virgin in her many incarnations, a faded picture of Pope John cut out from a magazine, flowers made from newspapers stuck into black pottery vases, and a large television, Kamal asked Señora Florencia if she knew anything about a long piece of heavy silk embroidered cloth which might have been in Señora Mary's possession.

Kamal tried to explain what a sari was and the importance of this particular sari, grateful that her mother had insisted that she take Spanish in high school and the first two years of college. "I have taught you Gujarati, Kamal. But when I am dead, you may have very little chance to speak it. And if you continue to speak only English, you will come to believe like the rest of the people around you that English is either the only language spoken on this earth or that it is the only language worth knowing. Learn Spanish. Maybe one day we can go to Peru. I want to see if a person from Peru would really be interested in writing about Parsis! Your Grandfather Tehmurasp had a book on Parsis which he insisted was written by a scholar from Peru."

Señora Florencia asked, "¿Una tela? ¿Un vestido de la India? !Que bueno! !Que bueno! ¿Tu eres de la India, no? ¿Dondé naciste? ¿Y tu Mama? Ah si. Tus ojos, son de la India, Señorita Kamal."

And then to Kamal's complete bewilderment, Señora Florencia asked, "¿Conoces tu la China Poblana?"

Kamal knew of "La China Poblana" only as a Mexican Indian restaurant which used to be in Berkeley, on San Pablo Avenue. She and her mother had frequented it until it closed down. The owners, cooks and servers were a Mexican woman from Puebla and her Indian husband from Goa. Dinaz and Kamal had always ordered the same dishes there: rice with crab curry and chicken enchiladas with a side of guacamole and a side of cilantro chutney. Katy loved being surprised by the fresh, green taste of cilantro, mint, lemon, and chilies in the chutney and the guacamole. Dinaz approved of the chutney because it possessed the right amount, just a hint, of shredded coconut and cashews in it. It was of course the same restaurant that

Carmelita, Ratna and I had gone to after Tracy Robertson's party

But no, Señora Florencia wasn't speaking of any restaurant. She was speaking of the original China Poblana: Mirrha, a princess who had been stolen from India by Spanish and Portuguese pirates, taken to the Philippines, then to China as they put together their cargo of spices and silks and ivory and sandalwood for New Spain. Mirrha had arrived with the cargo from Asia on the coast of what was to be named Mexico in 1620. Señora Florencia seemed sure about the date as well as the fact that the young girl who had eventually ended up in Puebla de los Angeles had been baptized, somewhere along the way, with the name Catarina de San Juan. She had been married for fourteen years, widowed, revered as a visionary and a saint by her new countrywomen and men, and sent up for canonization by her father confessor, a zealous believer in the saintliness of the woman from India, especially if they were of royal blood. She was condemned by the Inquisition for among other reasons, her reports of her conversations with Jesus. During one of those conversations, when the Resurrected Christ appeared before her not quite properly clad, Mirrha had gently scolded him and told him that she would have nothing to do with him until he appeared before her decently clothed. Mirrha's once scintillating, sequined, silk embroidered skirts and shawls from India had reputedly influenced the clothes worn by the China Poblanas. Señora Florencia told Kamal that she wasn't too sure about the clothes part. She had read in one of the biographies about Mirrha that her abductors had brought her to New Spain disguised in boy's clothing in order to protect her virginity, to keep her chaste and beautiful for the highest bidder. And according to the same biographer and Señora Florencia, Mirrha had always worn very humble, modest clothes.

While Señora Florencia spoke about La China, Kamal wondered if her Chinese great-great grandmother's gaaro was in this house or in San Diego or in San Francisco. She thought about the last piece of embroidery her mother had created especially for her. It was a wall hanging, nearly five feet long and two and a half feet wide, with lotus and almond-paisley designs from India, an enclosed French garden with a unicorn but no maiden, a many slope-roofed stylized pagoda from China, a house straight out of Grimm's Fairy Tales, and tile patterns from Alhambra all embroidered with sly, brilliant craft into a juxtaposed, linked pattern. Around the edge, Dinaz had cross-stitched: DO NOT EXPECT MIRACLES—SETTLE FOR COINCIDENCES. Looking at the paper flowers, the black vases, the rugs, the television, Kamal thought about that embroidered work against the wall of her own living room in San Francisco, and found herself telling Señora

Florencia all about her mother, her mother's headache, her longing to feel the monsoon rain in her garden on Malabar Hill and her death. Señora then got up from the couch covered with a gray rug with the Mitla pattern woven into it in red and blue and asked Kamal to follow her into the room behind the kitchen. She led Kamal to one of the tables which was covered with jars and bottles filled with dried leaves, twigs, seeds, and roots. Each container had a piece of paper wrapped around it with a thick rubber band. The name and uses of an herb, a healing plant, were written in beautiful, straight script in jet black ink on each piece of paper. Señora Florencia picked up a jar labeled Té Malabar and poured some of the contents into a small plastic bag. "Scatter these herbs on your mother's grave. It will help to cure her homesickness."

Kamal shook her head and told her that there was no grave. She then described her ash-scattering expedition. She went to the living room and returned with her "mother bag." The old woman nodded, plunged her hand into the bag, pulled out the plastic bag Kamal had been using for her mother's ashes and emptied them into a small clay bowl. She then added the Té Malabar to the ashes and carried the bowl to the other table in the room. As she lit three candles, Kamal leaned forward and grabbed the corner of the altar cloth nearly hidden under the bottles and jars and candles and statues.

It had been a very long time since Kamal had seen the maroon silk, threadbare and delicate, the white "spiders" carefully embroidered across the length and width of the sari.

Señora Florencia said, "I sent Señora Mary's belongings to her son in San Diego. But I kept this. She herself had spread it on this table as the altar cloth but I knew it was not hers. There is no feel, no touch of Señora Mary on this cloth. But if you touch it," she unclenched Kamal's hand freeing the sari corner, straightened out her hand and pushed it across the silk. "No, no. Do not become tense. There is nothing to fear. Close your eyes and be strong. Touch this silk. Don't you see her? A woman, she has the face of the Chinese women in my Rogelio's book with pictures from China. She is working on this cloth. She has tears in her eyes. I do not know why."

"Because one son will be sent away never to see her again."

"¿China está cerca de la India, no?"

Kamal explained to Señora Nunez, that no, China wasn't all that close to India. And without any warning, she began to cry. For the loss of her mother and for her own ignorance of the land her mother had left.

"This cloth," Señora Florencia said, "it is so full of life! But I must tell you, Señorita Kamal, I am sorry, but a piece is missing!"

Kamal knew about that missing piece. She told Señora Florencia that the sari had a piece missing from it even before it was given to Mary Crawford. It was missing even before she and her mother had moved to California and rented an apartment from Mary Crawford. A piece had been cut out in Wisconsin.

One March afternoon Kamal brought a note home from her teacher saying the class was putting on a fashion show and could Kamal dress in the costume of an Indian princess.

"I get to carry a bow and arrow! And wear moccasins! Real ones with beads and all!" Kamal had been thrilled.

Dinaz was appalled. Her lecture for the next fifteen minutes was garbled between explaining to her daughter about Indian "like me, like your father, like our families, like the Indian part of you," and the first people of the Americas, "as usual mis-named, mistreated by these conquerors." Her outrage at the word "costume" was part of the tirade.

"Costume-fostume! Indian princess-Indian frincess! And remind your teacher that you are an American. An American from India!"

As Kamal grew older, she lived in constant fear of her mother's habit of repeating words, Gujarati fashion. But Dinaz never made an embarrassing blunder.

"Doesn't she know that India is free? Independent since 1947! And what are we? Some kind of actors? Circus performers? We wear clothes just like everybody else. Not costumes. I will make you a jhabloo, a special Parsi dress for my special little Parsi girl in America. You are not too old or too big yet for a jhabloo."

But, according to Dinaz, a real jhabloo needed a Chinese embroidered silk cloth and so she had taken her scissors to the gaaro and cut off three-fourths of a yard. She had sewn the short straight sleeveless dress and crocheted a white silk cap for her daughter's tight black curls within two days. Alternating between singing, "Dolly mahri kevi tun," all the wonderful things she was going to do for her little doll, including sending her to school and college before getting her married, and "Avse naro vago lai ne," the bridegroom who whould arrive with a trousseau which would include necklaces of emeralds and rubies. She also told Kamal stories from the SHAH NAMA.

Kamal's favourite story from the SHAH NAMA was the story of Rhodabeh and Zaal. Rhodabeh who lived in a tower and who had very, very long hair. And when she liet it all down so that Zaal could climb up and meet her, he refused to do anything so dastardly. He kissed a lock of Rhodabeh's hair, threw the rope he carried in his saddle bag high inthe air, and lassoed a turret on the very first try and climbed up and into his beloved's window. And their son was the great hero, the dragon killer, Rustom. Rustom, who killed his own son, Sohrab. Unknowingly, Kamal, who refused to cry for Beth March, always sobbed loudly without any shame whenever her mother told her the story of Rustom and Sohrab. And of Rustom's wife, Sohrab's mother, Tehmineh, who died of grief within a year of her son's death.

That was in Wisconsin. In Mexico, many years later, Kamal said to Señora Florencia, "Don't worry, I know about the missing piece. My mother cut it out to make me a dress, when I was six years old."

"Yes, but I too cut a piece from this material. For Rogelio. I wanted to give him something to make him a bit more sensible. To guard him. He never thinks of protecting himself on this earth. The cold. The heat. He always wants to fly! He makes piñatas which he hangs up on high poles and never allows anyone to break them and bring them down to earth. Always to be left hanging up there, in the air. He talks about all those machines he says come from the stars in the sky. And he never wraps up his neck or covers his head when he goes out in the cold. He is always catching a cold. So I took a piece of this cloth because he said he liked it. No reason. Not because of the color or the touch of it. He said one evening when I was giving him some herbs from that table, that he liked this cloth. I gave him a piece of this cloth to wrap around his neck. It is light but warm, this silk. I will try and get it back for you and sew it on again, but as I told you, the last I heard from him he was going to Peru. And he always gives away everything..."

Kamal was not paying any attention. She was rubbing one of the spider designs on the cloth between her fingers.

"I never answered my mother's last question," she said, "about being a real American."

She picked up a thick, fat pink candle which had been stuck with serious intent into a small candlestick. She wondered if it were a gift of the illusive Rogelio. She put the candlestick back on the sari covered table.

"Señora Florencia, I already have a piece of this sari in the dress my mother made. Another piece is most probably in Peru. Let's just keep what's left of this sari here in Oaxaca with this portrait of an angel my mother loved. When you dream of la China Poblana, Mirrha-Catarina, maybe you will also dream of the rain falling on my mother's garden and of my Chinese great-great grandmother, whose name I don't know. And maybe one day I will come back and visit you for a longer time. And sit in your garden."

"Yes," said Señora Florencia, "You are right. This is a good place for this cloth to rest for some time. With an old woman, in her old woman's house, with an old woman's herbs and flowers and birds. Yes. This is a good place to rest."

But of course, it didn't rest there. A few minutes later, just as Kamal was leaving Señora Florencia's house, Roxanne, Sarosh, Carmelita and I turned up. We met Kamal. Kamal and Roxanne argued about the sari, and after they came to an agreement, Roxanne demanded to know why a Zoroastrian was carrying around human ashes and Kamal told us her story.

Sarosh took the zip-lock bag of ashes and tea from Señora Florencia and handed it to Roxanne. "At least some part of Dinaz Mehta should be given a home somewhere in India. Roxanne will take this bag back with her to Devinagar."

"I will?" asked Roxanne.

"Yes, you will. And don't tell any other Parsi that you are carrying any part of a dead body with you. Just be quiet about it. And now Kamal and I are going to the Mexicana office to change her ticket."

"!Como no, muchacho!" said Carmelita.

Sarosh laughed. A forty-two year old muchacho. He began to think of the letter he would write that night to Virbaiji, about Kamal Mehta, granddaughter of Khorshed Japanwallah Mehta, and Mexico. Not a word about the sari.

Carmelita and Señora Florencia began planning a trip to the yard good store for next morning to find an addition for the sari.

"It will most probably come from Taiwan or Korea. Or Hong Kong," muttered Roxanne.

"Or even India. Lots of textiles and clothes from India are sold in Mexico now," said Señora Florencia.

I hoped that at least for one day, one morning, the old woman with bare feet and her black butterfly would disappear. What use would she have for a yard goods store? She had worn the same clothes ever since she had first appeared to me nearly thirty years ago. The skirt, the embroidered blouse, the ribbons in her hair.

# XIV.

## Oaxaca, Mexico

### *Authentic Doughnuts and Sexy Roses*

It was not until the evening of Good Friday, five days after our arrival in Oaxaca, two days after our meeting with Señora Florencia and Kamal, that Carmelita took me to La Soledad. We had postponed our visit to Monte Alban.

Carmelita and I could hear the Bishop of Oaxaca speaking in the main courtyard of the church, as we walked outside, passing families eating tacos, tamales mole and a variety of white and pink puddings from the food stalls set up on the stone steps leading to the church. Children ran up and down the stairs, the braver ones balanced themselves on top of the rough stone walls framing the steps.Shoppers crowded the stalls selling religious articles, plastic souvenirs of Oaxaca, jewellery, and candy and toys.

As we entered the dark courtyard of the church, we became part of the large crowd of worshippers. While the Bishop prayed and preached and changed hats and caps, girls and boys in scout uniforms kept the crowds in place behind a rope fence. They were earnest and solemn and had probably never sold a cookie or sung a silly campfire song. Women and men listened, carried on quiet conversations, burped babies, flirted and changed places with the minimum of fuss. I was lulled into a sense of calm comfort until I found myself moving along with the crowd, following the image of the Virgin of La Soledad into the church.

The church was stripped of pews and benches. Mary was dressed in unadorned black and carried a white lace handkerchief in one hand, to catch her tears, and a white silk cloth in her other hand, to wipe her son's face as he walked towards his final destination. The crowds that had not bothered me in the courtyard terrified me when I was with them inside the church. I didn't want to be a part of the drama I was caught in, and yet I couldn't find a way to remain detached. The quiet, desperate passion surrounding me, the resigned grief, tears on people's faces, hands clenched around bouquets of flowers, around candles, around handkerchiefs demanded a responding emotion from me. There was a general acceptance of shared yet private sorrow that I dared not acknowledge. Theresa and Gregory Sanders and Lakewood, New Hampshire had not prepared me for this symbolic suffering, the silent intensity of mourning in that church in Oaxaca, Mexico. A young woman in terrifyingly high heels separated herself from the crowd and approached the Virgin. I caught a glimpse of her face and was reminded of Carmelita's stories of la llorona. I had never seen a face as devoid of expression as that young woman's. I felt overwhelmed by the sense of controlled sorrow that seemed to permeate her. She was neither lamenting loudly nor scaring anyone around her into death or insanity. I tried to move towards her but was shoved back roughly. It was the old barefoot woman moving me out of her way. The black butterfly was flying around the feet of the Virgin. Suddenly I had had enough of crowds, people mourning, the grieving statue, and the barefoot old woman. I grabbed Carmelita's hand and began to push my way out and away from the church.

Carmelita was quiet as we walked back through the stone-paved streets. We walked beyond the university, empty and quiet because of the holidays, beyond the shops preparing to close their doors, beyond the restaurants serving pizza and blaring rock and roll, beyond the German and French tourists still wearing their straw hats and shorts even as the evening turned cool. At every bougainvillea vine, every hibiscus bush, every tuberose cluster, Carmelita stopped. She closed her eyes and breathed. Once, twice, three times, four times. She wiped tears from her cheeks with the back of her right hand.

I broke the silence. "I am sorry I forced you to leave the church. But she touched me. In the church. And the black butterfly flew to the Virgin's feet."

"Is that what was happening? I wondered. I bet your Catholic church in New Hampshire never saw such crowds."

"Or such rituals or worship or fervor. Theresa Sanders once told me it was always difficult for her to attend Mass in Mexico. She felt embarrassed by what she called 'all the needless fuss.' Why are you crying? And breathing?"

"Katy, people who are alive always breathe."

I gave her a Kleenex.

"I am trying to breathe in the smells. These flowers. The cooking. The burning of the garden rubbish. The earth in love with the sun and now turning quite elegantly sensuous under the chill of the night. I need these smells, these textures, Katy. When I am in San Francisco, I always have an empty, cold place inside of me. I try to grow bougainvillea and hibiscus. But you know how it is there. The plants look as if they are doing you an enormous, grudging favor by growing for you! They need constant pampering. And there are seldom sexy roses in the US of A. And God knows, I really like that city. But it is never home. Even your wonderful house in Half Moon Bay is not an easy place to breathe in."

We passed by the Santo Domingo church and bade a very good night to the very young soldier at the army barracks behind the church, standing on solitary duty, his rifle under one arm and a boom box under the other. Mercedes Sosa was belting out, "Gracias a la Vida" from which I thought I heard the call of the buoys, the wind through the eucalyptus, the dark Pacific Ocean waves washing against the sand. I wanted to be wrapped safely in the familiar, silent, cold, fog of the California coast as it drifted across the cemetery and entered my garden. I missed the season of the red-tailed hawks. Walking through the mountain-locked city of Oaxaca, I hoped that Putlibai was at peace in the garden near the ocean and wondered if she and Rosario were talking to one another in their sleek, mermaid bodies even now as Carmelita and I entered Tía Lucía's house on Avenida Constitucion.

While Carmelita and I were visiting the La Soledad, Señora Florencia and Roxanne had found some doughnuts in a bakery three blocks from the zocalo. But Roxanne wasn't satisfied. They weren't real, honest-to-goodness, American doughnuts. And so, the very next evening, Carmelita and I found ourselves once again passing the army barracks and the same young soldier with his weapon and his music. This time Señora Florencia and Roxanne were also with us. We were in a search of authentic Norte Americano, Estados Unidosian doughnuts.

Roxanne loved doughnuts. She had discovered the imitation form of doughnuts—thick, cake rounds with frosting and jam—at the Niketan Hotel in Devinagar many years ago.

The idea of doughnuts had been brought to the Niketan by hippies. Actually by the mother of one of the hippies. The hippie in question was named Donald Douglas and he had arrived in Devinagar in 1965. He soon became known to everyone in Devinagar as Donald Duck. He loved his name and decided to stay forever in Devinagar when he discovered the warm beaches and the ease with which he could earn the few rupees he required for his simple needs. He either stood near the Hanuman Temple to beg for his living or he earned his money by singing the latest American war resistance and folk songs in front of the Niketan. He did both with great charm and goodwill. The citizens of Devinagar were appalled, fascinated, amazed, and embarrassed at the idea of a white man, an American at that, begging in the streets of Devinagar. It was mainly the embarrassment that put rupees in Donald's brass bowl.

Doughnuts were introduced to the Niketan and from there to many of the kitchens of Devinagar when Donald's mother, Mrs Frank Douglas, arrived to reclaim her son. She arrived with three dozen doughnuts, one dozen Snicker's bars, five packages of assorted American cookies, two pairs of new jeans, a family-size package of a dozen non-scented, soft-as-a-baby's-behind, toilet paper rolls and two sets of dark green, lush towels. Donald abandoned Devinagar for Sacramento, seduced by the doughnuts, his mother's love, and the idea of bathrooms with matched sets of towels, bathtubs with floating rubber duckies and flush toilets that worked. But before he left, he shared his mother's bounty with the citizens of Devinagar and the doughnuts caught on with the Hotel Niketan crowd. Mrs Douglas taught the art of making doughnuts to the Niketan chef as best as she could from what she remembered and what ingredients were available in Devinagar. Somehow, even when the doughnuts at the Niketan had the prerequisite hole in them, they resembled chunks of sponge cake and tasted vaguely of Anglo-Indian trifle and Indian gulab jammuns.

To her immense joy, Roxanne had discovered authentic American doughnuts in California during the few days she spent with me in Half Moon Bay before we left for Oaxaca. And after the Saturday late afternoon lunch at Tía Lucía's, she had announced that she craved doughnuts. Señora Florencia had heard that they served authentic doughnuts at the restaurant of the Hotel Camino Real. At one time the Hotel Camino Real had been a convent. And so Carmelita and I found ourselves accompanying Señora Florencia and Roxanne to the Hotel Camino Real.

As we entered the hotel, an old woman sitting at the entrance, selling blood red roses from a basket, got up, pushed her way through us, and went into the lobby. Señora Florencia recognized the woman. "Katy, your lady with the butterfly is here. She knows everything. Even Roxanne's desire for doughnuts. Let's see where she leads us."

I didn't want to follow the woman and I didn't particularly like doughnuts. I had once again felt the old woman's body touch me. I wanted to go to Señora Florencia's house and have steaming herb infusions placed on my knees.

The old woman and the maitre d' led us to a table away from the central patio with the tourist boutique. The four of us sat down facing the pomegranate trees and the night blooming flowers enclosed by old convent arches. We ordered doughnuts, pastries, and cups of Oaxaqueña chocolate. Roxanne and Carmelita went off to explore the faded frescoes and portraits decorating the walls. I heard Roxanne say, "Carmelita, these people are serious about their saintliness!" "Only in their portraits," replied Carmelita. Señora Florencia raised her eyes to the balcony where nuns had walked in sedate silence, and where now six giggling teenagers from San Diego ran in and out of rooms with dark, stout doors.

"Well, they bring us dollars," she said.

I was looking at the old woman sitting across from us on the rim of the low wall surrounding the well. Mosquitoes were flying around her bare feet.

Señora Florencia and I could see the scar on the woman's neck bleeding in the silence of that evening as a lone guitarist on one of the balconies played the opening bars of "Lagrimas para mi hermano" again and again. Neither of us said anything. Señora Florencia reached for my left hand.

The doughnuts, the cups of chocolate, Roxanne and Carmelita arrived at our table at the same time as a middle-aged man with a smile for Señora Florencia walked up to us. He picked up Señora Florencia, right out of her chair, and kissed her. She said, "Of course. It is time you were here. I am glad you didn't go away with those people from the other stars."

"What stars?" said Rogelio. "You travel more than those UFOs. I tried you at our house. Then at your friend, Señora Glafira's. She sent me to Señora Lucía's. She sent me to Hotel Presidente. But there is no Hotel Presidente anymore! There is this one which was Hotel Presidente but is now Hotel Camino Real. And the night manager in the lobby is very upset because someone has covered the floor of his immaculate, convent-hotel lobby with fresh red roses. It happened while he was answering the phone. I told him it could be a milagro, considering the time of the year, but he did not even want to think of things such as miracles." And then Rogelio noticed the doughnuts, the hot chocolate, and us.

Roxanne looked at him and said to Señora Florencia, "You don't have to worry about anything. He looks quite sane. He doesn't look like a man who has talked to space aliens. Maybe he has brought back that scarf and we can stitch it back on to the sari as well as the material we bought on Thursday."

Carmelita turned to me. She mistook my dazed look.

"I agree," she said. "Quite an amazing man! Look at our Señora Florencia! Transformed. Just being in the presence of her nephew."

Señora Florencia introduced us to Rogelio.

"This one with the crazy, beautiful hair lives in California. But she is

135

from here. She is Señorita Carmelita Gutierrez. Niece to Señora Lucía, goddaughter to Señora Glafira, granddaughter of the woman who braided her husband's tongue."

Rogelio hugged Carmelita and kissed her on both cheeks. "But I know you," he said. "We met when we were very young. And I was rude to you because at that time I wanted Tía Florencia and Señora Glafira all to myself."

"You did apologize." Carmelita reached over and ruffled his hair as if the man were still a young boy.

"This is Señorita Roxanne from India," said Señora Florencia. "She is a lawyer. There are two others from India. A man, Señor Sarosh and a lady, who was actually born in New York and is an architect in California, Señorita Kamal. But they are exploring Oaxaca on their own. You'll meet them soon."

"A lady lawyer from India! That wonderful land! Tagore! The sarod, the sitar! The Meenakshi temple! The great and wise emperor, Akbar!" And Rogelio kissed Roxanne's hand without any sign of affectation. She liked the gesture and the comments. And decided that he and Saleem would get along very well.

"And this is Señorita Katayun Cooper from California. She too has connections to India. You have come in time to help me cure her legs. Her knees do not want to work for her. Enough about those UFOs and politics. You should start the work you were sent to do. Be a curandero. And that Señor Sarosh wants to talk to you about that also. And your newspaper flowers have confused Señorita Katayun, whom we call. . ."

"Katayun? No, no. Katy. K-K-K-Katy."

Rogelio was no longer a charming, handsome man. Within a few seconds he had turned into a man who was furiously, quietly angry. It was a terrible anger. Cold, deep, and detached. And all of it was directed towards me. He turned away from me and said to Señora Florencia, "Tía, let us go to Monte Alban tomorrow morning. You and Señorita Katy. We will then speak of curing and healing."

"Not without me." Carmelita did not trust this man who had changed so drastically from laughter, hugs, kisses, charm, to anger. "I will come with you. And if Roxanne wishes, she will come." She decided that a lawyer might be needed. Carmelita lives in the United States and understands the need for lawyers. I wished that Ratna were with us. She might have said nothing but would have joined forces with Carmelita and Roxanne.

"Pick us up at Tía Lucía's tomorrow, morning," said Roxanne. "I want to be next to Katy if there is any curing or healing to be done by this man."

"Let's go back to Tía Lucía's house now. Señora Florencia and Rogelio,

136

we'll see you tomorrow morning." Carmelita led Roxanne and me out of the Hotel Camino Real and to her aunt's home.

# XV.

## Oaxaca and Monte Alban, Mexico

### *Tia Lucía's House and the House of the Black Butterflies*

If ever there was a house primed for haunting, it was Carmelita's Tía Lucía's house on the Avenida Constitucion. The "Casa de la Mujer: Rosario Castellano" across the street from Tía Lucía's house had a staunch, adobe wall with red geraniums in clay pots on its windowsills. Tía Lucía's house had a small garden with a broken down wrought iron fence facing the Avenida. The garden survived on its own. Neither Tía Lucía, nor her companion of many years Tía Elena, nor their neighbor, Señora Margo nor Señora Margo's daughter Lupita aged seven had ever tended the plants and trees. There was a stunted date palm in one corner of the garden and various plants grew in large pots that had, in the past, boasted gaily painted surfaces. The garden was glorious in March and April when the fiery jacaranda and the just as dramatic tavachina were in bloom.

Cats prowled around Tía Lucía's garden. They looked well fed and much loved. No one knew how many cats claimed Tía Lucía's garden as their own. And no cat had ever been seen to enter or exit the house itself. The house, surrounded by the garden and the cats, presented a dingy, comfortable face to the world. Inside every room, including the kitchen, had masks of papier-mâché, tin, wood and clay on the walls, in all the colours and with the look of having been molded over the faces of living, breathing creatures staring malevolently or dolefully at the world through their eye-slits.

The haunted quality struck me as soon as I entered Tía Lucía's front room. It wasn't just the masks that gave me that feeling. It was also the light. Sunshine filtered through lace curtains pulled against amber, green, and red stained glass windows, looking as if it had risen from the bottom of a sea through dark layers of water. It was the kind of light that brought to mind dramatic scenes of murders, torrid romances, or poisonous family feuds carried on around a dining table.

The afternoon we arrived from San Francisco via Guadalajara and Mexico in search of Mary Crawford, the family sar,i and someone whose name resembled "Maita," Tía Lucía, Tía Elena, Señora Margo, and Señora Margo's daughter, Lupita, were waiting for us in the room of the strange light. As soon as she saw me, Lupita, who had been hanging in the background, away from the smiles, the hugs and the talk, pointed at me and shouted, "Mama, mama! Tía Elena! That woman is the ghost." In Spanish, I came out as being 'la espectra, el fantasma."

Tía Lucía quieted Lupita. She introduced me to her and explained that I was an old and dear friend of Carmelita and stated my antecedents, "Her father was from India. But she grew up in the United States."

Lupita retreated. "No madrina, she is not a person. She is a ghost."

Carmelita looked towards Tía Elena. She explained later to Roxanne and me, Tía Elena was the one who really knew what was going on in that house. She had also, at one time, held well-attended seances in Merida.

Tía Elena smiled and shrugged. She and Lupita's mother, Señora Margo, had known for many years that Lupita saw ghosts and spirits everywhere. It wasn't something they encouraged but they didn't actively discourage it either. And for the last two years and a half, a woman with dark skin, brown eyes and long, dark hair had been seen by Lupita at the door of the house on Avenida Constitucion. Since the gates to Tía Lucía's garden were always left open, the woman would walk up to the house and knock at the front door. The knock would come usually come at a little after 7:30 in the morning. When Lupita answered the door, the woman would smile, start to speak, and then disappear. Or she would turn into some horrible creature. The terrified Lupita would slam the door in the woman-creature's face. If the knock on the door was answered by anyone else, there would be no one there.

Tía Lucía didn't believe in espectras or fantasmas. She explained away the mysterious knocks at her door as sounds from the street, which was increasingly filled with the noises of automobiles and trucks. She shook her head in disbelief when Lupita expressed her dismay at my being allowed to enter the house.

Tía Elena poured two glasses of lemon juice. She handed one to me and the other to Lupita.

"My friend Lucía stopped believing in the existence of ghosts, spirits, and eternity when she was in Europe. She studied in Austria and Switzerland. She became a psychoanalyst. She seldom goes to Mass and never to Confession. But she is a good woman and a very good friend."

"I am a healer, like my mother. That is enough for me," said Tía Lucía, the child fostered by the singing, braiding woman whose husband had sent children to her from all over North America. Tía Lucía had been sent from San Diego.

Now Lupita pointed behind me and said, "Dios mio. Hay otra. Una vieja. Sin zapatos. Con listones en sus trenzas."

"And there you have it," said Carmelita.

"And there you have what?" demanded Roxanne.

"This young girl just said that there is another one. An old woman. Without shoes. With ribbons in her braids."

"Well then, I suppose one does have it." Said Roxanne. "Katy's Auntie Agnes and my friend Nanibai have also seen Katy's old woman. I haven't. Have you?"

Carmelita shook her head. "But that does not mean that the old woman doesn't exist. I phoned Ratna before we left California and told her that we were coming to Oaxaca. She is staying with Katy's Auntie Agnes. Ratna said that she would be with us. In spirit. I wonder if little Lupita can see her also. Three strange beings. Katy, our live phantasm. The old woman, the dead ghost. And Ratna, an out of body visitation."

Roxanne listened to Carmelita with great seriousness, thought for a minute or so, and said, "I am sure Lupita can see all three of them. Is there such a creature as a 'dead' ghost and does Ratna have the habit of losing her hair pins?"

Carmelita looked at Roxanne and raised her eyebrow questioningly.

Roxanne laughed. "It's clear that you have to practice this raising of the eyebrow some more, Carmelita. You haven't quite gotten it yet." And then she went to her bag, rummaged inside it, found something, came back to Carmelita and opened her hand. Six black hairpins were in her palm.

"Are these Ratna's?" she asked.

Carmelita nodded. "Definitely. So she is sending us things, everyday stuff, to tell us that she is with us. Where did you find them?"

"All over the place, ever since we decided to follow the sari to Oaxaca, and especially on my pillow, before I went to bed in Katy's house, and here, on the bed, when Tía Lucía took me a few minutes ago to the bedroom to show me which bed she has allocated to me. They can't be mine, my hair certainly doesn't need these lethal looking things. They're not yours and Katy doesn't use these."

I opened my bag and brought out the chocolate Easter bunnies Roxanne and I had bought at Cunha's County Store, as renditions of "Easter Parade" were being played on the speakers. Roxanne had sung along with every version. The old woman had surprised me by picking out a bouquet of daffodils, pointing at my purse, taking the money I pulled out, paying for the flowers, accepting the change, and walking out of the store. I had watched as the sales lady had smiled at the old woman and told her, in Spanish, to have a nice day. It appeared that the sales ladies at Cunha's County Store and the old barefoot woman were acquainted.

Lupita seemed comforted by the edible rabbit from Half Moon Bay. She smiled at me and tentatively touched my hand. I, who seldom touched another human being, smiled at Lupita and hugged her. But even as I noticed her crooked teeth, sharp eyes, and the mouth that always seemed to be on the verge of trembling, as resembling my own teeth, eyes and mouth, I felt a jolt of pain through my legs. I tried to ignore it by counting the plastic barrettes in Lupita's long hair. There were at least three pink, four green and two yellow barrettes. A portrait of Lupita flying over houses, cathedrals, trees, and oceans took shape in my mind. And each barrette was in the image of the people and the ghosts Lupita encountered on her flights. I remembered Putlibai, she would have felt comfortable in Tía Lucía's home.

It was at this house of two psychics and one psychoanalyst that Rogelio appeared, seven days after our arrival in Oaxaca, at 8.30 on Sunday morning with his aunt sitting next to him in a white, red, and green Dodge van. Carmelita, Roxanne, and I were ready for Monte Alban. Kamal and Sarosh had gone off to Mitla and parts unknown to continue their courtship. They had yet to meet Rogelio. The excitement of new love had won over Sarosh's curiosity about the man from Peru.

The discovery of Kamal Mehta at Señora Florencia's house, the trip to La Soledad, the red roses scattered all over the lobby of Hotel Camino Real, the appearance of Rogelio seemed to have happened many months ago instead of only within the last week.

Even as he greeted Tía Lucía and Tía Elena with courtesy and gave little Lupita a hug and a box with a big blue bow, Rogelio looked grim and sad. He paid no attention to Carmelita when she said, "My friend Katy is the artist. She notices how people look. The beauty of a woman or a man seldom moves me. But you, hombre, take my breath away. You look just like my mother used to describe my grandfather. She said that even when he didn't speak his wonderful words, people stopped to look at him."

I felt trapped in the van, between Rogelio in front of me and the old barefoot woman behind me. There was no butterfly.

Roxanne was excited about going to Monte Alban. Señora Florencia, in the front passenger seat, constantly had to turn to look back to answer questions about the pyramids, the carvings, the paintings, the tunnels, the social, the economic conditions of contemporary Oaxaca, and her experiences as a curandera.

Rogelio spoke once. As the van began to climb the road to Monte Alban, he said, "We are going to Monte Alban so that K-K-K-Katy can see the black butterflies. We will see if they will cure her." I couldn't decide if the darkness in his voice was due to rage or sorrow.

Señora Florencia was unhappy with her beloved nephew.

"Rogelio, will you try and cure this woman? You have learned much from me and from all your travels. Señorita Katy has suffered for too many years.

Rogelio didn't answer her.

"And to think that only last evening the man was kissing cheeks and hands and picking up old women to hug them!" Roxanne was definitely not pleased with Rogelio.

As we entered Monte Alban, the carefully balanced landscape of ruins, mountains and valleys stunned me. I, who had been taught by the Sanderses, my school teachers in New Hampshire, and my art teachers at the University in California never to express beauty, or the lack of it, in trite, normal words, could only say, "It is beautiful. It scares me. I can't bear it."

Roxanne, completely at ease with ancient places, told Carmelita that a good dousing with buckets of water over the large expanse which spread from pyramid to pyramid to pyramid, from houses to tunnels to ball park, would make the heat rising from the dry earth more breathable.

There were no clouds in the sky and very few people at the ruins.

Roxanne stood in amazed, silent appreciation before the ancient fresco of the man with an erection at the base of the furthest pyramid. Carmelita said she was glad that at last something in Mexico had halted the tongue of the lady lawyer from Devinagar, India. She challenged Roxanne to race her up the pyramid stairs. Roxanne agreed to climb the pyramid if on the way Carmelita would explain to her the mysteries behind the steep stairs on ancient as well as contemporary edifices in Mexico.

Rogelio requested, quite politely, that I not follow Carmelita and Roxanne. I could hear the two women arguing over the steepness of the steps and the practice of human sacrifice.

Just as Roxanne's voice came down towards us at the bottom of the pyramid, "If any one thinks the practice has stopped. . .if any one doesn't believe that our economies sacrifice the poor at the altar . . . you should hear the stories Nanibai. . . ," Rogelio took my hand.

"It is time for you, Katy, to see the black butterflies and to talk of death. Those two are just making empty, hot words."

I decided to follow him since Señora Florencia was right behind me.

We walked to the house with the rectangular doorway facing the pyramid of the astronomers. Across the door there was a window overlooking the valley. The view was breathtaking. Anyone standing at the window would see enemies approaching, travelers climbing up to the mountain, visitors arriving. From the time the house was constructed, no one who entered that valley had been hidden from peering eyes at the window. Señora Florencia, puzzled at her nephew's behavior, entered the house, carefully stepping up and down the different levels. She walked through each room, and stood behind me as I stood looking out the window.

"Look Señora Florencia, black butterflies! Millions of them! Black with a small red dot on each wing!"

Señora Florencia shook her head and crossed herself.

I stared at the woman who was moving across the valley-sometimes in the form of a raven, sometimes as a butterfly, sometimes as a curtain of dust dragged across the valley by the wind, sometimes in her own form as an old barefoot woman with ribbons in her hair.

Rogelio too was staring out at the valley.

"Rogelio, I know you can see her. Your aunt has already seen her. I don't know who she is. You do. Tell me who is this woman?"

"You are demented. It is nothing but the wind." He let go of my hand. Then he pushed me away from him and against the low wall and said, "Murderer!"

Señora Florencia and I both saw the knife. Small, sharp, glittering and quick in Rogelio's hand as he moved towards me. He was allowed one small cut against my throat before the old woman rushed through the window and grabbed his arm. Rogelio looked at his arm, where he had been touched, he looked at the place where the old woman stood facing him, he dropped the knife and leaned out of the window and screamed out his sorrow. His lament carried across the valley like the terrible cry of a nocturnal creature let loose in the blinding light of that bright, cloudless morning.

Roxanne and Carmelita heard Rogelio's cry and ran down the pyramid, across to the house and into the house just as I spoke, "I am not a murderer."

Rogelio insisted, "Yes, K-K-K-Katy, you are a murderer."

Carmelita and Roxanne turned towards Rogelio but before they could do anything, Señora Florencia said, "Enough of this madness. We must first get Katy to my house." She quickly examined my wound. "No, it is not at all deep. Just needs to be cleaned up. But we must get her inside. Away from this heat. She is in shock. Rogelio has gone mad. He needs to be cured more than Katy. A curandero trying to kill! And I taught him how to heal when he was such a little boy. And never, never has he raised his hand to anyone. Not even when he was a little boy."

Carmelita got into the driver's seat. Rogelio climbed in beside her with the hesitating movements of an old exhausted man.

Roxanne and Señora Florencia sat in the back, their arms around me, constantly uttering Ave Marias and other mantras to the Virgin. I was the calmest of them all as I began to rub my knees. Right hand on left knee, left hand on right knee. If the old woman was in the car I did not see her.

Señora Florencia took care of my wound as soon as we reached her house. As I waited for a cup of the Té de Tila which Señora Florencia and Carmelita assured me would calm my nerves, I heard Carmelita yell at Rogelio, "If you ever raise your hand or your voice at Katy again, if you ever call her a murderer again, I will kill you. If you bring her pain, in any form, I will destroy you."

"No, Carmelita, I don't think I can ever try to harm her again. I missed my one chance. I am not a man who hurts others. And if I do harm her . . . if God gives me another chance. . .then take me to the police. Let them kill me. If you kill me, they will arrest you and then maybe kill you too."

His smile was the smile of the paintings and sculptures of the grinning skulls and death masks of Oaxaca, of all of Mexico.

"Oh no, they won't kill her," Roxanne said to Rogelio. "I will defend her. None of my clients have been sentenced to death and only two have received life imprisonment." Of course Roxanne's qualifications would be useless outside of India, but everyone knew that she would find a way to defend Carmelita.

I shuddered at the thought of what Theresa Sanders would say at all the melodramatic talk about murder and vengeance and court cases swirling around me, her beloved foster daughter.

Señora Florencia placed mugs of tea in front of Rogelio, Carmelita and Roxanne. And then she entered the bedroom to give me my cup of tea. There was silence as all of us drank one tea. Roxanne seemed to have forgotten that she hated any and all herb teas.

After a few minutes I heard Carmelita speaking in a softer, calmer voice.

"Hombre, what are you up to? Katy is my friend. She is the sister I had always prayed for. We have laughed and cried together. She has made my hair a part of her life and her work. She has painted my hair as red coral, as the dark branches of a winter tree leaning over the Pacific, as the wings of a large raven. We have listened to our dreams together. We have dreamed for one another. We have shared food, clothes, money, friends, houses. She, our friend Ratna, and I have prayed and cried over a woman from India whom we have buried in Katy's backyard."

I saw Rogelio raise his eyebrows and shake his head at the last piece of information. His smile was nearly normal. Carmelita couldn't stop trying to explain me to Rogelio. Roxanne kept nodding her head in agreement while she continued to sip her tea. She said, "You are absolutely right!" when Carmelita told Rogelio, "So Rogelio, Katy and I remain together. I will always be near her. Even though her father is dead, we don't know about her real mother, she has me. Her sister. Do not ever try to harm her again. Do not even think of it, even dream of it. I will know if you do."

Rogelio looked across the room at me. Señora Florencia entered the bedroom carrying a small tin brazier with copal sprinkled on a bed of live coals. She placed the brazier on the table which was covered with the Chinese sari. Everyone had been waiting for Kamal to remove the sari from the table and hand it over personally, officially, to Roxanne for the final adding on of the missing piece of material. The ghost of the barefoot old woman followed Señora Florencia into the room.

"No matter what both of you say, she is a murderer." It was a statement of fact. Rogelio said it without any anger.

"Look, Rogelio," I recognized Roxanne's lawyer voice. "You did not even know that Katy existed until yesterday. You must have confused her with someone else. She must remind you of someone. Tell me about this murder."

Rogelio shook his head. "I did know of her existence. I just didn't know where she was. And the murder—that is between the two of us."

Roxanne put down her mug and said, "Well, since this is going to be a long night, I will tell you a story about a murder. Not just a wild accusation with no explanations." She glared at Rogelio. "The story is about Katy's mother. I will tell you her story because I think that all of you, not just Katy, should hear what Nanibai told me before I left for America. I'll do it because I want to tell a story to keep myself awake and because our new friend Lupita sees ghosts and such things and because this man here who has accused our Katy of murder goes in search of UFOs and aliens and because Katy is followed around by that old woman whom I don't see and because Señora Florencia is a magical healer and because Carmelita . . ."

Carmelita said, "Me? Mujer, I am just a regular, normal human being. A beautician and nurse at your service."

Roxanne turned to Rogelio. "Remember that besides Carmelita, Katy also has me, my family, her Aunt Agnes, Nanibai, and Saleem. We are a formidable lot. We believe that the Goddess has the power of destruction and we will not hesitate to call on her."

I felt overwhelmed.

Carmelita said, "Amen." She sounded calmer.

"I was destroyed many years ago," muttered Rogelio as he went to the sink, poured out his tea and began to make coffee in a blue enameled saucepan.

"No Rogelio, you survived. If you use the destruction of others to destroy you, then you might as well be dead," said Señora Florencia. She pulled a chair from the kitchen into the bedroom, sat down beside me and said to Roxanne, who was in the kitchen, "Tell us about Katy's mother."

# XVI.

## Devinagar, India Recalled in Oaxaca, Mexico

*Roxanne Japanwallah Tells Us the Story of Maala, my Mother*

I wondered if Señora Florencia had any idea of how long and complicated Roxanne's stories could be. Roxanne began with a deceptively straightforward statement. "Nanibai told me about Katy's mother Maala the night before I left Devinagar to come to California."

One afternoon, about two years after Nanibai had set up the Devinagar Thieves Union with herself as the President of the Union, she had gone to the Empress Victoria Market to keep an eye on the members of the Union and to buy some vegetables for herself. Roxanne was barely four years old at that time. The market was renamed Kamala Nehru Market after Independence.

Nanibai was checking up on the members because one of the rules she had made for the Union was that none of the members could steal from the vendors in the market. She didn't want the storekeepers to alert their patrons who would then protect their pockets and bags and purses with extra vigilance. Picking the shoppers' pockets and purses was allowed. The Union didn't condone undue physical violence or consorting with the police. Getting what one wanted through the use of trickery was encouraged.

As Nanibai was buying onions and potatoes inside the market that afternoon, she happened to look across towards the meat section. Fresh meat had been brought in that morning and she could smell the thick, sweet smell of blood. A wall of flies stretched across the walkway separating the butchers from the rest of the market. Nanibai saw a young woman on the other side of that wall of flies. She was wearing a green sari, she was pregnant, and she was trembling. She couldn't move forward and seemed to have forgotten that she could move backwards, away from the flies.

Nanibai walked through the flies, took the woman by her hand, and brought her to her hut on the edge of town. Nanibai's hut was about half an hour's walk from the street of the Hanuman temple. It was the street where many years later Donald Douglas begged and sang his songs of freedom, lovers with silver daggers, flowers that had disappeared, unnatural rain, the house to be avoided in New Orleans, and a magic dragon named puff. Some of the Devinagar children had asked him if the dragon was a cream puff or a curried chicken puff. These delicacies were sometimes found at the Niketan. Donald didn't understand the question and talked about puffs of smoke and fire.

The woman said nothing until Nanibai sat her down and gave her some milk and two chappatis. Nanibai told her guest that pregnant women needed lots of milk, lots of green vegetables, especially spinach, and lots of chappatis with good ghee on them. Nanibai didn't know if any of this was true. She had never been pregnant. The woman thanked Nanibai and said simply, "My name is Maala."

My mother's name, according to Roxanne when she told us the story in Señora Florencia's house, meant a garland of flowers, a string of pearls, a gold necklace, a necklace of diamonds. According to Nanibai's account my mother was an astoundingly lovely woman. All the beauties of classical India: Sita and Parvati and Ahlya and Sarasvati and Lakshmi and Kannagi were incarnated in Maala. And according to Nanibai, Maala was not of this world.

"Not another alien!" groaned Carmelita when Roxanne came to that point in her story.

"*Another* alien?" asked Roxanne.

Carmelita pointed at Rogelio. He laughed. "I look for aliens. Now and then. But I am human." He passed around a basket of breads and a plate of Oaxaqueña cheese he had peeled into flat strings. He looked questioningly at me from the kitchen. I shook my head. I wasn't hungry. Not when I was about to hear about my mother. I noticed the beauty of Rogelio's hands and the soft gray and black of his hair.

Carmelita said to Roxanne, "Katy is certainly of this world. No one who is not of this earth can cook or paint as well as she does."

"A part of her is certainly human. As we know it. According to Nanibai."

I told the two women to stop discussing me. This was my mother's story, not mine.

On the second day of her life with Nanibai, Maala told the older woman a strange story. She said that she was the eldest of four sisters. She didn't know where she came from but said that she and her three sisters, just the four of them and no one else, lived in a house in a place far away. Maybe in the sky or at the bottom of the sea or at the center of the earth. Maybe another country. Maala didn't know. Maala and her sisters lived for one reason alone. To create the world. Everyday. Every single night they dreamed of designs and patterns for the tapestries they wove. And every morning their hands and eyes were ready to turn the yarns and the cloth and the threads and the paints that were always present in their house into the patterns and designs they had dreamed. They didn't know where their ideas came from because they had no books, no pictures, no companions, no contact with anyone or anything outside their home and their garden. As they worked, they told stories about their particular part of the pattern and about their dreams to one another. Sometimes their work blended into the larger pattern of their combined work and sometimes the four sisters looked with horror upon their colors, lines and textures, which seemed to scream against one another, trying to tear apart the tapestry they had created.

They did not know why they wove and stitched and painted and did not have any idea as to what happened eventually to their work. All they knew was that they created a tapestry, a flowing fabric during the daylight hours, and just as the light began to disappear, their work moved away from their hands, spilled out of their home over the high garden wall and disappeared. Carmelita was delighted by the image, "Right out of Remedios Varo." I shuddered. It reminded me of a giant, patchwork serpent slithering away.

One day they decided that the image of the oldest sister should be worked right into the tapestry. Maala's form, her voice, her presence were woven, embroidered, painted into the pattern they had been allotted by their dreams. Maala didn't work that day. She sat completely still while her three sisters placed her into the fabric. She was to travel with that day's work and see where at least one part of the sisters' creation, the part with her in it, went.

At the end of that day, Maala's sisters had trapped her within their weaving and then sent their weaving off, out of their home and down a waterfall to the part of the earth that happened to be India. She later discovered that her special task on the weaving and the painting had always included India and that the two youngest sisters' work included Portugal, Spain and the Americas.

Maala began her life in India as a schoolteacher in Mysore. She had come to India with her name and some knowledge about Indian history, music and languages. She was a successful teacher. She also knew what to say to people when they asked her who she was. Not lies but not quite the truth. From Mysore she went to Old Delhi. After that she decided to travel to Kashmir. And then one late afternoon she arrived in Devinagar on the Arabian Sea.

As she was passing by Our Lady of Fatima church in Devinagar, she saw a little boy with his school bag, sitting on the sidewalk crying into his shirt-sleeve. He had fallen down and scraped his elbow. She picked him up, wiped his tears, examined his elbow, told him that he would be OK and he should eat his favorite food—which he told her was rice with yogurt and raisins—for many more years, and accompanied him to his home. The boy's mother ran out to the front verandah, hugged the boy and scolded Maala for bringing the boy home later than usual. She thought Maala was her son's ayah. All ayahs looked alike to Mrs Lalacji. She had decided that all her son's ayahs, and there had been many of them though he was only seven years old, would be called Maria. Even if their names were Maria or Mumtaz or Meghna or Maala or Meera or Shanta or Anuradha or Fawzia or Nasreen or Shireen or Natasha or Rosie. They were all Maria.

The boy knew his ayahs' real names and he knew that Maala was not his latest ayah. He had left the school compound before his current ayah had arrived to take him home. And since this was the fifth time that had happened in two weeks, and since the ayah did not want to deal with the parents' anger again, she had gone off to find another job.

Maala and the boy realized that it was useless trying to change Mrs Lalacji's mind and Maala became the latest Maria, the ayah. She didn't think it would be very different from being a teacher.

Roxanne had agreed with Nanibai that it was Maala's karma that led her to that boy and that house. Apparently with all her special knowledge, Maala had no idea about sex and lust and taking care of herself. She had not paid any attention to how babies were produced. I am sure she and her sisters had put that in their patterns. How else would they have had a world to weave? For whom? But those four women, according to what Maala had said to Nanibai, had not even seen a man. Except in their dreams and in their weaving. Maala told Nanibai that men were the biggest surprise for her when she found herself in Mysore. When she had seen men in the fabrics she and her sisters created, they seemed to be just another kind of women. But she discovered, the second day she was on earth, that there were numerous things wrong with that idea. And in the Lalacjis' home she found out an important difference. Mr Lalacji's favorite nephew raped her when she accepted his invitation to listen to music in his room on the new gramophone his uncle had given him. When he attempted to repeat his performance a week later, Maala was no longer naive or trusting. She told him that she would report him to Mrs Lalacji. He laughed, pulled the sari covering her breasts, thrust ten rupees down her blouse and went off. A few months later, Mrs Lalacji realized that this Maria was pregnant. She told her to leave and found another Maria for her son. When Maala tried to explain the situation, her mistress called her a whore. Mr Lalacji decided to find out for himself exactly what had tempted his nephew. Maala fought back, he accused her of being a thief and threw her out of the house.

Maala was sick and unhappy and wanted to return to her sisters. But she did not know how to go back. She had not found the exact place where the four sisters' weaving touched the earth in India. And she knew with great certainty that she couldn't go back with her baby. There was room and work for four women only and not one more person, not even a child, in her old home. She became depressed and confused. She had not experienced such feelings before. They frightened her. She began to wander around Devinagar and on the seashore calling out to her sisters. The fishermen and their families stayed away from her.

One afternoon she was sitting at the entrance to the Empress Victoria Market, thin, dirty, scared and pregnant, when the man I later knew as my father, Freddy Cooper, saw her. He gave her some money and told her to go into the market and find something to eat. He had just come back after some years away from Devinagar.

He told her, "Get some food in you. It will give you strength. Here's some money for the food. After you eat something, go to the Cooper house. It is not very far from here. Tell them that Freddy Sahib sent you. Ask for my sister. Her name is Agnesmai. She will take care of you and your baby. Don't be afraid. We won't harm you. Go now and get some food."

But then, according to Roxanne's version of Nanibai's story, when Maala came into the market she stopped at the wall of flies. The smell and the sounds reminded her of the pain she had felt when the man had raped her. She couldn't move. A few minutes later, Nanibai rescued her, took her home and told her that Freddy and Agnes were good people. But Maala wanted to stay with Nanibai, away from the town and the seashore, away from people who hurt her or pitied her. Nanibai told everyone that Maala was her sister's daughter whose husband had died in a war. Somewhere. Someplace. Nanibai told Roxanne that she gave this explanation for Maala's presence in her hut because "there are always sisters and sisters always have daughters and there are always wars and men are always dying in wars."

After her baby was born, Maala started to have dreams with the designs and patterns for her part of the tapestry. She told Nanibai that she had to leave. But before leaving, she went to Agnes to ask her if she would take care of the baby. Maala had realized that Nanibai could be arrested at any time and put in jail. After all, Nanibai was a thief. Maala said, "Nanibai, you have been my mother. I touch your feet. But I love this little baby I gave birth to. I want her to learn how to read and write. I want her to earn enough money so that she never has to beg or steal or stay quiet when someone treats her with disrespect."

Nanibai reminded her of Freddy Cooper's offer. She told Maala, "Go to his sister Agnes and talk to her. Tell her your story. She will understand. She will find a good home for this baby. And I too will keep an eye on her as she grows up."

But Maala and the baby never made it to the Cooper home. Mrs Lalacji saw Maala and the baby near the Market. She said loudly to a friend who was with her that the baby would be a dirty, evil woman just like her mother. Maala put the baby in the lap of the woman who had sat outside the market selling fish ever since anyone could remember. She grabbed the fish cleaning knife from the woman's basket and attacked Mrs Lalacji. Roxanne, who was not there but who had seen many other fights, said that it was "quite a tamasha. Lots of noise and action. Quite a drama." Mrs Lalacji and her friend were screaming, people were rushing around, Maala was crying and trying to put the knife through the woman who had insulted her child. Someone recognized Maala as Nanibai's niece and pulled her away from Mrs Lalacji. Maala picked up her baby and returned to Nanibai's hut.

Maala couldn't stop crying. She cried for her baby and she cried for her sisters. She tried to nurse her baby but she couldn't do it. She dreamed of patterns and designs until she said she was going crazy. One morning Nanibai woke up and found her gone. She had left the baby behind. A few hours later, Nanibai found Maala in front of the Lalacjis' house. She was dead. Nanibai saw the place on her head where she had been hit hard.

When she told Maala's story to Roxanne, Nanibai said, "Roxanne, my dear friend Roxanne, you were not a lawyer then. You were a child. Otherwise we would have found the person who killed my Maala and punished him. But, I tell you Roxanne, even if you had been a lawyer then, we could have done nothing. I brought Maala to my hut and before my eyes and the eyes of the two other women who had come to help me prepare her for the pyre, Maala's body disappeared." Roxanne told Nanibai that such things never—or at least very seldom—happened. Nanibai looked at Roxanne and continued her story without any further discussion about Maala's disappearance.

Two days after Maala's death and disappearance, Nanibai heard through her network of informants that Freddy needed a newborn baby. She took Maala's baby to Freddy. She went all the way to his apartment in Bombay. She told him Maala's story. He said, "Poor Maala. I will give her baby to my friend Margaret Shriver. She will take care of her. She is a very nice English lady. I promise you Nanibai, that whatever happens, I will see to it that this baby, whom I will call Katy, after my mother, will be taken care of with love. But please Nanibai don't tell people about disappearing bodies. With all the political problems right now, someone might accuse you of murder."

"Why Katy? Your mother's name was Katayun?" Nanibai asked him.

Freddy looked embarrassed. "Because, you see, Nanibai, I will give the baby to Miss Margaret and she will tell my father that the baby is his. And then he will marry her and even if she can't love me, she will always be grateful to me. And if the baby is hers, the name should be English. And I sometimes called my mother Katy."

Nanibai told him that he was absolutely crazy if he thought that his father would believe that the dark baby she was giving him came from a memsaheb. She told him that he should just forget about his love and Margaret Shriver's gratitude and his ambition to train people to work for those who had ruled over all of them. She advised him to take the baby, little Katy, to his sister Agnes.

But he paid no attention to Nanibai and went off with the baby. Agnes told Nanibai that Freddy had gone to America with a baby he said was his and the memsaheb's. Some years later she informed Nanibai that Freddy had died in America and the girl was given to some foreigners to bring up. She was very sad about that. "And then," Nanibai had ended her story, "Katy came back to us. And she looks like Maala. Not one trace of those Lalacjis, except maybe the nose. And now Roxanne, you are going all that way across the sea, you are going to fly through the sky to that country to see Katy. Tell her that old women will always help her. Even old women who are dead."

Roxanne said, "And that is the story Nanibai told me only recently. And so you see, Katy did have a mother and a father. No miracle-firacle there."

Roxanne had moved towards me during the last part of her presentation of Nanibai's story. After the story she went back into the kitchen, asked for a cup of hot, black tea with sugar and milk. She wondered aloud how long it would take her to tell Sarosh and Kamal, who had arrived during her recitation of Maala's story, about the events of that morning in Monte Alban.

"And so all of you now know that Katy did have a mother who loved her very much. And forget about the man who was her biological father. He died, according to Nanibai, during a tiger hunt. Unfortunately the tiger didn't eat him up. One of his fellow hunters shot him because he was drunk and making too much noise and disturbing the hunt. But Katy, he did participate in giving you life and as far as I am concerned, my world without you would not be as exciting as it has been, and my old friend Freddy was a true father to you."

"Explain yourself," said Carmelita.

"Carmelita, you are getting to sound like me!" said Roxanne. "This—once again according to Nanibai—is what happened. Edulji-Eddie, he who was Fareidun-Freddy and Agnes' father, laughed at Margaret's offering of the baby and told her he would marry her but sans baby and so Margaret took the baby Katy back to Devinagar. She returned baby Katy to Freddy and went off to England. Not to be heard from again until that letter for Katy from her solicitor. I suppose our Katy must have left some impression on her. Even as a tiny baby. Freddy was soon shipped off to spy schools in England and America. And he took Katy with him wherever he went. He took care of her, loved her, and told everyone that she was his daughter. He wouldn't answer any questions about the baby's mother and when people started whispering that Katy was Margaret's baby, he just smiled. I suspect that he was a spectacular failure at spying and was then used as a middleman, a manager for that Anglo-American plantation in somewhere in Mexico.

"Near the Pacific coast of the State of Oaxaca," said Rogelio. He poured himself his fourth cup of coffee. The last traces of the copal had blended with the fragrance of the coffee and the roses.

Roxanne looked at her watch. She told us that it was the time of night when the bell in the sanctuary of an agiari would be rung to mark the change in the twenty-four hour cycle of life. The cycle that did not end with the setting of the sun. Roxanne said that she felt a longing to hear the deep sound of that bell echoing, spiraling into the darkness, to smell the sandalwood and the loban burning faithfully in the silver urn, to stand within the refuge of prayers, the rituals, the repetition of the names of famous teachers and priests, the names of the not-to-be-forgotten high priests, and of noble, virtuous ancestors transformed into the pure, angelic guardians, the Asho Farohars. She spoke of those names carried from Iran to India to Pakistan to China to Japan to the Americas to Europe to Africa, to Australia and back to India to Iran. Recited by Zoroastrians in their endless travels. She spoke of my father Freddy Cooper, dead in a place whose name he had not even heard of in his home in Devinagar. A place where his name would not be repeated in any prayers for the dead. She looked at me, she looked at Kamal and Sarosh and then at the sari, the gift of our common ancestress. Neither a Zoroastrian nor from India. India, China, Mexico woven together in an embroidered length of silk. And we saw Roxanne gently shaking her head in wonder.

I smelled the dusty red roses at the window of Señora Florencia's room and thought of the Jashan ceremony in the livingroom of my aunt's home. Roxanne's Grandmother Meheramai had arranged the Jashan in thanksgiving and celebration of my first visit to my ancestral home. I remembered the fragrance of the red roses on the silver tray in front of the silver urn that held the sandalwood fire. Silver, reds, whites and the soft gray smoke. The mobed seated in front of the tray, his white, starched robe spread around him, his voice coming through the white, starched cloth covering his mouth and nose. I was fascinated by his hand as he picked up the roses, one by one, his movements following a secret, perfected rhythm, touching each rose to his eyes before separating the petals. It evoked the memory of the passionate fragrance of the roses of Iran, the luxurious garlands of India, the startling beauty of roses covering baskets held proudly on the heads of women in the zocalo and the parks of Oaxaca, Mercedes Sosa's voice raised in exultation expressing gratitude to life near a hotel that was to see a miracle of roses, Carmen weeping in joy over the flowers of her tierra, the roses encased in plastic at the Benito Juarez airport and the roses I had planted on the edges of Putlibai's grave.

The mobed had prayed continuously, sometimes softly, under his breath, sometimes chanting clearly the cadences of ancient hymns and prayers. I had wondered if my father had ever been as moved to tears as I had been by the ceremony, a ceremony he must have witnessed many times. I wondered if Maala, my mother, had woven the ceremony into her tapestry especially for me, her daughter. As a gift to me on my first visit to the place of my birth.

I saw Rogelio watching me from the kitchen and turned my eyes to the roses again. A large brown spider was resting in the middle of a web stretched across a corner of the window. I turned my face and looked at the white spider patterns on the maroon sari. And I knew the truth behind Rogelio's words.

# XVII.

## The Place of the Black Butterflies, Oaxaca, Mexico

### *Rogelio's Abuela and His Hermano*

As I watched the brown spider spinning its web across Señora Florencia's window, suddenly I remembered an afternoon when I was nearly eleven years old. It was before I had gone to live in New Hampshire with Theresa and Gregory Sanders. My father and I were living in the house on the finca. I remembered the tree growing at the far edge of the large garden that spread from our house to the river. I remembered the spider web and I heard myself scream.

Rogelio was the first one to reach me. He sat down on the floor, took my head gently between his hands and would not allow me to look away from him. Señora Florencia and Carmelita tried to hold me. They stroked me on my head, my breasts and my arms. Roxanne kept repeating, "Katy dear, it is alright. Whatever it is, we will help you. We are all here." Kamal and Sarosh stood at the foot of the bed and began to massage my legs. From the knees to the feet. Kamal was crying silently. Sarosh was reciting the "Yatha Ahu Vairyo." Virbaiji had taught it to him when she had adopted him. She had told him that the recitation of the ancient Zoroastrian prayer would help any human being overcome any difficulty, any obstacle.

I looked at Rogelio and said, "I told them."

"Yes Katy, you did. And they came to the Place of the Black Butterflies. Because you told them."

"They killed my father."

"They killed my grandmother and my brother."

"They shot my father. Flies came all over his face."

"They sliced open my grandmother's neck. After they forced her to see them kill her grandson. They hanged him from a tree and then they butchered him. I saw it all. From the top of the tree against which they had tied my grandmother."

I pulled Rogelio's hands away from my face. "I loved them. I am sorry."

"You told them. You are also their murderer."

Señora Florencia came around the bed and slapped Rogelio.

"You poor, stupid man. Your anger has made you evil. Blind. Come back to your senses. She is not a murderer."

Rogelio took my hand and held it fast as he told me how he had watched me from the time my father and I had arrived at the finca. But he had to be hidden from us because ever since he was a child he had been the messenger between his abuela, his beloved grandmother, and the men and women who fought against the landowners. At first he had taken messages from his grandmother to her son, his uncle, who moved around working from one finca to another. Rogelio's father had gone off to Canada after Rogelio's mother died. To make money, he said. No one had heard from him. When Rogelio's uncle who was fighting for the workers in the fields was killed, Rogelio became the messenger between his older brother, Lucío, and their grandmother. Lucío had taken over his uncle's work and it was Lucío who taught Rogelio to read and write. But when it became very dangerous and Rogelio could not meet his brother to give him messages, their grandmother taught Rogelio to make signs with leaves and sticks and stones. When his abuela or some other worker gave him a message for his brother, he would leave a sign for Lucío with stones, twigs and leaves. And all the time that he was going from one place to another, one person to another, he was always to be hidden from us, the father and daughter who lived in the main house.

Sitting on the floor beside the bed in Señora Florencia's house, Rogelio said to me, "I wanted to come out and play with you, Katy. I heard your father singing to you once when my abuela had hidden me in the kitchen. You and your father were on the verandah and he was singing 'K-K-K-Katy' to you again and again and you were giggling and making up songs about your father and my brother Lucío. I wanted to be your friend because you loved my grandmother and hugged her all the time and because my brother told me that you were a wonderful girl. You were intelligent and strong and brave and loved everyone and one day he would marry you. I could see you but you never saw me."

I said, "Rogelio, I didn't even know you existed!"

"I know. And that day, the day you have now remembered, I saw those men coming to your house, I saw my grandmother running away and I followed her, to the place only she, you, and I knew was Lucío's hiding place. And I saw them hang my brother, put a knife to his body before he was dead and then put the same knife to my grandmother's throat."

Carmelita said, "Rogelio, calm yourself, mi hermano. Let her tell her story. You both must be healed. We have heard your story. She must now tell her story. I do not want her to die. Either from your sorrow, at your hand, or because of her own pain."

And Roxanne added, "For God's sake, she went to live with the Sanderses when she was eleven years old. Whatever happened, whatever she did, she was only a child! Shut up Rogelio and not one more word against Katy. And Señora Florencia no more slapping this man. He seems confused, but not at all dangerous. And the slap seems to have caused you too much sorrow. Rogelio go wipe your aunt's tears."

Roxanne's voice was the best defense against the pain and the bewilderment surrounding us in that little room.

Sarosh spoke quietly, "Rogelio, if you saw everything, did you see Freddy falling to the ground? Dying? That is one of the few things Katy has remembered earlier."

Kamal went to Rogelio and began to massage his shoulders. Rogelio continued to hold my hand.

I answered Sarosh. "No. There is nothing more to say. They killed Freddy and I told them about that place, the secret one that only I and Lucío and his grandmother knew. And then one of the men who had come to the house took me to the truck and gave me to Mr Sanders. The others went to the Place of the Black Butterflies. I saw them going there. Mr Sanders took me to his house in Mexico City and then he and Mrs Sanders took me to New Hampshire. And they loved me and treated me like their daughter all their lives."

Rogelio said, "I know that it was Katy who told those men. They were some kind of soldiers. One of them told my abuela that Katy had told them about that place. He told her while he was tying her to the tree. That is when I promised myself that I would find Katy and kill her. In revenge for the murders of my brother and my abuela. Because Katy had told the men where my brother and abuela were hiding. I didn't see Freddy being killed but they also told abuela that they had shot him and no one was going to bury him. She said that the workers would bury him, and she asked what they had done with the little girl."

I was looking at the old woman with the ribbons and no shoes standing next to the table covered with the sari, the smoke from the copal wrapping itself around her. But the old woman wasn't looking at me any more. She was looking at her grandson.

Rogelio said, "When my grandmother spoke of you, the men laughed and said, 'She is now with that American man. On her way to America.' My grandmother cursed them and said that she was happy they were going to kill her because she had not been able to protect you from them. I think Lucío was conscious enough to have heard them. She turned towards him and said, 'Lucío go in peace now. These men will never know peace. And I will always protect our Katy.' They killed her soon afterwards. She didn't know I was hiding above her. I was terrified. I did not make a sound. I did not even cry then. But I promised myself that one day that I would find Katy, to punish her, kill her for telling those men about the secret place. Katy, why were those men laughing? What did they do to you, besides killing your father in front of you and forever damning themselves for that."

I told him, "It is no longer of any importance."

"You have remembered all that happened, haven't you?" asked Carmelita.

"Yes. But it doesn't matter."

But that was not satisfactory for Señora Florencia. She saw me clenching my hands and trying to hold my mouth steady, not only because of Rogelio's story and my own memories but also because I was trying not to cry out in pain. My legs were trembling under the covers.

"It is time to tell us what you remember, querida," she said to me.

"Not in this room. Not at this hour. Tomorrow in the afternoon. When it is bright. I will try and tell you what I remembered tonight. I will tell you in Tía Lucía's house. The house which will one day belong to Carmelita."

And I fell asleep in Señora Florencia's bed in that house in Colonia Jalatlaco filled with the strange flowers and piñatas made of newspapers.

# XVIII.

## Oaxaca

### *Memories of my Father's Home in Mexico*
### *The Spider's Web*

I told my story the next afternoon to Carmelita, Roxanne, Kamal, Sarosh, Señora Florencia, Tía Lucía, Tía Elena, Señora Margo, Lupita, and Rogelio, as we all sat around the large table in Tía Lucía's dining room. I sat at one end of the table while Señora Florencia sat across from me at the other end. A dancer's mask from Monte Alban painted gold stared at me from the wall behind Señora Florencia. I addressed my story to Señora Florencia in English. Carmelita and Rogelio took turns translating my words.

I said, "When I heard Roxanne speaking about the sound of the bell in the agiari, I looked at the red roses and brown spider in the middle of its web on Señora Florencia's window and that white silk pattern of the sari on Señora Florencia's altar. I thought of my mother but I really didn't remember my mother, Maala of Nanibai's story, or even Margaret of the photograph. I did not remember India or New Hampshire or California. But I did remember my life with my father in the house on the finca."

I remembered each room of that house. The placement of the furniture, the movement of the curtains, the sounds of the people, the exact shades of green and brown and red and blue of the plants, the trees, the flowers, the birds, the insects and the two cats of the finca. The memories were as vivid as the dreams Carmelita and I talked about. The colors, the sounds, the smells. I even remembered my father in his version of a safari suit and his English-sahib pith helmet as he sat with me and taught me to read and write and paint and sing on the verandah of our house.

I thought of him as he walked among the workers, smiling and talking to everyone, even those who barely nodded to him. He had sometimes taken me with him, and told me, "Remember, Katy, when all is said and done, this is a beautiful land. And the people are equal to all that is good in this land. This is now our home. Yours and mine. It has given us so much happiness." He would sometimes stammer as he told me this. And I would take a deep breath and smell the brown earth and the thick green growth and the translucent pink roses that grew all around the verandah and the thick petalled red roses that grew at the banks of the river across from our house.

I looked straight at Rogelio who was sitting near Señora Florencia. "I now remember her. The lady with the ribbons and the butterfly. I used to call her 'Lita because I had decided that the woman with all those wrinkles on her face and the gold-brown eyes who took care of me, my father, and our house-she was so calm, so polite, so tender--was my very special grandmama, my abuelita."

My voice changed. I sounded like a very little girl as I talked about my life with my father and 'Lita. I tried to clear my throat, to recover my adult voice, but I couldn't get it back.

As long as I had my father Freddy, my 'Lita, and my two cats, I was happy. But to make me really, really happy, 'Lita's grandson, Lucío, had to be present. I didn't know that Lucío had a little brother, Rogelio. Lucío and I were great friends. He used to carry me on his shoulders until I was six years old. When I was six, I told him that I was going to marry him when I was as old as he was that day. I was sitting on his shoulders and pulling his ears at that time. He put me down, took both my hands in his right hand and told me that he was sixteen and that he would wait for me to marry him when I was sixteen. He said, "In ten more years I will ask your father for your hand and I will offer him three cows and two donkeys for you." I told him that I would bring my two cats with me when we got married. Lucío said he would think about it. He didn't like cats all that much. We decided that we would leave Mr Green, the parrot, with my father to keep him company.

I looked away from Rogelio, from everyone at that table, as I described how when I was ten years old, Lucío and I were no longer the kind of friends we had been in the past. I had turned shy and Lucío had his secrets. But even then I had known that Lucío was a leader among the workers. Right after my ninth birthday, Lucío had started talking to me very seriously about justice for the workers who grew the food for the owners of the fincas, the ranches, the haciendas, the factories, the cities. The people who grew food for everyone. His words were simple and clear. His voice was very beautiful.

I had heard an old man say to 'Lita that her grandson Lucío was a warrior. I had liked that. I didn't like what my father's employer, Mr Sanders called Lucío. A troublemaker.

Mr Sanders used to say to my father, "Maybe you should get someone else than this old woman to take care of Katy and the house. That Lucío is a troublemaker and he is that old woman's nephew, or grandson or some sort of relative. You know how these people are. Very confused and complex blood ties." My father would answer, "Maybe we should give the workers better money. Good housing. A school. A hospital." Mr Sanders would laugh. "Might as well bring in good, expensive European or American workers if you are to spend so much money. Or forget about fincas and plantations and factories in this part of the world, Freddy." My father did not like to hear Mr Sanders say this.

When I spoke about these conversations between the two men, Roxanne said, "Freddy will always be your father, Katayun. Maybe Margaret Shriver, giving you back to him so carelessly, running off once and for all with his father, cured him at last of his reverence for our late rulers. Good for Fareidun-Freddy." Roxanne was happy. A man she had liked, but not always approved of, had at last come to his senses, even though he had to leave home for that to happen.

I tried to smile. "My father said good things about the workers to Mr Sanders. But whenever Mr Sanders spoke about 'Lita or Lucío, my father would look very uneasily at the four armed men who always accompanied his boss.

One day, I saw my father talking quietly to 'Lita. From that day on Lucío didn't come to the house and kept his distance from me when I went out with my father. But whenever I caught Lucío's eye in the fields or on the road, he would grin at me. I had great anxieties about myself those years. I didn't know if Lucío saw me as plain or downright ugly. I had become uneasy about my face and body. I didn't look like the girls in the books and magazines Mrs. Sanders sent me as presents from Mexico City. And the young girls I saw around me at the finca seemed so much more womanly and robust and happy with their bodies than I was. Even the girls who were my age seemed to be grownup. When I complained about my lack of beauty and physical maturity to 'Lita, she said "Just wait a few more years and then everyone will see what I know!" 'Lita had asked my father to send for some special rainbow-colored ribbons from Mexico City and had woven them through my hair a few months before my eleventh birthday.

One month before my eleventh birthday, Lucío disappeared from my world. I asked my father about Lucío and he said, "It is better for him to be gone from here." 'Lita said the same but I was not satisfied. When I told 'Lita that I had dreamed that Lucío was dead, she took me to a grove of trees across the bridge, on the opposite bank of the river. She called it "The Place of the Black Butterflies," although there were no butterflies of any color, shape, or size in the grove. This is where 'Lita used to meet Lucío to tell him the latest news about our finca, about the other fincas, about the workers who could be trusted to help him fight, about those who preferred that he be taken away by the soldiers. Lucío was waiting for her. He was surprised to see me and when 'Lita told him about my anxiety about him, he told me not to worry.

When I asked about the butterfly name for the butterfly-less grove, 'Lita said, "That is what this place has always been called. Maybe many years ago there were butterflies here."

Lucío said, "Most probably thousands of years ago." He and I laughed but 'Lita remained quiet. She looked very worried. I went with her two more times to the butterfly place. I noticed that besides the news she gave him, 'Lita gave Lucío food and also what looked like guns wrapped in sheets. She told my father that she was taking the sheets to the river to wash and that I was accompanying her because it was good for me to be outdoors and under the trees on the bank of the river. As far as I know, my father didn't ask why some of the sheets never returned from the river. But once, while he was sharing the afternoon meal on the verandah with 'Lita and me, he said, "Be careful, Señora 'Lita. Don't go too far from this place. There have been soldiers on some of the other fincas. There have been shootings and deaths. Tell Lucío to stay far from here. I don't want him around Katy or you. He will learn that there is nothing like justice or peace in this world. And very little love. Tell him not to be a fool and lose what he has. You. My little Katy. Even I like him a lot." And 'Lita said, "Yes, Señor Federico."

For the next three days 'Lita worked around the house looking very anxious. She barely talked to me. She didn't even sing as she worked. Then on the fourth day she asked me to write a letter to Lucío. It was to be from her and it was to tell him all that Señor Federico had said. I had a lot of trouble writing the letter because although I spoke Spanish, no one had taught me to read or write Spanish. I wrote the letter as well as I could and 'Lita took it to the butterfly place the next day. She would not let me accompany her. She said that it was too dangerous. And anyway Lucío wouldn't be there. He was to be at the grove three days later but she didn't want us to be there at that time. She was going to leave the letter hidden in one of the trees were Lucío would be sure to find it.

Three days after 'Lita left the letter in our secret place, she decided to teach me how to arrange roses in the crystal vase my father had brought from Mexico. I looked out of the window and pointed to the military truck that had stopped across the bridge and the men who were coming out of it. 'Lita quickly pulled me towards her, kissed me, made the sign of the cross over me, took off her apron, threw it in the dirty laundry basket and ran out of the house from the back door. The men from the truck could not see her.

Mr Sanders came towards the house. This time seven men in uniforms accompanied him. They had rifles and guns. Two of the men who seemed to be some sort of leaders, wore dark glasses, military hats, and pistols at their hips.

As soon as the men entered the house, they asked my father to call 'Lita. When 'Lita did not appear, two of the men searched our small house. One of the men in the dark glasses told my father that 'Lita had to be found and handed over to them. He also told me go to the verandah and sit quietly there. I heard Mr Sanders tell the man that his friend and employee, Mr Cooper, was not really responsible for 'Lita and that he was sure Mr Cooper had no knowledge of where the woman was. He blamed 'Lita's disappearance on the number of men who had come along and the noise they had made as they crossed the bridge. "You scared her off," Mr Sanders told the man with the glasses who was giving the orders.

One of the soldiers came out of the house and pointed at me as I sat on the white rattan chair. I was trying very hard to be quiet. I thought I looked quite proud and dignified. Like the British princesses my father always told me about. They had short hair but my hair was long. It was neatly braided and tied at the ends with rainbow ribbons, and I was wearing my favorite yellow cotton dress with the red flowers; my feet in sparkling white shoes with brown buckles were demurely crossed at the ankles. I was actually looking down at those shoes and remembering my argument with 'Lita and my father earlier that morning. 'Lita never wore shoes. She said that since she had gotten bunions on both her feet from the too-tight shoes she had worn as a young woman, she could not wear shoes again. Sandals, sometimes, but never shoes. But both she and my father insisted that I always wear shoes, even in the house. I was not even allowed to wear well-ventilated zapatos. I had to wear closed shoes with buttons or laces, the kind which my father and Mrs. Sanders always assured 'Lita and me, all well-brought-up little ladies wore.

I told my audience in Tía Lucía's house, "Those shoes always seemed to give me blisters or heat rashes."

I didn't pay attention to Tía Lucía when she said, "Ah, now we under-stand the pain in Katy's knees and that old woman without shoes that Lupita says she has seen. Deeply embedded memories. No ghosts."

I was looking straight at Señora Florencia as I said, "When that soldier pointed at me, I looked at my father. My father said, 'She doesn't know anything.' But the soldiers decided that I did know where the old woman had gone. When one of them approached me and began to pull me out of the chair, my father grabbed me and ran out of the door. I could hear Mr Sanders shouting, 'Freddy, stop. They won't harm you. We'll search the grounds for the woman.' One of the soldiers nearly caught my father and me. My father was still carrying me. But the man stopped and aimed his rifle as soon as he saw my father lean down to pick up a rock. I heard a sound I did not recognize. But I knew that something had hit my father. He fell down, pushed me away from him and stammered to me to run to Mr Sanders. But I could not run. I watched the blood flow out of the head, the mouth, the ears, the nose of the man I loved. The man I called Daddy and Papa and Padre and Father and sometimes even Freddy-Daddy was bleeding to death in front of me. The soldier pulled me up by one of my braids and said, 'See what will happen to you if you don't tell us where the old woman is? We will shoot you too, and you too will have blood and flies all over you. Better tell us quickly.' He didn't let go of my braid. He kept on yanking at it and yelling, 'Tell us. Where is that old woman?' And I kept on looking at my father and the blood and the flies that had begun to cover him and crawl all over him. A thin white serpent emerged from his mouth and disappeared into the earth, or into the air. I don't know where it went."

"Enough!" Rogelio, Roxanne, and Carmelita shouted together.

Kamal ran to the kitchen and brought a glass of water. Sarosh and Lupita came to me and held me. The four older women had tears running down their cheeks but they did not move from their chairs.

Rogelio took the glass of water from Kamal and brought it to me. "Drink this." He had not shed a single tear. But his face, his eyes were of a man who had wept every tear he could weep. He said, "No more. Forget what I said. I spoke in anger and in ignorance. You are not a murderer. Do not tell us any more. Please forgive me, Katy."

Señora Florencia said, "Katy, tell us what happened. All of it, querida. Keep your eyes on me. Rogelio, do not stop her. Go on, querida."

I took the glass from Rogelio but could drink only a few sips of the water. "Mr Sanders ran to me and tried to take me away from the man. 'Leave her alone,' he said. 'She is just a child. Let me take her away. It is enough.

She has seen her father killed in front of her eyes. She doesn't have any one else in the world. Give her to me. I'll take her away. You can search for the woman. She couldn't have gone too far.'

"I even heard one of the soldier say, 'Pobrecita. Let him take her away. And we should do something about burying this poor man.' I saw that this man who spoke was the second man with the dark glasses, but he did not have a dead voice, like the other man with the glasses. That other man, the man with the dead voice, yelled and said there was no room for pity when criminals were around. He told his companion in the dark glasses to take Mr Sanders away and to wait in the truck across the river. Mr Sanders's hand was pulled away from my arm and I heard a scream that seemed to go on and on. All the birds had fallen silent just as they had done at the time when my father had taken me to the fields to see the eclipse. The birds had all become quiet then, when the eclipse covered the sunlight. I knelt down and took my father's hand. I did not cry. I just screamed."

When many years later, Gregory Sanders was dying in New Hampshire, he had taken my hand and told me what he had told his wife four days after my father's murder. He returned to his home in Mexico City from our finca with me. I had not said a single word since I was dumped on his lap in the truck. Gregory Sanders told his wife, "Theresa, when that child's scream rose to the skies and went on and on, I felt it circling the world and then coming back to my ears. It seemed as if she would never stop. How could such a tiny girl produce such a sound? But then there was silence. And then those other screams. How was I to know what they were about? Those men were on our side. We helped them. They helped us. We worked together. How could I even imagine? And what could I have done? We had always worked together. For so many years. They would not even listen to Colonel Jimenez when he tried to get that child away from her dead father."

Gregory told me that Theresa didn't ask any questions, hadn't demanded any details. She only said, "We will take care of her. She is now our child. We will allow no one, no one, to hurt her again."

When Gregory Sanders had known that he would die within ten hours, he had taken my hand, kissed it and said, "Katy, our child. We, Theresa and I, have loved you. I thank you for taking care of both of us with such kindness these last two years. Thank you for being with me here while I am dying here in our house in Lakewood where we brought you so many years ago. I could have loved you more. So much more. Forgive me. I couldn't love you more. It was that scream. That sound. I couldn't do anything. The workers who had come running couldn't do anything. They had no power. That scream. I have never stopped hearing it. I have been singing louder and louder to try to push the scream behind all the tunes and the words. It has not worked."

He died two hours later. At that time I had no idea what he had been talking about. All I guessed from his words was that he hadn't been able to prevent my father's death or my witnessing it.

In New Hampshire, holding my dying foster father's hand, I did not remember what I remembered a few years later in Señora Florencia's room. I did not remember that day when my father was shot and Mr Sanders had yelled to me before he was led away to the truck, "Katy dear, tell them where the woman is. The one you call 'Lita. We all know that you know where she is. We know that she took you with her when she went to meet that Lucío. They are bad people, child. They are wicked, bad people. Your poor Daddy was killed because of them. He would tell you to tell them. Some of the good people who worked for us, your friends, told us that you know. Tell them, child."

I couldn't tell them. Not because I was strong or stubborn but because I knew that my father was a good man and the men with Mr Sanders had made blood come out of him. I knew that 'Lita was good and Lucío was good. They loved me and I didn't want the soldiers to kill them.

And now, in Tía Lucía's house, I understood what Gregory Sanders had been talking about. I said to Señora Florencia, "I didn't tell them where 'Lita and Lucío were. But I couldn't stop screaming and holding on to my father's hand. Until the soldier who was still holding my braid pulled me up again and dragged me against a tree growing on the riverbank near the bridge. It was across the garden. I became silent then. I could see the house and the verandah and the pink roses and Mr Green's round perch swinging in the breeze. I couldn't really see my father's face. And anyway it was already covered up with flies and ants and insects. The soldier slapped me again and again."

Carmelita was nearly sobbing. "Señora Florencia, this is enough. Tell her to stop. Katy, stop. Please! Mother of God where were you?"

Señora Florencia shook her head. I looked at my friends. They were weeping. Lupita was patting Rogelio's back as he sat slumped over the table, his face hidden in his hands. I looked at Rogelio's hands. And even as I relived my experience of the past for the people around me, I became aware of how much Rogelio's hands resembled my own hands. Strong, capable hands of an artist. Hands that had never been raised to hurt any creature. Except once. To hurt me. Because as a child watching his brother and his grandmother being butchered he had vowed vengeance on the person he thought had betrayed them. I thought of Putlibai's hands clapping as she sang and as she picked up a small stone in my backyard, replacing it carefully on the soil before coming into my house to share the evening meal with me. I felt Putlibai's arm around me, supporting me as I sat in the chair in Tía Lucía's dining room, telling my story to Señora Florencia, hearing it being translated for her by Carmelita and Rogelio. I wondered if the woman who had given me birth and dreamed of a wonderful future for me had woven Putlibai into my life, to help me as I recaptured my memories of my years with Freddy Cooper.

I said, "I had never, ever been slapped or beaten in my life and I was so taken aback by the gesture and the pain that I stood quietly against the tree, completely in shock. The men with the rifles and the pistols kept on yelling at me to tell them about 'Lita and Lucío and the hiding place. I heard one of them say, 'She knows. She knows. Just look at her eyes!'

The man in the dark glasses who was in charge turned towards the small group of workers, men and women, who had gathered a few feet from the tree. He told them to go away. When they didn't move, he asked one of the soldiers to shoot at them. The first two shots drove the people to the verandah of the house. The soldiers forced them to leave even that shelter. I don't think any of them saw the soldier dragging me down to the ground, towards the roots of the tree.

The women and men forced to leave the verandah and then the area around the house did not see the soldier drag me to the foot of the tree. But as they went towards their homes and before they closed their doors, I am sure they heard me scream. Once, twice. And somehow I knew that some of them cried and that most of them prayed as they heard my screams.

Two of the soldiers grabbed my legs, one man to each leg. When one man pulled my left knee away from my right leg and the other man pulled my right knee away from my left leg I began to scream again. And then I couldn't scream any more. I was silent as someone pushed a finger into my vagina which had not yet experienced the cycle of bleeding, as someone began pinching and pulling on my nipples around which my breasts had not yet begun to grow. All I could do was look up at the branches of the tree. It was then that I noticed a brown spider high up on one of the branches. It was so calm and so quick as it wove a web! As I looked at the spider, I found myself sitting on the branch below the web. I could see the spider up close then. I watched the strands of the web meeting together. The web became larger and larger. A woman with a tapestry flowing from her hands was sitting in the middle of it. She was painting and embroidering on a long, narrow piece of cloth. She looked at me but I couldn't reach her. There seemed to be a curtain between us. I could see her through that curtain and I could hear her. She said, "Be patient. Have courage." And then she disappeared. The web became a small regular spider web again.

I looked through the branches and the leaves and saw the river, the bridge, the truck on the other side of the river. From my branch I could see Mr Sanders sitting in the truck, the other man with the glasses sitting next to him. Both men had tears running down onto their shirtfronts and neither man was looking towards the tree where I was sitting. I was up above in the branches looking up at the spider and across at the truck and at the same time I was down on the ground, my head against the trunk.

When the man with the glasses and the dead voice entered my body, I screamed again. As he pushed himself against me, into me, his glasses fell off and I noticed his eyes. They were a beautiful gray with a blue rim around the gray. I had met him at one of Theresa Sanders' sparties and he had told us that his mother's family had come to Mexico from France after the First World War. His father's family had come to Mexico from Spain in the seventeenth century. He was very proud of his European ancestry. He had told Freddy "I have no Indian blood in me!" When I recognized the man, I was no longer looking down at myself from the tree. I was on the ground and I began to turn my face. They hadn't held down my face. I looked at the men who were holding my legs, the other men watching what was being done to me. I looked at the men's eyes. Most of them were brown like mine. One pair was very dark. Black just like Lucío's eyes. I was no longer silent. I was whimpering and crying."

I began to cry as I looked at the dancer's mask on Tía Lucía's wall. I felt sliced through with terror and horror. Tía Lucía motioned to everyone at the table to sit quietly. She came to me and held me as I remembered how my world had turned incomprehensible under that bright sky. The birds were still silent when the two men pushed my knees further apart and put their full weight on them and leaned into my face, hissing, "Tell us. Tell us where that woman is. Or we will do this to you again and again and then we will kill you."

I said, "Rogelio, please lift your head. Look at me."

I looked straight at him and said, "I told them about the place. I told them that 'Lita and Lucío were there. And they let me go. One of them took me to Mr Sanders and told him that he could now take me away."

I was making an effort not to lean down and rub my knees. Right hand on my left knee, left hand on my right knee.

Rogelio stood up, walked over to me and knelt down next to my chair. He took my left hand and cupped it carefully in his right hand, passed his strength to me and said, "I didn't see my grandmother yesterday in Monte Alban but I knew she was there. She stopped my hand from killing you. And she loosened my tongue so that I could speak. Things I had never told anyone before. Not even to my Tía Florencia. Forgive me for my words of anger and hatred." He touched my neck where Señora Florencia had placed the small Band-Aid. "Tía, how could I ever have raised my hand at her? At anyone. But especially to her."

I could only say, "Your words made me remember what happened that day. But Rogelio, they also reminded me of the happiness of the days before that terrible day."

"Yes," Rogelio said. "When I make my newspaper piñatas, and flowers, I remember the messages Lucío taught me to make with stones and leaves and branches. And I also remember how I used to wish I could play with you instead of learning about messages, and reading and writing and the ways to fight injustice from Lucío. I loved my brother, but I thought you would be more fun to be with, Katy. That was so many years ago. But not very far from this city."

Roxanne, my cousin, said, "Katayun Cooper, listen to me. We, all of us, are proud of you. We love you. If you will allow me, I will tell your story to Agnesmai."

"Don't tell her that we don't know if anyone ever buried my father."

"Be at peace, querida. The people of the finca would have buried your father," Señora Florencia assured me.

Carmelita pulled out a packet of Kleenex from her skirt pocket, came over to me, wiped my face, and then wiped Rogelio's face. She then passed the packet around the table. She didn't wipe the tears from her own face. But she reached into her pocket again and pulled out four black hairpins. She looked at them with some bemusement and then shook her head and gave them to me.

Lupita came to me and took one of the hairpins in her hand and looked at it with great curiosity.

She asked Carmelita, "This belongs to the other lady from India, doesn't it? The one who wears the sari? She is the lady who sings very beautifully. I want to dance when I hear her!"

When Carmelita translated Lupita's statement, Roxanne said, "And there you have it. Once again. An amazing child."

"And now," said Tía Elena, "we need to eat. Katy, you need to get your strength back." Tía Lucía asked Lupita and Carmelita to help her bring in the food.

Before going to the kitchen, Lupita hugged me. "We will pray for your father and for Rogelio's brother and that old lady. I don't think you will see her again, Señorita Katy. But I will. She likes me and she will teach me many things. And if she wants to tell you or Rogelio anything, she will tell me first."

Tía Lucía shook her head. "First learn to live in this world, child. Come on we need to heat the soup. See if you can do it without it boiling over!"

# XIX.

## Oaxaca—Devinagar

### *Miriam's Mantle With Sleeves*

Kamal's return to California was postponed once again. We all decided that instead of formal prayers, we would remember my father, 'Lita, and Lucío with an evening devoted to telling stories and painting and, of course, making things with old newspapers. We had decided on the stories because I had remembered that my father used to love stories. He would challenge 'Lita and me to tell the most horrifying ghost stories we could think of and then he would enter the competition with stories so gruesome that the old woman and I would alternate between laughing nervously or screaming. 'Lita would make the sign of the cross and say, "Madre de Dios! Señor Federico, where do you get such ideas!" For 'Lita and Lucío, we decided to sing songs, any songs, because Rogelio said that his grandmother and his brother loved to sing. And I remembered how before Lucío began to move further and further away from the house and the finca, he would teach us verses from popular love songs which he would inevitably turn into songs of revolution and resistance.

Señora Florencia brought the sari and the extra piece to the memorial evening at Tía Lucía's house. Señora Florencia and Señora Margo began to join the two pieces together. Rogelio apologized for leaving the sari-scarf in Peru. He said he had lost it. But none of us believed him. We were sure he had given it away.

Roxanne asked Carmelita to write a letter to Ratna, explaining what had happened to me, to all of us. Carmelita held up two of the hairpins that had appeared in her skirt pocket the previous day and said, "What for? Our friend Ratna, unbeknownst to us, has all these skills of strange travel and knowledge. Why should I write to her?"

Carmelita seemed a bit miffed at Ratna.

Roxanne said, "All these extraordinary skills and events are helpful. But one has to take precautions, some kind of tangible backups for them. A letter will take some time to reach Ratna in India but it might be more straightforward than other, less orthodox, ways."

Sarosh said, "Roxanne, take the letter and the remainder of Dinaz's ashes back with you. You always travel light. A letter and a plastic bag with a few ashes won't weight you down. Tell the customs officials that they are ashes or medicine. Make your choice according to what you think the official will believe. But be sure they don't think that you are carrying some type of exotic drugs from America to India."

Carmelita began writing a long letter to Ratna. Every few minutes she would say, "Who wants to tell Ratna about Roxanne's search for authentic doughnuts in Oaxaca?" Or "Who wants to describe Rogelio?" Or "Roxanne, I think you are the best person to write about Sarosh and Kamal and all those sex, lust, and love goings-on between those two." Or "Do you think I should summarize Katy's story or write it in detail?"

We all contributed to the letter. Lupita drew a picture for Ratna. A mermaid combing her long black hair and singing to her mermaid baby. I drew a picture of Lupita dancing with the trees on the bluffs on Poplar Beach in Half Moon Bay, her hair entangled in the branches.

Kamal bought a beautiful necklace of black luminescent Oaxaca onyx for me in remembrance of both our mothers.

Kamal and Sarosh had wanted to look for a Zoroastrian priest to marry them as part of the celebration.

Roxanne yelled, "Sarosh, forget this silly business about marriage-farriage. Looking for mobeds in Oaxaca for a Zoroastrian wedding! No one is stopping you and Kamal from doing whatever you two have been doing these last few days. And if you must become conservative before you are old, get married in our Mumbai. Otherwise, your mother, who also happens to be my great-aunt, good old Virbaiji Japanwallah Dubash, will never forgive me. Here I am, all the way across the earth in Oaxaca, just to take back a sari so that she will leave us in peace. What do you think will happen if I go back and say about her beloved son, 'Your vahlo dikro got married in Mexico.' And I have to go back soon otherwise that doom-foom thing will begin again and my sister will be a nervous wreck."

And so we held the memorial three days after I told my story. A memorial in which writing a letter became the central event.

Carmelita looked up from the letter-collage she was creating for Ratna. "Katy, do you remember the story Ratna once told us about the mantle of

Allah? Did she say that it was maroon or purple?"

I was trying to persuade Rogelio to make regular piñatas and fill them with candies and let children as well as adults break them. I didn't remember the color of the mantle of Allah. I did remember that it had large sleeves. "Can it be a mantle if it had sleeves?" I asked.

Sarosh was trying to use watercolors to paint a portrait of Lupita. He wasn't very happy with the outcome and everyone was giving him conflicting advice about how he could improve his artistic skills. He was laughing and saying, "I am just a western-trained doctor. What do I know about art and songs and stories and healing! But I can tell you about the history of western medicine."

We weren't fooled. Sarosh had talked to Rogelio and Señora Florencia for many long hours about the various medical systems of India. Señora Florencia had taken to addressing Sarosh as "el señor curandero de la India."

When Sarosh heard the exchange between Carmelita and myself about Allah's mantle, he asked, "Is that the story about the hand, the palm of Allah?"

"Allah's palm might have been present. I don't remember the story too well."

"Who wants to hear the story?" Sarosh asked.

Carmelita translated his question.

Señora Florencia laughed. "Just tell the story, hombre. Don't ask about who wants to hear it. If anyone wants to hear it, they will listen."

Sarosh asked Carmelita to be his official translator. He said, "Katy's Aunt Agnes told me this story. She said she heard it from a Sufi healer whom Roxanne's Grandmother Meheramai once brought to Agnes. He was to try and make her walk again. 'Instead of healing me, he told me a wonderful story,' Agnes said to me during one of my visits to Devinagar. She insisted that it was a special Devinagar Sufi story. Here it is.

"Once upon a time, Miriam met Allah as He was walking in the Garden of Paradise. Allah was unhappy with the human race because brothers and sisters were wounding and maiming and killing one another. "With their arms and their tools, their words and even with their thoughts," He told Miriam. She comforted Him and walked with Him. He blessed Her for Her words and Her smile and said, "Miriam, since you have walked the seven important steps of wisdom and friendship with Me, I will always remember you and the comfort and kindness you brought to Me." And she said, "I will make a special cloak for You and it will comfort You whenever You need comfort."

"Miriam wove Allah a wonderful cloak. It was a simple cloak made of white muslin and it had very wide sleeves.

"Allah wears the cloak whenever He judges a soul.

"And this is what He does. Allah summons the dead person to come into His presence. Then He picks up the person in His right hand. Whoever it is, man, woman or child, this dead person has to stand in Allah's open palm and speak about the life he or she led on earth. Everything has to be told. Nothing can be hidden. No act, no word, no thought. Good, bad, helpful, harmful, stupid, intelligent, embarrassing, noble, evil. Everything has to be told. And as the person recites her or his life, long or short, fortunate or unfortunate, blessed or cursed, happy, sad or average, the whole world, all the people, all the angels, all the demons, all the saints, all the animals, all the plants, all the universe listens to the person's story. If a person tries to lie, Allah thunders out "It is a lie!" If the person tries to stop, Allah shouts out, "Continue your story!" If the person tries to hide from the eyes of Allah, Allah shouts again, "You can not hide from Me. Look at Me as you speak." Sometimes the stories are interesting, sometimes they are boring, sometimes funny, sometimes pathetic. Sometimes a person tries to bargain with Allah, asks for pity or blames Allah. And Allah says, "I am the Judge. Do not think I have your emotions. Continue your story." And at last the story ends. Then Allah says very gently, "You are My creation. You can now rest." And no matter how good or bad or mediocre or interesting the person has been, Allah smiles at that person with great tenderness and love. He then very carefully places the person inside the wide refuge of the sleeve of His cloak. He protects the soul from the harshness of the world's judgment that does not have even one grain of sand's understanding of Allah's will, His plans for the universe. And Allah says to the soul, "Rest now in Miriam's gift. Her Cloak of Compassion. Go now where you will remember how to dance once again to the music and the rhythms you have forgotten how to hear, the music and the rhythms that have disappeared even from your imagination. Take refuge within compassion."

"And" finished Sarosh, "this was the story Katy's Aunt Agnes told me one evening, some years ago when I was visiting my cousins Roxanne and her sister Gulnar in Devinagar."

I looked at the sari with the white spiders in the hands of Carmelita, Señora Florencia and Señora Margo and I thought of the hands of the woman who had embroidered the silk patterns onto the sari. I wish I could have been with Kamal when her mother, Dinaz, had sewn the jhabloo for her daughter, singing songs and telling stories, and also when she had waved her hands smelling of spices and shrimp at the man who had dared to question who she was. I remembered Putlibai as she clapped her hands together while she sang her mother's songs. I wondered if I would ever see La Soledad's hands again holding pieces of cloth to dry her son's face, to wipe her own tears. I looked around the table at the hands of the adults, the children. I looked at my hands trying to fashion flowers out of newspapers. I wondered if my hands resembled the hands of my mother Maala. I looked up. Rogelio grinned at me. I said, "Who needs UFOs and Aliens and customs officials and border patrols, when we have a sari and stories and ghosts that travel around the world, back and forth, back and forth Asia to the Americas, the Americas to Asia."

Carmelita laughed. "And maybe from Machu Picchu to the stars. Katy, you are becoming a poet in your middle-middle age."

And as usual my cousin Roxanne had the last word. "All of us, Coopers, Japanwallahs, Mehtas are poets. Poetic story tellers. Maybe we should change our names to Poeticvaatwallas. Always have been. Always will be."

That night I dreamed of a spider web. A gray-blue eye with a white eyelid sat in the middle of the web. Each strand of the web was beaded with blood. It was a web that stretched across the many branches of a tree with hundreds of trunks. A young man and an old woman were hanging on that tree, the fibers growing from one of the branches twisted around their necks. A news reporter's digital recording of the scream of a child watching his mother being raped and slaughtered as they tried to flee a war ricocheted back and forth between the trunks of that tree. I forced myself to remember the mantle that Miriam wove for God, to somehow bring it into the dream, but it eluded me.